A SOLDIER'S VOW

KATE CONDIE

D1528159

To my grandparents, whose cabin started it all.

---

*A*ll her life, the folks in town had seen themselves as better than her. The problem was Fay had seen it too. She watched their skirts swirl on the dance floor. Colorful calicos she couldn't afford and partners who no longer sought her out. But if she wanted her plan to work, she had to be as good as them. Better, even. She'd accomplished the small feat of convincing them she thought herself better, yet no wealthy man had come along proposing marriage and solving all her family's financial problems. Instead she was stuck in this small town with folks who deemed her lofty dreams unfathomable and so treated them—and her—to scoffs and cold shoulders. She couldn't even resent them for it.

The song ended and as the dancers cleared the floor, Fay's gaze snagged on two tall men entering the building. She'd never seen either of them. Her friend, Edna, broke away from her partner and returned to Fay's side.

Fay gripped Edna's arm. "Who are *they*? Both of them are as tall as Ponderosas." Brothers? But one had lighter coloring and a wave to his short hair, while the other had darker, stick-straight hair. A lock had come loose and fell across his forehead, nearly touching his eyes.

The two men made their way through the crowd of townspeople, nodding polite smiles as they did so. Finally, they stopped in front of Fay's employer, Della Graham, and the dark-haired one embraced Della, kissing her cheek. Realization hit Fay like a bucket of well water.

The flush in her cheeks turned to rage. "That one is Garrick Hampton. The weasel."

Fay wanted to find her brother and demand he throw Garrick from the dance, or at least knock a tooth loose.

Edna spoke, pulling Fay from her wicked daydream. "Della's brother?"

"And the reason my sister had to move to Oregon." The nerve he had, to show his face here after nearly getting Fay's brother-in-law killed.

The last Fay had heard, Garrick had joined a company fighting Spaniards on some island. She thought he'd be gone forever. Seeing him now was something she'd not even thought to pray for protection against.

Just then, their eyes met. His grew tight, as though he was studying her, or maybe he hated her as much as she hated him. Then the fool nodded to Della and took a purposeful step toward Fay. She disentangled herself from Edna's arm and disappeared into the crowd in search of her brother, Hugh.

She could feel Garrick's eyes burning a hole through the spot between her shoulder blades. She couldn't face him. Not yet. Not until she got her emotions under control. Otherwise she'd make a scene, and the people in this one-horse town would think even less of her. They already saw her as a haughty fortune-seeker. And so she might be.

When her sister had refused to marry any of the town men, they'd still tried to win Eloise over. But now Fay was seventeen and of marriageable age, none of the men pursued her. It was possible she'd said too much to too many folks and now everyone thought her as shallow as a saucer.

Well, so be it. She didn't want to marry any of them anyway. She hoped to be taken far away from here and given a life of luxury. Something like the Grahams' life in Chicago, with servants and closed carriages. Mostly, though, she wanted enough food to fill everyone's bellies and fabric to cover growing bodies.

Memories of being taunted for her too-short dresses still made her cheeks heat. They'd teased her for her destitution then, and now they shamed her for her dreams. Folks were impossible to please. What was the point in trying?

She spotted her brother, Hugh, dancing with the blacksmith's daughter. Fay shook her head and waited for the song to end. Hugh caught her gaze and his eyebrows slanted. Fay found a spot in the shadows and crossed her arms. Waiting.

Finally, Hugh came to her. "Why are you scowling at the world?"

"Garrick Hampton is here."

Hugh straightened, using his height to look over the crowd. Now that she was looking, she decided Garrick was not too tall after all. Probably only the same height as her brothers, which was a head and a half taller than Fay, but not so tall as to draw any attention. Garrick and his companion had only caught her eye because they were newcomers, and not because there was anything special about them. Certainly Garrick was a low-down cuss of a

3

man, no matter how long he'd been gone. The Spaniards probably surrendered just so they wouldn't have to look at his ugly mug.

Too far. Now she was lying to herself. Because no matter how much she loathed the man, she couldn't deny that he was far more handsome than she remembered. Before, his feet had been too big for his chicken legs and his beard patchy. Now he had a clean-shaven face, but the ghost of a full beard darkened his jawline, refusing to be tamed by a razor.

Hugh's voice drew her back from the image of Garrick's square jaw. "Back for good? Or just a visit?"

"Maybe he's wounded and came here to die." Wishful thinking, she knew, especially when she'd watched him walk into the dance with the grace of a stallion. But what business did he have here? He wasn't a Graham, only an in-law. Aster Ridge was full already with Graham offspring. He'd have to buy his own land somewhere, and soldiers didn't earn enough to start a life after just one little tiny war.

"Fay," Hugh chided. "You better settle that temper. No doubt you'll be serving him breakfast come Monday."

A growl rose up Fay's throat, but she kept it back. She'd once witnessed an encounter between a Billings shop owner and his employee. The employee had knocked a glass jar from a shelf, an honest accident, and the employer demanded she work to pay it back. The girl refused and quit on the spot, waltzing from the store with her head as high as a princess.

Fay wished she had the leverage to quit with her head high. But there was little employment in Dragonfly Creek and nothing that paid as well as the Grahams. Besides, she liked working for the Grahams. Della was nothing like her weasel of a brother.

Speaking of brothers.

Fay elbowed Hugh. "You're just going to let him stay and dance with Edna? I swear, sometimes I wonder if you fancy her at all."

Hugh's brows moved the tiniest bit closer together as he watched Garrick and Edna dance. "He's not dangerous. If anything, Aaron was the dangerous one."

Fay's chest grew tight at the mention of their sister's husband. She'd spent plenty of time angry with Aaron, too. Angry at him for being an outlaw and taking her sister to live a thousand miles from home. But it was no good being angry with someone so far away. Much better to take her rage out on someone who was here, someone like Garrick.

He had, after all, loathed the idea of Eloise marrying Aaron. True, it hadn't been a love match, not for her at least. She'd married him to pay the hospital bill for their eldest brother's sickness. But Garrick, ever the hero, had decided it was his job to prevent the marriage, and when he couldn't do that, he'd left town. Everyone thought that was the last of him until a bounty hunter had turned up with questions regarding Aaron's whereabouts. It was no mystery where the man had gotten his information.

The song ended, and Garrick and Edna went to Della's side. Garrick mirrored Hugh's method of looking out over the crowd. Fay sank into the shadows and out of his sight, only to find herself among the young children playing on the chairs that had been pushed to the side for the dance.

Fay had never played here like this. As long as she could remember, her father hadn't the use of his legs, so a country dance was out of the question. What need had their mother to attend without her husband when she had five little ones to keep in line? Fay didn't blame Mama, but she couldn't stop the prick in her chest, mourning the bits of childhood lost to her forever. Their family was never going to be like the rest of this town. They were too poor. Too sorry. Too... pitiable.

Fay wouldn't be any of those things. She would rise above everyone who had ever hurt her. Starting with Garrick Hampton.

GARRICK HAMPTON HADN'T THOUGHT to return, at least not so soon. The Spanish War had practically been a single battle, one that was mostly fought by a regiment of negroes, the glory claimed by the whites.

It wasn't as though racism was a new concept to him. Out here it was whites against Native's. Same story, different cover. Only the men he'd fought alongside overseas had been fighting for this country. A country whose press refused to assign any glory to the ones most deserving. Instead, they'd printed a photo of his white regiment, lauding them for their swift victory. It still made him sick. His companion, Stimps, understood. He had been fighting this inner battle all his life down south in Texas. Slavery might be abolished, but equality remained a mirage.

Garrick stood at his sister's side while all the young people, and plenty of the older ones, danced on the floor. He scanned the room, waiting for Fay to reappear. At first, he'd thought he'd seen Eloise, but even after three years her image was still sharp in his mind. He'd only needed one second more to discern Fay's sharper features and lighter hair. One second was all he got, too, for she turned away, and he hadn't seen her since. Fay and Eloise had never looked so alike to him before. It was probably only memory and wishful thinking that had made him think she was Eloise.

Eloise was gone. Della had written to him once he'd settled. She'd told him what happened, how Eloise ran away with Aaron when the bounty hunter had come for him, as though she had truly loved the man. The thought still confused and sliced at Garrick. If he had known she'd loved Aaron, he would never have turned him in. Garrick had thought her an unwilling victim of circumstances. He should have known a girl with as much fire as Eloise would make the best out of any situation.

As much as he looked, he never found Fay again. After the dance, he and Stimps left with the crowd and moved toward Della's wagon. Little had changed around here. Besides his niece growing up a bit, getting old enough to beg to ride with him on his horse, much remained the same.

As they rode back to Aster Ridge, Della hardly stopped smiling, touching Garrick like she believed he was some phantom about to steal away into the black night.

"You two can have the guesthouse," she said. "Willem and Lydia have finished their place further along the valley." Della gestured south, but the sun was long set, and Garrick saw nothing but moonlight shining on darkened ground.

Garrick and Stimps put away the horses and brought their tack into the guesthouse, a habit formed during travel. Here, there was no need to sleep with one's belongings beneath them for safekeeping, but the habit remained nonetheless.

Stimps raised the lantern and eyed the space. "Nice place your family has."

Garrick nodded, seeing it through new eyes. When he'd been here before, he'd slept in a bedroom in the main house. Eaten with Della as a member of the family. He knew she still loved him, but did she resent him for his foolishness regarding Eloise? Would he and Stimps be invited in for meals, or would they be expected to fend for themselves out here like farmhands?

"Bedrooms are this way."

Once they were both settled in their own rooms, Garrick lay on his bed, fingers woven together behind his head. Maybe he should continue down to Texas with Stimps. A fresh start might be best. He didn't know what he would do here anyway. He was a soldier, trained only for fighting. According to those in his regiment, he was even quite good at it, but excelling at conflict wasn't something to be proud of. The last thing he wanted in life was to resemble his father. A man can only fight so long until he's washed up and angry with the world. Some days Garrick thought he was already walking that lonely path. He wasn't about to give into it entirely.

2

*H*er brother was missing.

He was delivering Edna to the train station so she could spend Christmas with her mama in Chicago. The trip should have taken Hugh two days, but today was three and he had yet to return or send word.

Fay urged her horse faster, but the beast was old and had traveled far today, and while Lady quickened her pace for a few steps, she slowed once more. Sleet fell around them, filling the brim of Fay's hat until the cheap felt gave way and sent a pile of slush into her lap. She brushed at it, but it didn't matter. She was soaked through already, her jaw pained with the effort of stilling the chattering.

She passed home, the yellow light shining brightly, beckoning her to partake of the warm fire. Lady even quickened her steps as she recognized how close her own shelter stood, but Fay would not return, not without word of Hugh or, in the least, without chasing down every possibility.

With each squelching hoof print, she continued deeper into the valley belonging to Della and Bastien. Fay chastised herself. She should have gone there first, then into town, then further along the route. As she'd ridden the road to Billings, she'd expected to find Hugh around every bend. When the sun had set completely, Fay knew it was time to turn around. The last thing Mama needed was *two* missing children.

As she came upon the main house at Aster Ridge, her heart sank. All the lights were doused. She chewed her lip, content to let Lady walk as slowly as she wished while Fay summoned the courage to wake her employers and ask if they'd had any word of Hugh.

He had never returned late, not in any storm, and this wasn't even the worst one he'd driven the coach in. A shiver jerked through her as her body ached for any stimulation to bring heat back to her frozen limbs.

Fay glanced further into the valley, at the other homes that peppered the wide, white expanse. None were lit because none had family lost in a storm. As her gaze scanned the valley, it snagged on the guesthouse. The heat her body had been craving filled her chest. It wasn't the warmth of comfort that burned within, but hatred.

She didn't mind waking *him*. In fact, she'd take joy if some critter had built its house outside the guesthouse and made noise all night every night. Perhaps then Garrick would leave once more, and this time he might stay gone.

She rode Lady up to the hitching post and slid off. Her knees were stiff from being bent in the stirrups, and as she straightened them, they ached with the weight of her drenched skirts. With quick steps, she strode to Della's front door, and with quiet hands, tried the latch. Locked. The children would be asleep, and if she wasn't keen to wake Della and Bastien, the last thing Fay wanted was to wake the children.

Under the cover of the porch, she removed her hat and flicked the collected water off before squishing it back on. Slushy snow still rained down from the sky, but it was drier than it had been a few hours ago, becoming more of a true snow. The valley would be blanketed come morning, and Hugh might be out there, cold and fighting his way back to them.

She stomped across the yard to the guesthouse. With icy knuckles, she rapped on the door, wincing at the way the contact rang through her bones. She waited, shifting from one foot to the other. Now that she was off the horse and using her feet and legs, discomfort bit at her toes like little pricks of a needle. She vowed if she ever searched for one of her brothers again, she would wear a pair of their old boots. And socks. Maybe two pairs.

The door opened, and Garrick blinked at her, his brows tight in a glare. Of anger or confusion? "Fay?" His voice was scratchy, as though he were still dreaming.

She shifted her feet on the step. "The main house is locked, and I don't want to wake the children."

"What are you doing here?" He passed a hand over his dark hair and glanced over her head, no doubt noting the dark windows at Della's. "Did you come alone?"

"Hugh isn't back. He should have been back. I thought you might have had word." Well, not him exactly, but someone on this homestead. She stared at his bare feet. No doubt the frigid wind that pulled on his loose shirt came as quite a shock compared to the warmth of his bed. That same warmth called to Fay, but she would not answer.

"Could he have been waylaid in Dragonfly Creek?"

Fay shook her head. Just a few hours ago she'd stumbled into the nearest post office, hoping for word he'd been snowed in at Billings. "That's why I'm here at this hour. Nobody I spoke to in Dragonfly Creek has seen or heard from him. I took the road to Billings as far as I could before the sun set."

He pulled his jacket from the wall and stepped into his boots, striding past Fay and leading the way to Della's front door. Fay stayed close at his heels.

He tried the latch.

"I told you. It's locked."

He glanced at her over his shoulder. "You shouldn't be traveling that road by yourself."

Fay set her jaw and glared. "And who should accompany me? Pa in his chair? Or perhaps Lachlan, who is emptying his stomach back at the house?" It felt good to release some of her emotion on this man. Both the stress and worry of today, but also the hatred she'd bottled against him. She'd been forced to make meals, clear dishes, and serve this brute all week.

He narrowed his eyes. "They don't know you're out, do they?"

"Ma knows." Fay straightened. "I can handle myself." She patted her pocket and the pistol that rested against her thigh.

His gaze brushed down the length of her, noting the spot where her hand touched. "I hope you're a decent shot." Garrick started for the side of the house.

"I am," Fay said, more to herself since his back was to her. She followed him once more, skidding to a halt when he stopped just outside Bastien and Della's bedroom window. He tapped softly on the glass with a beat that could only be human, then waited. Fay shifted her feet again, the pain increasing the longer she was off Lady's back and using her own legs to carry her around the slippery earth. The curtains fluttered and Bastien's face appeared. To his credit, he blinked at them for only a moment before jerking his head in the direction of the front door.

Garrick spun and bumped into Fay. Her frozen feet weren't as nimble as normal, and with pinwheeling arms, she started to fall.

Garrick caught her belt and pulled her to rights again. This close, Fay thought she saw a touch of concern behind his glare, but she couldn't be sure through the dark. She shrugged him off and took the lead on the path to the door, if it could even be called a path, concealed as it was with white.

The front door latch clicked, and Fay rushed to meet Bastien. Garrick's boots came to a squelching stop behind her as she relayed everything.

Bastien stared at the ground, his face tight with thought, before he waved them in. "We figured he'd been waylaid by the storm. Might be worse in Billings. Come inside. You're wet through."

Fay swallowed her cold. She didn't need to be warmed. She needed a plan to find her brother. Plus, it was her job to tend the children inside, and she was all too aware how difficult it was to get them to sleep. "I don't want to wake everyone."

Garrick cleared his throat, and Fay jolted. She'd forgotten about him.

"We can use the guesthouse," he said. "Stimps won't wake for anything but a bugle or the sun."

Bastien nodded, and Fay followed Garrick to the guesthouse. As soon as the door was closed behind them,

Fay let out a sigh of gratitude at the warmth that enveloped her. She swayed toward the stove's welcome heat.

Garrick opened the stove door with a soft creak and threw a log inside. He fiddled with the flue before turning to Fay. "Better remove your boots. They're dripping."

Fay blinked at him, unwilling to be curt in Bastien's presence. But if the man thought adding a log to a fire on a cold night was akin to an olive branch extended as recompense for shredding her family to pieces, he had a few things wrong in that big head of his.

Bastien approached the fire and gestured for Fay to sit in the armchair. "The post office didn't have word?"

Fay walked to the chair, stretching her fingers nearer to the glorious warmth of the stove, but didn't sit. "None from Hugh, and they've had other wires come through."

Bastien nodded, and she could almost see the cogs turning in his mind. "He's most likely waylaid in town. There's no reason to believe anything bad has happened to him. He's a grown man, and he knows this territory better than any of us."

Garrick stepped nearer and stretched a hand out to her. "Give me your boots. They're wet, and they can't be comfortable." He turned to Bastien. "She's been all over the county tonight."

Bastien surveyed Fay's soggy form. "Alone?"

Fay harrumphed and threw Garrick an annoyed look. "Lachlan's still enduring a spell. I have Papa's pistol in my pocket." Bastien was right. Hugh did know the forests. But she couldn't ignore the feeling in her gut, nor the fact that Mama had allowed Fay to search for him. She hadn't said so, but Mama felt uneasy too. Fay was certain of it.

Garrick snapped his fingers. "Your boots."

A hateful flush climbed up her neck as she leaned down and reached for the buttons on her boots. As soon as she tried, she realized her frozen fingers were useless. They felt as tight and fat as sausages and equally inept at working the tiny buttons. She put her fingertips to her mouth, huffing warm air onto her skin. Then she tried again, but one hot breath couldn't undo the chill of several hours of riding.

Garrick knelt at her feet, knocking her hand aside. He pushed her skirt away and undid the buttons with ease, slipping off first one boot, then the other.

He placed them close to the fire and stirred the flames, adding one more log. Fay curled her toes, the water in her stockings dripping onto the floor. She didn't need to be sorry to anyone though. It was Fay's job to clean this floor.

Bastien cleared his throat. "If he's out in this, we can be comforted, knowing he can sleep in the coach. He won't be without shelter."

Fay nodded, but her chin quivered. That steady beat in her belly refused to be convinced.

Bastien took Fay's hand between his own warmer ones. "There's naught to be done at this time of night. We'll make a plan in the morning. You should sleep here. We've room in the house." He glanced down at Garrick, who still knelt by Fay's feet. "Can you put her horse in the stable?"

Fay stood once more, shaking her head. "No. Ma will be worried. I can't stay."

Garrick buttoned his jacket. "I'll ride over and let her know."

Fay pinned him with a stare. "I can ride home."

"Without boots?" Garrick took a step back, swinging a

hand toward her boots, barely warmed and surely not at all dried. "If you can get them back on."

Fay drew a long breath before sitting down and struggling into her boots. Her wet stockings clung to the leather. Eventually she took off the knit wool that no longer granted any warmth and slid her bare foot inside. Fay ached to get home and into dry clothes. To stand *in* the fireplace if that's what it took to thaw her icy skin. When she stood again, she found Garrick staring down at her with an amused expression. If he enjoyed watching her struggle, he should have stuck around after he'd run her sister off to Oregon; he would have had the time of his life watching Fay suffer loneliness.

She gave Bastien a weak smile. "Thank you for your help." Then she turned to glare at Garrick. She hoped her expression conveyed all the iciness of the storm outside.

Garrick smiled at Bastien over Fay's shoulder. "I'll walk her home. I doubt that horse has much speed left anyhow." Fay wanted to jump up and into his line of sight, to tell him to stop looking over her with that stupid towering height.

Before Fay could form a coherent argument, Garrick pulled his hat off the peg and was out the door again. He unwrapped Lady's reins from the post and held them in his hands, smiling at Fay as she came closer.

As she passed him, she said, "I can take myself home."

Garrick leaned closer. "Bastien wouldn't think of it, and do you really want your *employer* to walk you home on a night like this?" He glanced up at the sky, and Fay took pleasure in noting his damp hair. He hadn't worn his hat when they'd gone to get Bastien. If he was going to walk her home, at least he'd be uncomfortable while doing it. Fay wanted every excuse to teach this man that saving Morris women was as lost a cause as it had been three years ago when he'd tried helping Eloise.

With wet stockings in her hand, Fay climbed onto Lady. She reached her free hand out for the reins, but Garrick just turned away.

Bastien exited the guesthouse and gave Fay a grim smile. "We'll work this out in the morning. We've plenty of men around here to go searching."

Fay nodded, gratitude swelling in her chest. Her own family was less than capable. Fay had done her best, but as usual, a Morris' best was just not enough.

3

_G_arrick rose before the sun, stepping into his trousers and heading into the main house. He wasn't a core member of this family, and if he didn't insert himself, he'd be excluded from the search party for Hugh.

The smell of fried meat filled the air, and Garrick removed his hat and boots as quickly as he could. Fay was a decent cook, but his sister, Della, was the best.

But when he rounded the corner into the kitchen, he was shocked to find Fay was the one at the stove. He figured she'd be at home sleeping or comforting her mama. He cleared his throat, and she jumped at the noise. Her gaze flicked down him and back up, but her frown stayed, like an employer who surveyed a prospect and found him decidedly lacking.

Ignoring the dent in his pride, he said, "He didn't come home then?"

She gave him a stiff shake of her head and turned back to stirring the pan of hash.

The front latch clicked, and Garrick sighed with relief. He didn't know who it was, but he didn't like being in this house alone with Fay. Too many memories of her sister and all he had done to ruin their family.

Bastien walked in with his brother Willem and his brother-in-law Thomas behind him. Garrick tried not to feel sorry for himself, though he doubted Bastien had bothered to knock on the guesthouse door while rallying the troops.

Fay breezed past him with a sizzling pan of hash. She threw a cloth pad on the table and set the pan on top. The men found their seats, and Garrick joined them, as though he too had been collected by Bastien. Fay returned with a plate of biscuits and set them near Bastien.

"Thank you, Fay. You really can go home. Della will be out soon, and I'm sure your mama wants your company."

"I'll be on my way in a bit." Fay gave him a prim smile and planted her feet. She wasn't going anywhere until she was good and ready.

The men heaped their plates full and talked of forests and ridges Garrick had never heard of. He wasn't familiar with this territory, not like these men were. He'd spent a few long months of his life in Aster Ridge, but that had been years ago. It was no wonder he hadn't been summoned for this meeting.

He leaned on his forearms. "Stimps and I can take the road to Billings. I was going to escort him there anyway so he could take a train home. We could inquire at the train station and see what day they arrived." He lowered his voice. "*If* they arrived."

He glanced at Fay to find her listening intently, her arms crossed and her eyes wide. Careless to pretend she wasn't eavesdropping. He couldn't really blame her. This was her brother missing. She could have lost a few toes to frostbite in last night's attempt to find him. Etiquette likely wasn't high on her list. And truly, Bastien seemed a lot less cavalier this morning. Perhaps he had expected Hugh home last night and was now as worried as Fay.

Willem cleared his throat. "I'm going to Billings. Hugh has my coach, and if I can find that, it will tell us more than any ticket master at the train station."

Bastien nodded as he swallowed down his bite. "Normally we'd send Willem first, but with this weather, we should spread out right away." He glanced at Garrick. "You and Stimps can take the east side of the road. When you get close, he can break off and go to Billings while you cover the rest of your section." He swiveled his gaze to the rest of the group. "What do you say? Three days? One out, and two to search our way back?"

His words were met with nods of agreement. Garrick couldn't help but admire the man. These weren't his children, and yet he was a sort of patriarch of this valley. Even stiff-backed Fay had come to him when she wasn't able to solve the trouble.

Garrick stood, ready to wake Stimps and be on their way, but Bastien lifted a hand. "Do you think you can follow a map?"

Garrick nodded, trying not to be stung by such a basic query. Of course he could read a map. He wasn't the youth he'd been the last time he'd lived under Bastien's roof. He sucked his tooth, unsure if he wanted to stick around and prove as much to this man, or if he'd rather cut his losses and leave, find a place where nobody knew him. A place where they needed what he was built for: fighting.

Bastien stood and walked to his desk. He pulled out a

folded piece of paper and spread it wide. The men pushed the food out of the way to accommodate the large map. Bastien pointed to a few places, naming those same ridges as before. Garrick could see them now, in proximity to Aster Ridge. The men would all search in a perfect fan with Aster Ridge as the starting point. Garrick would have the section that ran east along the road, then he would travel south for a bit, then west back to Aster Ridge.

Bastien glanced up at Garrick. "Can you draw this, sketch your section? I don't want you lost too."

Garrick nodded. When it came to skill with his hands, fists were usually his choice, but he was sure he could draw this map, get the basic geography right. It would help him to remember the landscape anyhow.

Bastien pushed the map closer.

Garrick took it and folded it back up, then stood. "I'll go wake Stimps."

He didn't look at Fay as he left, but he felt her there all the same. Hatred pulsed off her. Why shouldn't she hate him? The last time he'd tried to help, he'd only destroyed. He was bred for wounding, not healing. Not even kind Della had been able to gentle her words when she'd written to him regarding the havoc he'd left in his departure.

He pushed into the guesthouse to find Stimps already up and pulling on his socks. He glanced up with a smile when Garrick entered. "So we're braving breakfast at the main house?"

"Hugh is missing."

Stimps' smile fell. "Missing?"

"He should have been back by now and there's been no word from him."

Stimps nodded. "Are we going to help with the

search?"

"We've been assigned a route near Billings. Are you ready to see your family?"

His friend stilled his hands and took a slow breath. "I'm ready."

Garrick gave Stimps a sad smile, attempting to assess whether Stimps truly wanted to go back to Texas. He could have gone home right from their base on the east coast, but he'd chosen to accompany Garrick. Clearly, Garrick wasn't the only one reluctant to return to the world he had left behind.

Garrick paused, wondering if he should just join Stimps on the train to Texas. But no, he'd broken up the Morris family once. He would do all he could to bring Hugh back to them. Then he could leave, go to Texas or to the plains of Africa. It didn't much matter where he went, but he didn't belong here. Della had her new family, and Fay's hostility showed no signs of ebbing.

As much as his heart might wish it to be, this wasn't his home. It was time he found out where that was.

———

HE HAD DEFINITELY OVERESTIMATED his drawing skills. Stimps had packed and gone into the main house for breakfast, and Garrick still cursed over his attempt to duplicate the map.

The door opened, and without looking up Garrick sighed and leaned back in his chair. "I'll never get this thing right. Will you give it a try?"

Silence. He turned to find not Stimps, but Fay, with two lumpy bundles in her hands. "Grub for the journey."

He eyed the leather bundles, weighing the likeliness that one of them was filled with poison.

She set them down and crept closer, eyeing his drawing. She uncrossed one arm to point at his pitiful sketch. "Thunder Ridge is too close. And Grasshopper Valley stretches further west."

Garrick scooted his chair back and held the pencil out to her.

She slid it from his grip with a polite grace he hadn't thought her capable of. She knelt in front of the table, her arms resting on its top. Her hair was lighter and straighter than Eloise's, and Fay's face was sharper somehow, her chin coming to a point, so her whole face resembled a native's arrowhead.

She sketched light lines, showing where the valley should end, and darker lines where the ridge should have been. She stared at it a minute more, chewing her lip. "You'll want to stay below the ridge. There's no easy way down from the top, not on our side."

"Thank you." Garrick dared. "For the food and for the help with this map."

She turned, and he could just see her profile. "I pray one of you returns with him."

Garrick was quiet for a moment, unused to her politeness, unsure what to say to soothe her worry. Any promise he made would be as empty as his boots standing by the entry. "At the very least, we'll have answers. Stimps and I will check the train station."

Fay nodded, her throat bobbing as she flattened her palms on the table and pressed to standing. He wanted to reach out, to ease her heart like he'd tried to ease her cold feet last night. He glanced down suddenly to see she was wearing the same boots. "Have those boots already dried?"

She shifted her feet so her skirt hid the worn leather. "I packed enough food for each of you for three days. Just in case Stimps decides not to break off and go to Billings."

Stimps entered the guesthouse, stomping snow off his boots. "Horses are ready." His face lit when his gaze fell upon their guest. "Fay, as always, that meal was delicious." He patted his stomach for emphasis.

Fay turned, and the moment she stepped away Garrick knew whatever had tried to heal between them had snapped again. He drew a slow breath. It was Garrick's duty to do a thorough search, to ensure Hugh wasn't in his section, but he wanted so badly to bring him back. He wanted to take away one reason for Fay's hatred, to earn her gratitude, however brief it might be.

She walked by Stimps and murmured, "You're welcome."

Garrick watched her boots. Though they didn't leave wet marks on the polished wood floor, he was certain they were still damp and uncomfortable. She may not be the reflection of her sister, but she had that same self-sacrificing attitude when it came to her family. Garrick's stomach clenched at the memory of Eloise selling herself in marriage to a bandit, all for the sake of her brother.

"Ready?" Stimps face shone with a familiar excitement, the same he'd had the day they climbed off the ship and into boats that would take them to the shore of the island. That day Garrick had been equally thrilled at the prospect of fighting, of proving his valor and strength. He should have known he would excel at violence. His pa had shown him little else throughout childhood, and the few months he'd spent at Aster Ridge, before he had made a mess of Eloise's life, hadn't been enough to make him into a good man.

He shouldered his pack and nodded to Stimps. "Let's go find Hugh."

4

_____

Fay waited until her mother's soft snore started before she stepped into her brothers' old boots. They'd been worn by each of her three brothers in turn, and now they were weathered and too long in the toe for Fay's feet, but with three pairs of socks and a bit of fabric wrapped around the arch, the rest fit quite comfortably, not to mention her feet would be far warmer than they'd been when she'd searched the county last night.

All the Graham men, Garrick and Stimps included, had set off this morning. Before they'd gone, Fay had helped Garrick draw his map, and as she did so, she realized Pete Corbin's cabin sat within Garrick's section. She'd gone out there several times over the years when she was riding the trap lines with Hugh. Would she still be able to find it without the guidance of her brothers?

If any of the other men had Garrick's section, Fay would have felt sure that they would come across Pete's cabin, but Garrick hardly knew these woods, and he was just as likely to get lost as he was to find the moon in a cloudless sky.

On the off-chance Garrick *did* find the cabin, would he be able to get close enough to ask about Hugh? Pete could be cagey, and odds were he wouldn't trust a strange man wandering onto his property.

No. As the day wore on, Fay knew she couldn't trust her brother's best chance of coming home to this interloper.

So she adjusted the breeches she'd borrowed from her brother Otto's old trunk and tried to forget how it would look if she came across anyone she knew while wearing this getup. She wouldn't. She was following Garrick and Stimps' trail, and with what little Garrick knew of this country, he would likely have his nose so deep into his map he'd never realize she followed them. Why Bastien even included him in the search was beyond her understanding. He should have been tasked to stay home and protect the women.

Hiking her pack higher on her shoulder, Fay set her note on her night table. She'd considered keeping her whereabouts a secret for fear they'd send someone after her. But who else was there? It wasn't hard-headedness that had Fay taking this duty upon herself. She was all that was left. Papa had told her more than once—a woman gets no mistakes in the forest. With the snow falling hard and fast, she'd be a fool to hide her route. She kissed the tips of her fingers and ran them along the wall as she passed her parents' bedroom and left out the front door.

She entered the small barn they had kept when they sold the majority of their land. It was also where she'd hidden her supplies once she got the idea to set off unaccompanied for Pete's. She wrapped a kerchief around her head, tucking her braid inside. Then she pulled the brimmed hat over top. With her breeches and hair pulled up, she likely looked like a boy. Around these parts, that could only benefit her, but it wouldn't protect her entirely. Her attention went to the pistol on her belt, heavy with the weighty comfort of protection. She was a sure enough shot, and she hoped a moving target wouldn't be too different. Their horse, Lady, nickered in greeting, and Fay pulled an apple from her coat pocket. "Here, girl."

The horse lipped the fruit from Fay's palm, sniffing around, wanting more. There was never more, not around here, and the poor animal didn't have the sense to understand.

Fay saddled and packed the horse. When everything was set, she stood for a moment, one hand on either end of the saddle, taking slow breaths. She'd been through these woods more than any of the men out there. If she didn't take this horse, surely her brother Lachlan would crawl from his sickbed and do it in her place. She was well outfitted with food and warm clothing and would be gone for two days at the most. If Hugh wasn't at Pete Corbin's cabin, she would come home and wait for news from the others.

But Hugh *was* at the cabin. Some sisterly sense told her so. That sense was what drove her forward. But a small sliver of doubt waved its tiny hand, asking her why that sense hadn't kicked in before the men had left, back when she could have told Bastien and sent him to search Garrick's route. Was she grasping at straws here? Putting herself at risk? The line between hope and foolishness was a thin one, and just now Fay wasn't sure which side she stood on.

She climbed onto the horse, her large pack almost a backrest behind her. The breeches she wore were certainly more comfortable to ride in, and they would keep her legs warmer than a drafty skirt. When it was time to rest, she would wish for some petticoats to use as a blanket. She pushed that thought away. She'd brought blankets. She didn't need a frilly skirt getting in her way.

She urged the horse forward, watching as she passed the darkened house. She hadn't expected resistance, but perhaps a small part of her wanted to be stopped. If only Lachlan were well, this wouldn't be her responsibility. She touched the barrel of the pistol at her hip, feeling the cold even through her gloves. Another pistol was stowed in her pack, and a long rifle nestled in the scabbard in front of her right knee. She'd never used a gun on a man before, but a determination deep in her chest told her if it came down to her life, or even Hugh's, she could fire a shot.

GARRICK WOKE UP COLD, the tips of his ears and nose numb and his fingers struggling to work properly. As he and Stimps packed their camp, he remembered Cuba and the sickly warm air that stuck in his throat and made him feel like he was choking. "It's warmer at your home in Texas, right?"

Stimps laughed. "A bit." Stimps had borrowed a pair of Bastien's gloves and so far hadn't complained about the frigid air.

Garrick glanced at his own gloved hands. Two fingers lost to a factory blade, the very accident that had brought him to Aster Ridge. In his short time here, he had learned a thing or two about what a family could be, what it should be. He thought of his niece and nephew, so young and innocent. Little Violet loved and accepted Garrick as her family, even though she couldn't possibly remember him from the last time he'd lived out here.

He tried telling himself it was the children who made this feel like home, that being anywhere besides a barrack full of grown and grumpy men would bring with it a sense of contentment. Maybe, so long as he didn't go back to that life, he could find that feeling wherever he decided to settle.

Once they were packed, Garrick pulled out the map. Stimps wasn't in a hurry to get to Billings, so they had started on the section furthest from the road, and today they would sweep across to Billings. Stimps would buy himself a ticket home, and Garrick would weave his way back to Aster Ridge.

"More of the same?" Stimps came over and inspected the paper map; even with Fay's help it remained roughly drawn, but Garrick could still picture the original map in his mind. They would be entering a forest today, and the riding would be slower than yesterday as they picked through trees and tried to keep their bearings under the canopy.

"Yep." Garrick sighed. If he could ignore the white blanket of snow and the pine trees, it almost felt like they were back in Cuba with their regiment, mapping their way from the white sand beach and into the fighting. Imagining Cuba brought a certain comfort—the comfort of imminent victory—but Garrick didn't hunger for battle the way some did. Even though battle was the only thing he excelled at. Fighting might be his most developed skill, but it was time he found something he was better at than putting bullets through men's hearts.

They climbed onto their horses, and Garrick glanced at his friend. Stimps had a life waiting for him, acquired skills just waiting to be shaped into a future. Perhaps Garrick should join Stimps in Texas. Though he was reluctant to return, something about that place had made Stimps into the content fellow he was today. Garrick could use a dose or two of whatever it was.

With every pass along the map, Garrick lost a bit of hope. Finding a trace of Hugh or Edna in this wide swath of earth would be a miracle. They reached a clearing and scanned the treetops. As though to prove him wrong, a thin trail of smoke rose from the tree line.

Garrick laughed outright and gaped at Stimps. "Who'd'a thought?"

Stimps grinned back, and they kicked their horses faster, heading toward what he hoped was a cold, yet unharmed, Hugh. A fire didn't feed itself. If there was smoke, there was a person.

When he reached the camp, Garrick found a small boy packing up his things. The fire had burned out and it was the smoking logs that had been so visible to Garrick and Stimps.

"Boy, we're looking for my friend, and possibly his lady companion."

The boy froze but didn't turn. Perhaps he was some sort of mute. His horse, a dingy brown with three white boots, was tethered to a tree, and for a moment Garrick thought he recognized the beast.

"You from Dragonfly Creek?" he asked. For who else did he know in this territory?

The boy turned slowly, and Garrick got a good look at his face for the first time. He laughed, a great booming laugh that caused a dusting of snow to fall from the branches above.

As his laughter died away, he hit the pommel of his

saddle with the heel of his hand. "Fay Morris. I can honestly say you're the last person I thought to meet out here." He ran his gaze down the length of her getup. She surely did pass as a boy, with her skinny legs and hair tucked into her hat.

Fay fussed with a buckle on her pack. "I had no intention of meeting up with you either. I thought I was ahead of you."

Garrick glanced back the way they'd come. "You *were* ahead of us, but we saw your smoke." She must have set off just after them, or continued riding when he and Stimps bedded down for the night.

Fay glared at the smoking logs with such power Garrick thought they might burst into flames once more.

She hefted her things onto her horse. "There's an old trapper, lives out in these parts." She buckled her things into the saddle, and Garrick sat on his horse, watching her with a wry smile on his face. "He's one of those paranoid folks and would likely shoot you on sight. He knows me, and I know where his cabin is."

Garrick chuckled again. "D'you have a change of clothes? Surely he won't recognize you in those." Even as he spoke, he was beginning to appreciate her new silhouette, different as it was. Seeing her legs like this was almost indecent, but he couldn't convince himself to look away. Just then, he remembered Stimps and shot his friend a look to see if he, too, was appreciating what he saw. Stimps looked out into the trees, where Garrick should be looking too. After all, Hugh was just as likely anywhere in these woods as he was at this Pete fellow's cabin.

Fay took down her tarp from where it hung on a rope from the trees, meant as cover from falling snow, and laid it out on the ground. Garrick dismounted and picked up one end, helping to fold it like a large quilt, meeting corners together until it was taut, then they walked toward one another and Garrick took her corners. She took his too, and they stood there in the world's most pointless faceoff.

This close, he could see her gloves, pinched and caved in at the tips, were too long for her fingers. Hopefully they were at least warm. "Why didn't you tell me? You could have marked the location of his cabin on my map."

"I already said I didn't think of it until everyone had left. There was nobody else to send." She tugged on her corners as she spoke.

Her voice cracked, and Garrick released his hold on the tarp, bending to pick up the bottom and repeat the step. "Is Lachlan still in bad shape?"

Fay's jaw clenched, the little muscles under her ears popping out. "He's not doing well. He's a fool who refuses to take his medicine."

Garrick stepped back as Fay finished folding the tarp against her middle. "You mean the medicine Eloise married Aaron for?"

Fay shot Garrick a scathing look. "Yes, but he doesn't know about that. He would hate to learn of it, even though Eloise is now *extremely* happy."

Garrick's gaze shot to Fay's face. Was she trying to convince him or herself? He untied the rope from the trees and passed it to Fay. "Why would he care what she did to get him the medicine, if it all worked out so well in the end?"

Fay shook her head. "You wouldn't understand." She laid her tarp over the rest of her gear and tied it down with the frayed rope.

"Try me."

"I don't want to *try you*." Her words mocked his, as though his phrase hailed from another world. "My family is none of your affair." She jiggled her gear, checking if it was secure. With such a flimsy rope, it was looser than Garrick would have allowed, but she must have deemed it satisfactory, because she walked over and kicked dirt and snow over the fire.

"Whose boots are you wearing?" They were altogether too large. Surprising she didn't trip on the toes as she walked.

She ignored him, mounted her horse, and kicked the beast into motion. Garrick glanced at Stimps, but his friend only shrugged.

Garrick climbed on his own horse and rode closer to Stimps, lowering his voice. "I don't want her out here alone, but I can tell you she ain't going to ask us to follow."

Stimps nodded. "Follow her."

Garrick did a double take.

Stimps laughed. "You two take our section. I'll continue to Billings and speak with the station master. Then I'll send a wire to Aster Ridge letting them know she found you."

Garrick glowered at his friend. "I can't imagine knowing she's with me will be any consolation for her family."

Stimps clapped Garrick on the back. "You don't need me, and as keen as I am to watch the two of you ignore one another for the next two days, I think I'll be better off on my own."

Garrick watched Fay's retreating form. She moved quickly, and he didn't have time to flounder in his decision.

He huffed. "All right. Tell them what she said about Pete's cabin. If he's not there, we'll weave through the rest of our section." Garrick touched his jacket near the pocket where he kept the map. He slipped it out and held it toward Stimps. "Take this."

Stimps shook his head. "I suspect finding the road will be a sight easier than whatever you two are up to."

Stimps grinned and touched the brim of his hat, a gesture both familiar and uniquely Stimps. When his friend turned around, Garrick put the map back in his pocket and urged his horse quickly after Fay's mount.

When he pulled up beside her, he asked, "When did you leave? If you were so close behind us, why not just ride hard and tell me so I could go?"

"I told you, Pete would probably shoot you, and that's where Hugh is." Fay's horse moved forward so they weren't side by side anymore.

"At Pete's?"

Silence.

Garrick urged his horse to Fay's side once more and pulled the map from his inner pocket. He held it out. "Mark the spot."

"No."

Garrick gave a disbelieving scoff. "No? And why ever not?"

She turned a hateful look at him. "Maybe I should let you get shot. But I'm not marking the spot and turning around. Someone living has to help Hugh make it back. There's a reason he's not home."

Her voice lost its anger, and by the time she'd finished speaking, her words were laced tight with fear.

"I don't have any intention of forcing you to go home." The forest grew thicker around them, the trees wider and more numerous, the branches hanging lower and heavier. His horse took him away from her to avoid one. He spoke louder to span the distance. "I doubt I could anyway. But if you show me where it is, I'll have an idea how far away they are, or maybe I can even help you find your way there."

Fay glanced at the map from the corner of her eye. "I don't think I could show you on the map. It's just"—she waved her hand north—"there."

"You don't know where it is." Garrick wanted to laugh, but his horse weaved around another tree. These dense woods were going to be slow traveling indeed. How did Fay even know where she was going?

When he was able to move to Fay's side again, her chin had lifted a bit higher.

"I know enough," she said. "So long as we're close during the day, we'll see the smoke. Same way you found me."

Garrick put the map back in his pocket, not at all content with her reasoning. The map would come in handy when she got them completely lost.

He snuck another glance at her. She really did remind him of Eloise, but she was still different. To know the difference, he would need to study her for far longer than was socially acceptable, but he was more than up to the task. He thought of Fay's earlier statement, about Eloise being happy.

"If she's happy," he ventured, "I'm glad." He watched her, waiting for a response.

But she trained her gaze forward as though she were participating in a competition that required all her focus.

"I loved her."

Fay swung her head toward Garrick. "Wh—" Before

she'd finished the word, realization dawned on her face, and she gaped at him. "Eloise? You loved her?"

Garrick laughed. "It's true. I did, or at least I thought I did."

He recalled those days so well. It felt like they were the start to his life. He'd been miserable in Omaha with his pa. Miserable working in that dank factory all day, rarely feeling the sun on his face. He never would have expected that losing two of his fingers would be the best thing that ever happened to him, the luckiest thing. For that was why Della and Bastien had come to get him, practically forcing him to come with them to Aster Ridge.

Pa had refused to pay for medicine, and Garrick had been facing the loss of his entire hand to infection until Bastien had hauled him from his father's home and to a doctor. Garrick didn't recall much except the fever that had burned day and night. Eventually, the pain in his hand had gone, the red swelling disappearing.

The doctor had told Garrick he would keep his hand, and Garrick had been overwhelmed with relief. What was a man without a hand? Fingers, he could live without, could fight in a war without. But a hand? With only one, there wasn't much he could do. It only strengthened Garrick's resolve to be grateful to his sister and her husband for what they'd done for him. And it strengthened his regret, too, for causing the Morrises more grief than they'd already experienced.

"D'you write to her?" he asked.

Fay's responding look was like a campfire, held back only by a circle of rocks but wishing it could jump out and consume him. "Wouldn't you like to know?"

She kicked her horse faster, and Garrick stayed back.

Finally, Fay drew her horse to a stop, and Garrick did

the same. She dropped her reins and pressed the tips of her fingers into her eyebrows.

"I'm lost." Fay spoke the words with a mix of irritation and defeat.

Garrick pulled the map out. "Can you show me—"

"I can't. I've only ever been out here while trailing Hugh. Never alone. I guess I didn't pay as much attention as I thought I did."

Garrick opened the map and looked around them, trying to discern where they were. There was a large outcropping to his left. "If we climb to the top of that, we'll have a view of the valley. Maybe you'll recognize something."

Fay sighed, a low sound that seemed to stretch out to the very edge of the forest, and nudged her horse in the direction Garrick had suggested. He trailed her, unable to look away from the defeat of her drooping shoulders.

She let her horse have its head, and too soon she pulled to a stop and pointed. "Tracks."

Garrick pulled up at her side and saw several hoof prints in the snow. He whipped his head around, looking to spot whoever had made these tracks. The hooves were shoed, so it wasn't wild horses. These mounts had riders. "Too many to be Hugh."

Fay stared harder. "The coach had a team of four. Could be he has the horses and not the coach."

Garrick didn't want to argue, not when they'd finally found neutral ground. "Either way, we should tether our mounts and go on foot to see where they lead. There's no way to know if friend or foe made those tracks." He turned his horse around, leading it away from the tracks and to a large pine tree. The forest floor beneath its branches was sparsely dusted with snow. The limbs above would provide coverage for their horses while he and Fay investigated the tracks on foot.

By the crunch of fresh snow, he knew Fay had followed. When he reached the tree, he slid off Dusty and wrapped her reins around a low branch. He pulled his rifle from its scabbard and tucked it under his arm. Fay reined to a stop beside him.

Opening the shotgun, he slid a shell into each barrel. He'd barely closed the chamber when Fay fell against him and knocked the firearm from his grip. With quick hands, he caught her under her arms and hauled her back up, but when he tried to remove his hands, she slipped deeper into him.

He looked down the front of her to find her boot stuck in the stirrup. At the commotion, her horse took two steps forward and, tangled, they stumbled along with it. He held Fay up with one hand and with the other loosened her foot from the stirrup. Once her feet were both on the ground, she moved away from him like he was a rattler.

He put his hands up, palms out. "I promise I didn't do anything to your boot." He pointed down. "They look too big anyhow. Can you even walk?"

She turned and opened her saddlebag, but he could see the flush on her cheeks. "My own clothing ain't fit for tracking." She lowered her voice as though she was no longer talking to him. "I never went out in the winter. Ma said it was inappropriate."

"She's right. You could have twisted an ankle. Or what if your horse got spooked just now? Took off with you attached? Your family would be down two children."

"Four." She turned to him, stuffing bullets into her pocket. "Don't forget Eloise and Otto."

Garrick scoffed and led the way back to the tracks.

With quick feet, Fay matched his stride. He reached the tracks and veered right to follow their direction. "You can hardly blame me for Otto. He's probably better off with Eloise, wherever she is, anyhow. What was he going to do here? Work for your family's welfare his entire life?"

Fay flinched and Garrick wanted to regret his words. Only he didn't. It wasn't right or fair, the way the Morrises sacrificed for their family. It wasn't right how Eloise had sold herself and everyone around her was perfectly content to let her.

"Eloise needed someone on her side," he said.

Fay jogged ahead and turned to face Garrick. "Do you think you're some kind of savior? My family is separated because of you." Her words held venom, laced with a sliver of truth.

"Families separate!" Garrick took a calming breath and stepped around her. With a lowered voice, he continued. "It's natural for people to marry and move away from their parents."

"Not mine."

Garrick gave a hard laugh. "That's precisely the problem."

Before she could say any more, he stopped. The tracks continued around the mountain, but he and Fay's original intent had been to climb this outcropping. "We should go up. If those are Hugh's tracks, we might spot him anyhow."

Fay's mouth pinched into a hard line. He could almost hear the battle within—fight with him or find her brother?

5

*A*nger choked her into silence. The man didn't regret a single thing. He actually had the gall to think she should feel grateful to him. At least he had the sense not to say it outright, but she could see it in the hard set of his jaw and the way his words danced around—but never actually touched on—an apology.

He wanted forgiveness, but he felt no remorse.

She stepped around him, leading the way up the slope that led to the outcrop. She refused to speak to him, but he was right. Going up to the outcrop was the most sensible course of action. She would see where they were within the forest and possibly even see where the tracks led.

She started to climb, but couldn't find purchase with the slick sole of her boots. Her too-short feet meant only the toe of the shoe gripped on the smaller steps, and the bit of shoe that had no foot inside bent far too easily, causing her to slip and hit her knees on the snowy rocks. Climbing wouldn't be easy with these boots.

Garrick wasn't doing much better. She could hear him

scrambling his way up too, though certainly with less difficulty than her. Her pa's words rang in her head—*a man gets one mistake in the woods, but a woman gets none.*

She'd already made a mistake, for they should have found Pete's cabin by now. She prayed this outcrop would tell her where they were, tell her how to find Hugh.

As she climbed her way up, her thoughts turned to her brother. Had he made a mistake too? He was the best of them. He set up traps all winter long, his usual trap line traversing at least this deep into the woods. If he wasn't at Pete's then he was dead somewhere, buried in snow or possibly unburied by the wildlife that saw him as a mere meal. Fay's stomach roiled and she slowed, covering her mouth with the back of her hand until the sick feeling passed.

Hugh wasn't dead. He was with Pete.

Perhaps he was hurt. That might explain his delay. Hurt, but alive, especially if he was with Pete. Pete had lived in these woods for most of his life. Though Fay had only been to his cabin a handful of times, and not at all recently, she'd heard her brothers talk about him enough to know that Pete knew cures and remedies. If Hugh was with Pete, Hugh was alive. She would feel it if he were dead. Wouldn't she feel it?

Garrick's voice rose from behind her, tight and angry. "If Eloise and Aaron hadn't left, they'd have been found out eventually."

Fay clenched her jaw. Why couldn't he just leave it well enough alone?

He continued. "What life was there for them here? A life of hiding? Would you all have pretended she wasn't married? What about when a baby came? Say she was a tainted woman? Say she'd been attacked? And the second baby?" He gave a hard laugh. "They're better gone than they ever would have been here."

He'd obviously thought about this as he hiked. How often had he thought of Eloise and Aaron? He mentioned that he *had* loved Eloise, but had he never *stopped* loving her sister? It was a pitiable thought and rather than argue, Fay crawled up a large boulder and stopped, looking down at Garrick as he did the same.

Garrick wasn't done though. "You want to hate me? Fine. Blame everything on me. Heck, pretend I gave Lachlan malaria too. Might as well add that I make his medicine too expensive for him to accept. But don't say I didn't try to do right by Eloise. I gave her an out, which none of *you* were doing. You all fawned over Aaron and practically offered her up as bait on a trapline. Don't hate me for trying to cut the tether."

He reached the top and rose to stand next to her, too close on this rock. Though large to climb onto, the open, level surface was tight, and their boots nearly brushed toes.

Fay spun and crawled up the next boulder. They were close to the top now. Almost all the foliage had disappeared, replaced by wide swaths of speckled granite.

Had they offered Eloise up? Back then, Fay would have gladly taken her sister's place. She even recalled having been a bit jealous. But she had been too young to know what marriage really meant.

These days, the girls her age all had beaus. One even got married last summer. If everything had happened three years later, would Fay have been the one to marry Aaron? Would she have wanted to? It no longer sounded like some grand adventure, marrying a handsome outlaw and living in hiding. It sounded lonely, and Fay had had enough of loneliness.

But Eloise did sound truly happy in her letters. She and Aaron had two baby boys, and Otto was there, as well as Aaron's younger brother. They'd created their own life, far from the needs of their family here. Perhaps Garrick was right. Otto was better off gone, but what about the rest of them? Fay couldn't leave, not unless she married a rich man willing to care for her family's financial needs. And how would Pa feel about that?

Hugh couldn't go, or else when Lachlan got one of his spells, who would tend the farm, small as it was these days? They just needed to tell Lachlan about the money. Let him sort out his own feelings about Eloise marrying Aaron for Lachlan's sake. Make him quit trying to ration it, make him take it regularly so he wouldn't have *any* spells. So he could live a normal life. But if he was off living, who stayed home to care for their parents? Hugh?

Eloise had the right of it. Marry a man with money and see the family is cared for. Only Fay wouldn't just marry the first man to fall into her life. She would choose well—someone who had enough to carry them through any illness or any storm. Her father would have to swallow his pride, not that he had overmuch to begin with.

Fay would try for a husband in earnest once the holidays were over and Willem's wealthy ranch guests started coming again. She would talk with Lydia and possibly even Willem and find out which one was the best man for marriage. If it took too long, she could lower her standards. He didn't have to be young so long as he wasn't too old.

She glanced back at Garrick. His wide hands gripped the rock before he climbed onto it. She rushed to stay at least one spot ahead of him to avoid that closeness. She shouldn't even be out here with him, and it was only for Hugh's sake that she didn't desert him now.

Men like him, young and strong, didn't have fortunes. At least not yet. Whomever she married would have to be rich or young. He wouldn't be both. She'd make her peace with that in time. She'd never been loved by a man of any age. Old or young, love was probably much the same.

Finally, she reached the top. Her hat had fallen back, hanging by its string, so she lifted a flattened palm to shield her eyes from the afternoon sun. She pointed and turned to Garrick, whose chest stretched with a deep intake of breath. "There. That's Pete's cabin."

He twisted and pointed in the other direction. "Then whose fire is that?"

Fay followed the point of his arm. On the other side of the outcrop, another trail of smoke lifted from the trees. Her heart soared to see the wispy gray line snaking its way from the tip of the pines. She'd been right that those tracks must have been Hugh leading the horses. Who knew where the coach was? It didn't matter now anyway. She almost laughed as her heart lifted with relief. "It must be Hugh."

She drew a deep breath and cupped her hands on either side of her mouth to shout his name. Before she was able to release the call, thick arms wound around her and squeezed the breath back out.

"Shh!" His mouth pressed against her head, and his hot breath ruffled her hair. "We don't know if it's Hugh. You can't go shouting at any sign of life."

She tried to hit his ribs with her elbows, but he stood too close for her to gain any momentum. "It could be him." She pushed at his arms, demanding to be freed.

Garrick released her, and both frustration and relief coursed through her to find his footing remained sure. He'd even kept the rifle in his hand, a feat that would have been impossible for her. The top of this rock was the last place she wanted to tussle with any man.

He set the butt of his rifle on the ground and twisted it as he stared at the mystery fire. "We'll go check it out. We know the way to Pete's if it's not Hugh."

He led the way this time, and each rock Fay stumbled on tumbled down for Garrick to contend with. Perhaps on the way up he'd been more sure-footed than she thought, only tripping on whatever she set loose.

Going down was harder anyhow, because both large and small rocks peppered the ground, waiting to slide further with every heavy footstep. Handling this hike in a dress would have meant using at least one of her hands to hold up her skirts, and she needed all the balance she could get. Thank the heavens she wore Otto's pants.

Just as she finished this thought, the rock below her gave way. She groped for something to cling to, to stop her descent. She caught nothing but air and found herself skating down the hill. She slammed into Garrick's back, and the collision sent him sliding down too.

Fay's feet went out from under her, and she fell roughly to her bottom, still sliding with the cascade of rocks and snow and bodies. It wasn't until Garrick collided with a tree trunk and she had collided against the bottom half of his legs that they stopped. She touched her cheek, unsure what had hit her face. Garrick's knee or her own fist?

He held out a gloved hand and hauled her to her feet, brushing at her back.

She frowned at a cut on his ear. "You're bleeding."

He raised his hand and touched the wound, his glove coming away bloody.

"Let me see." She reached out, but he pushed her hand away.

He wiped his glove on his pants. "I've had worse."

Fay blinked as he turned and continued down. Not blaming her, yet not forgiving her either.

Near the bottom, they had one last large rock to make it over. Rather than brave the foliage surrounding it, Garrick walked over the top and leaped down so only the top of his head showed over the boulder.

Fay walked to the edge of the boulder. Garrick stood below, his arms outstretched as though he expected her to leap into his arms like some princess being rescued from a tower. She wanted to refuse the offer, but the sun hung low in the sky and would be setting in a few hours. They had no time for pride. She sat down on the top, the snow-covered boulder's icy temperature soaking through her clothes as she scooted herself to the edge. Bracing her hands on his shoulders, she jumped. His hands caught her waist, and he set her down gently, like an autumn leaf falling from a tree.

She blinked at him, positive that, despite the tumble she'd just caused a few minutes ago, she'd never felt so graceful in all her life. He turned away, and she tried to shake off the feeling. This was no time to contemplate feeling like a lady. But she couldn't stop herself from wondering: was this what all the girls felt when they had a beau? Cared for, watched over?

They'd barely made it a hundred yards into the forest at the base of the outcropping when a guffaw sounded through the trees, far closer than Fay felt comfortable with. Garrick ducked down, one knee flat on the snowy earth and both hands pressed to the ground. He froze as stiff as the Grahams' lake. Fay lifted onto her toes, stretching her neck to see through the foliage to whoever made the harsh laugh.

A gargled sound came from below, and she glanced at Garrick in time to see him reach for her boot. His hand swallowed it as his fingers curled around the empty toe box and tugged. Her too large boot cut easily through the powdery snow, like the blade on a sled, and Fay crashed to the ground with an "oof." Garrick pulled her close, pressing a gloved hand to her mouth and silencing her protest.

"That's not Hugh," he mouthed, releasing his hold.

Fay's gaze flicked behind him, then back to meet his eyes. She'd know Hugh's laugh anywhere, and that wasn't him. She shook her head.

The voice came again, closer this time. "Probably halfway to Billings by now. We'll never find him there."

Garrick rose with the quiet stealth of a bobcat and lifted Fay under her arms. He hauled her like a sack of flour, and her feet had barely found traction in the powdery snow when he shoved her, back first, into a tangle of branches. Each bare twig clawed at her hair and clothes as she crashed through the bush until her body made contact with the ground. Along with the jarring impact, her hat tumbled off and her braid fell onto her shoulder with a flop, but Garrick wasn't done. He kept pushing her, his body pressing against hers as though he thought two could fit in this briar patch.

The knowledge that there were strangers out there and she didn't know where they were had her scrabbling deeper into the prickly foliage. She dug her heels into the pine needle strewn forest floor as she scooted her way backward. Eventually she made it through the mess of branches and into a small opening created by a boulder and a large conifer tree. She continued backward until her spine rested against the tree's trunk. Around her, its boughs hung low with the weight of snow, undisturbed by Fay since she'd come through the other side, and offering her some semblance of cover.

Before she had time to really appreciate her position, Garrick pushed through too, catching his boot on a lower branch of the bush and stumbling to the ground. Fay grabbed his jacket, pulling him in with her. He was practically on top of her when a voice came again. Still closer. Fay froze, her arms draped over his shoulders and her fists full of his jacket.

"We should go to Billings to sell this before someone reports it missing."

Garrick stilled, and Fay couldn't protest for propriety's sake, even though he lay on his side with his hips between her legs and his head against her shoulder. His rifle, gripped in one hand, lay along the length of his leg. On the ground of their entry point lay Fay's sad-looking hat, rolled in the snow and pine needles, crushed first by herself and then by Garrick.

Though the strangers were no longer speaking, Fay could hear the faint squeak of boots in fresh snow. Her breathing turned shallow, and it had nothing to do with the weight of Garrick's torso heavy on her ribs.

Garrick didn't move, not even to pull his legs up, as they listened to the steps of at least one man and his companion. When the sounds grew fainter, then disappeared entirely, Fay uncurled her aching knuckles and released her grip on his jacket. Garrick lifted himself onto his elbow but didn't move further for another several minutes.

Fay sat still, listening, wishing she could twitch her ears like a white-tailed doe.

Finally, Garrick nodded and lifted off her. He pulled the rifle up and checked the barrel and stock.

"Whatever they taught you in the army, you sure can hold onto a gun." Fay whispered the words, but a tremble still came through.

Garrick glanced at her, the whites of his eyes bright in the shadowy dark of their cover. "I think they're gone, but we ought to stay for a bit, hope they don't stumble upon our tracks or our horses."

Fay gulped. She'd not thought beyond their immediate danger.

He set the gun across his lap. "Think we can make it to Pete's before nightfall?"

"Depends on how long we stay here." She glanced around, realizing they could have accidentally tucked themselves away into the den of some creature. Luckily, most of the larger and sharp-toothed animals were asleep for the winter by now.

Garrick kept his back to her, and she could picture his face, serious and scanning the forest beyond their cover. Her brothers had always been protective of her, but it had always felt like a hindrance. They protected her by telling her she couldn't go with them or insisting she keep back so she didn't get hurt.

She didn't mind Garrick's protective posture though, his arms taut as they held the gun. Was this what it would be like to be protected by a beau, an equal, rather than a bossy older brother?

She scanned the forest, trying to see what made him

so tense. "They spoke of selling something in Billings. Do you think…"

"Bandits." Garrick nodded, plucking her hat from the ground and brushing it off. As he tried to reshape it, he added, "There's all sorts out here. The further west you go, the fewer people you encounter, but the ones you do are increasingly lawless."

Fay swallowed at how naive she'd been to set off on her own. All her life, she'd had a companion, either in her brothers or Mama and Eloise. Those months after Eloise left had been so lonely, and yet she'd truly never been alone. She'd always had her remaining family around. In her mind, she'd ridden through this forest enough times to be able to do it herself. She'd hardly paused to consider what being a lone rider could have entailed.

"We should go soon." Garrick passed Fay her hat. "If they do cross our tracks, they'll lead them right to us. May as well face them standing."

Fay set the sorry excuse for millinery on her head, tucking her hair inside the band as they crawled out from their hiding place.

Climbing out was far easier than the roundabout way they'd gone in. Fay brushed snow from her clothes and shivered as a gust of icy wind cut through the trees. The climb had soaked her front, and now sliding along the ground had soaked her backside.

One look at Garrick's legs told her he was in the same predicament. She could see the swell of muscles above his knees and the sinewy way they wrapped upward toward his backside.

Garrick turned, and Fay snapped her eyes to his face, chewing her lip as she tried to discern whether he'd seen where she'd been looking. This was no time to appreciate the shape of a man. Wet clothes were anything but trivial. If they didn't find Pete's house soon, they might find themselves in far more trouble than being found by bandits. Wet clothes in the winter could spell the death of them both.

Fay kept her eyes at an appropriate level as she followed Garrick to the base of the outcrop. Then they walked around the bottom. He kept the rifle in both hands, ready to shoot at any moment, and he kept glancing back at Fay. Was he scanning the forest, or making sure she still followed behind him?

His movements put her on edge, and by the time they found their horses, Fay wanted to dig her heels in and ride hard for Pete's. Their horses nickered in greeting, and Garrick shushed his mount. Fay did the same, glancing around the forest. With the threat of lawless strangers near, not finding Hugh no longer felt like the worst prospect.

Garrick waited while Fay climbed onto her horse. Then he climbed on his own and nodded in the direction of Pete's cabin. "Think you can find it?"

Fay nodded. "We'll move quickly."

She kicked Lady's flank and they were off.

6

*G*arrick watched her as they rode. She turned her head slightly, just enough to let him know she felt his gaze on her back, and she didn't want it, especially if her sodden pants revealed as much as his. *Look elsewhere, Garrick Hampton.*

Apparently, he took her glance as an invitation for conversation. "Do you share Eloise's commitment to never marrying?"

Eloise. It was always Eloise. He wasn't the only man enamored with her sister. She wondered vaguely if Eloise still collected admirers, even out in Oregon with a husband and a baby on each hip.

"You still love her," she said, the tone of her voice an accusation.

Garrick's horse caught up, and he rode at her side. Too bad they were out of the thick woods, where they would have been forced to ride single file like school children. She recognized a mountain peak and knew they were close to Pete's and on the right path.

"I don't love her."

Fay barked a laugh, unsure why it sounded so harsh. He had the right of it; Eloise *was* better off away from here. She'd given her sacrifice for the family and made it out from the soft cage of their home. Fay wasn't so naive to truly think her home a prison. She'd seen people being carted down lanes in walled coaches with only bars for windows. Seen others hanging from trees whose only crime was the color of their skin.

No, her home was no prison. Merely an island. One with no natural resources, which meant that anytime she left their island she had to return, lest the family starve in her absence.

"Have you got a beau?" Garrick's voice sounded deeper than usual, drawing her back into the bright valley, beautiful and wide. The glistening snow winked sunlight at them with each step.

Fay might have laughed if any man except Garrick had asked that question. It sounded too much like the lines men gave to the girls in town to check if they were spoken for. Heaven knew Garrick wasn't hiding a flame for a girl like her. She considered her answer, trying for something light and witty, but the truth hurt too badly.

"No," was all she could manage.

Garrick sniffed, and Fay risked a look to see if he smiled. He didn't. He sat tall in the saddle. Taller than she remembered. And his neck had thickened so he no longer looked like a wooden doll with a too-large head. Now he was perfectly proportioned and broad everywhere. If they had met at that dance for the first time, everything might be different. Fay might be enamored with him. Smitten even.

"You're not keen on marrying?" His gaze slid sideways.

Fay straightened, focusing once more on the bright sky. "I'm keen enough."

She should have said more, said she didn't *want* any of the men in town. They were too rough, too dumb, too impressed by girls as vapid as Ginny Price. But exhaustion consumed her, and what did it matter what Garrick thought? He was a soldier and would be gone in a minute, down to his friend in Texas, or so the Aster Ridge rumor mill said. Once Christmas had come and gone, she probably wouldn't see him for another three years. Maybe never, if she married and left before he came back.

Garrick leaned forward in his saddle until Fay met his inquiring gaze. He squinted one of his eyes smaller than the other as he watched her. "There's some bit you're not saying."

Fay laughed, his expression too much and his mind keener than she remembered. "You lookin' to be hired as sheriff?"

Garrick smirked but removed his intimidating stare. "I learned to read people while I was gone."

"Cards?" Ma would have been scandalized, or maybe it was exactly what her low opinion would expect from Garrick.

Garrick smiled. "A little. Boxing mostly."

Fay's breath caught in her throat. Her body cringed at the thought of his violence. He must have been an intimidating opponent, large as he was. "You need to read folks before you take a swing at them?"

Garrick's gaze pinned her again, and this new knowledge lent him a dangerous edge. Her legs tightened on Lady's sides, and the horse took the cue to move a bit faster. "The reading is for the gambling aspect, not the fighting part."

Ah, so he fought for money. "Did you like fighting?"

Garrick shifted in the saddle. They'd been riding for a short time. No reason he should be feeling discomfort unless the subject matter bothered him. Fay tucked her lips between her teeth so the smile didn't give her away.

Garrick stilled. "It was something to do. Made me a fair bit of money too."

Fay let out a breath, the cloudy puff of air larger from being held so deep in her chest. "You did it for the money."

Garrick shrugged. "Sometimes."

"Did you like it or not?"

"I was good at it."

Strangely, Fay understood his logic. He was still frightening. She could imagine those long arms swinging at another person, pummeling him the way she'd seen boys at school do to one another. But liking something because he was good at it... Fay felt the truth of it.

She had never been good at the household things. Eloise had resented her for it, Fay knew, but Fay wasn't good at any of it.

She was good at school though, at learning. All of it—mathematics, reading, writing. She even excelled at debate, which wasn't exactly something her teachers taught her, but rather something she'd learned from Ginny. But Fay still wasn't sure if she'd ever really won when it came to that girl, whose retractable claws were sharper than her teeth.

"If a man," Garrick said, once again breaking into her reverie, "with money came along, would you consider marriage?"

Fay glanced at him, then down at her horse's mane. "If the right man came along, I wouldn't hesitate." She'd answered vague enough. Good. Garrick didn't have to know *right* meant *rich*.

Garrick guffawed, scaring a large crow from a tree. "You Morris women and your money. What about love?"

The comment sliced Fay's pride. "What about love? Are you in love?"

Garrick's face darkened. "I'm not in love, but I intend to be when I marry."

Fay scoffed. As sure as the sun rose, this man still loved her sister. She'd seen it time and time again. Men, boys really, asking Fay questions, trying to learn things about Eloise that would make her sister fall into their arms. Pathetic.

Once Eloise had gone, they'd turned their attention to Fay, but it hadn't taken long for them to realize Fay couldn't compare. They'd lost interest and moved along to some other woman to bestow their affection.

"You think I still love her."

Fay met his furious gaze. "Right as rain. You've hardly stopped talking about her since you got here."

Garrick opened his mouth and a cloud of hot air spread before him. He closed his mouth and faced forward once again, with something like confusion knitting his brows.

Fay allowed a wide smile to spread across her face. This was the type of debate she liked—winning, leaving her foe in silen—

"If I have been talking about her, it's because here, you, this whole state reminds me of her. It's just...odd for her to be gone."

Fay's heart sank, then rose again, beating with rage. "You think it's 'odd' to be without her. What about me? She was *everything* to me. When she left, I had nothing.

No sister, no friends. I needed her, and I couldn't even write to her because we didn't know where they'd gone or whether someone was monitoring our mail."

"No friends?"

Fay let out a frustrated growl. Was that even important? It wasn't the point of her tirade.

"If you rail at everyone the way you keep doing to me, I can't say I blame them." Garrick faced forward again, taking his eyes from her for possibly the first time since they'd left their hideout.

Fay wouldn't listen to any more. She kicked her horse faster. She heard Dusty's hooves behind her and urged her horse into a run. A stupid thing in this wide valley. Lady could catch her hoof in a hole, but tears threatened to spill, and only the wind in her face kept them inside.

As she rode, she saw a bit of smoke rising from the treetops. Pete's place.

She slowed her horse and wiped at her eyes. It didn't matter if Garrick thought her just as awful a person as the rest of the people in Dragonfly Creek. None of it mattered; their opinions weren't going to seal her destiny.

Garrick caught up and pointed to the smoke. "That the place?"

Fay nodded.

"Good tracking."

Fay lowered her brows. "I didn't track the place." She rolled her eyes to the sky at his ignorance. The fact that Garrick had been included on this rescue mission at all would have been comical if it hadn't been her brother's life on the line. Garrick knew nothing about living out here.

Yet the way he'd protected her earlier still had her mind buzzing with fanciful imaginations. Of what it would be like for a man to swear before God to honor and protect her his whole life. Not Garrick, of course, but a man like him. What would it be like for him to hold her in his arms, not because her boot was caught, but because he wanted the feel of her entangled in him.

A bark sounded, and Fay smiled. Pete's dog, Bee, would soon greet them with a wagging tail and a few licks to the face. She pushed away her foolish dreams for the practical reality. Whoever she married would be a far cry from Garrick, and good thing, too.

A crack split the air, causing both Garrick and Fay's horses to rear back and whinny. Fay held Lady in place with every muscle in her legs. She looked around for whoever had fired the gun.

"Who's there?" a disembodied voice called.

Fay's heart stuck in her throat as she tried to settle Lady. She removed her hat, letting it rest on the pommel of her saddle and revealing her auburn hair. She hitched her voice loud enough so Pete could hear it from wherever he stood. "It's Fay. I'm lookin' for Hugh. Gone missing three days ago."

"You've got company," Pete called, still not showing himself to them. *Paranoid Pete.* She'd heard folks in town say he belonged in the asylum down south. Fay had always assumed they just didn't know him, but perhaps she didn't know him as well as she thought.

"My companion, Garrick Hampton."

"Tell him to get his hands off his pistol and put 'em in the air."

Fay turned to Garrick.

He held her gaze as though trying to communicate something with just his eyes. Still he held tight to the handle of his pistol.

Pete's voice came again. "He's in my sights. I'll shoot him in five seconds if his hands aren't touchin' the trees. Five... four..."

Fay's eyes widened as she pleaded, "Put your hands in the air. This ain't a battle. We're on this man's land. He has every right to shoot us dead."

Garrick slowly raised his hands. "I thought you knew this man." His whisper sounded harsh.

Fay let out a ragged breath. For the first time, she wondered if Pete would even recognize her. "I know him."

"Forgive me if your word is a bit questionable at the moment."

Fay turned away, fuming. No, Garrick was most definitely not the type of man she would ever marry. Disagreeable and selfish. Thick arms and a handsome face wouldn't do anything for her family, and it did nothing for her now.

When he called out again, Pete's voice had lost some of its anxious tone. "Leave your horses there."

Garrick and Fay stared at one another, then Garrick dismounted. Fay swung her right leg by instinct without thinking of her too large boots and her left one's tendency to stick in the stirrup upon dismount. She hovered for a split second, twisting her left boot and trying to sense whether it was going to give her trouble once her right foot hit on the ground.

Garrick's warm hands found her waist through her baggy men's shirt, and he gripped her tight, lifting her weight off the stirrup so she was able to work her boot free. Once her feet touched the snow-covered ground, he braced his hands on each of their horses' saddles and twisted so he stood like a wall between her and the forest where Pete hid.

Fay glared at him and tried to duck under his arm. He caught her and pulled her to him, close enough that her face brushed against the lapel of his coat. "We aren't safe here. Let's just ask if he's seen Hugh and turn our horses around." His mouth hovered so close to her hair, every word sending a wave of heat across her scalp.

Another call from Pete made her flinch. "He got a gun on you? Is that why he's holding you so close?"

Fay almost laughed. She'd noticed how close they were, and she could never claim he held her against her will. That would have to mean she didn't want him near, didn't want to grab his jacket and haul him closer, didn't hope to feel the heat of his breath along her skin. Her gaze snagged on a thin red line that ran from his neck under his ear and onto his cheek. A mark from their tussle with their hiding spot. She curled her fingers, ensuring she didn't reach up and touch it.

Garrick stepped back, as though four inches could erase what Pete had witnessed. His eyes searched hers, and she could almost hear him questioning how much she trusted Pete.

Instead of answering Garrick, Fay hitched her voice higher and called to the trees. "Pete, my brother is missin'. Stop the shenanigans and let us by."

"Not until I'm sure you know this man. I've got a bead on him. Just say the word and I'll fire a shot."

Garrick's eyes bulged, and he raised his hands high.

"He's my husband. That's why he's standing so close." The moment the words were out, Fay wanted to claw them back in again. This was what she got for letting her mind run away from her. For letting herself imagine what it would be like to marry someone like Garrick, someone as broad as a brick wall standing between her and danger.

Pete's reply came through the trees. "Tether your horses there. Tell your man to leave that rifle in its scabbard and keep his pistol holstered so long as he's on my property."

Fay moved to step forward, but Garrick lowered his hands and straightened his shoulders, giving the impression he had no intention of letting her pass. "You stay behind me." He shook his head slowly. "I don't know what you were thinking, bringing us here."

"I was thinking about Hugh." And, she told herself, that was why that impulsive lie had jumped from her lips. It wasn't that she *wanted* a fake marriage to this man. She simply felt desperate to speak with Pete. Fay tried to push past Garrick, but she may as well have been pushing at the trunk of a hundred-foot pine.

Garrick took Lady's reins from Fay, and as he tethered their mounts, Fay removed her gloves and breathed on her chilled fingers. When Garrick returned, he caught her hand and led her toward Pete's voice.

Fay looked at their hands to confirm what her numb fingers hadn't been able to identify. Garrick's hands were bare too. His fingers were rosy, and before she'd thought much about it, she'd curled her hand into his warm palm. It didn't seem fair that he was so warm, as though his body maintained a temperature higher than the rest of the human race. He tightened his hold on her, sharing more of his warmth, and Fay couldn't help but try to gauge whether the gesture was meant as a comfort or a threat.

He was right that she'd been hasty in her decision to come. She didn't know Pete as well as she'd let on. What if Hugh hadn't made it here? What if he'd come across those men and they'd done unspeakable things? What if Pete had encountered them too, and that was why Pete was so on edge just now? Or what if Pete had lost part of his humanity, alone in these woods, and she and Garrick weren't safe with him? She'd never known Pete like Lachlan and Hugh had. They'd known him before he'd lost his family. Fay had been a little girl when Pete had left for these woods.

Fay wrapped her other hand around Garrick's and squeezed. She whispered, "We'll be in and out real quick..." Fay couldn't finish her thought out loud. She'd assumed Pete would accept a stranger on her word and presence alone. She wasn't so sure now, and she didn't want to take any chances.

7

———

*G*arrick held tight to Fay's hand, trying to discern if the squeeze she gave him was apprehension or irritation at his protective impulse. *Protective* was a new emotion. For so long, he'd been driven by self-preservation. First in his father's home, then again in the war. Besides Eloise, the last time he'd felt protective over a woman, it had been for Della, and when she'd needed him, he'd been too young and helpless to be of any use. He wasn't young now and he'd made a vow to himself: Never again would a woman be harmed on his watch.

As they made their way through the woods and into a clearing, a cabin came into view. A rough trapper stood at the top of the stairs leading to his porch. His beard looked less like hair and more like the icicles hanging off his roof. But Garrick's gaze didn't linger on the man's face, because next he spotted the rifle in Pete's hands. Garrick's hands twitched, empty as they were.

Pete leaned forward, studying them through eyes hidden between the shade of his hat and the whiskers on his face. "Fay Morris, you say?"

Fay drew a breath, but Garrick squeezed her hand and leaned forward. "Hampton now. I'm her husband, Garrick." Repeating her lie twisted his stomach, but Garrick had never before been opposed to a white lie, and this one most certainly was harmless.

Though he couldn't see Pete's eyes, Garrick could feel the shift in the man's gaze. "You've a bit of your ma in your face." He picked at his teeth. "You two are lookin' for Hugh and his lady?"

Fay shot forward. "Yes!"

Garrick caught her arm and pulled her tight to his side. She shot him a look, but he kept his eyes on the danger ahead of them. "You've seen them?"

"Left on horseback this mornin'."

Fay let out a strangled sob. "And they're both well?" She tightened her grip on his fingers, and with her other hand she caught his wrist.

Pete gave a stiff nod. "Well 'nough. Took my horse with 'em. Their own is dead yonder. Shot." He jerked his chin at the forest to his right.

Garrick took a step backward, closer to Fay. "Thanks, mister. We'll be on our way then."

"May as well sleep the night." Pete's voice sounded softer now, far less frightening than when he was hollering through the woods.

Garrick eyed the darkening sky and glanced back at Fay, thinking of the men they'd come across. It was lucky they hadn't been found. Perhaps the men would have just shared a fire and gone their own way. But it wasn't a chance he was keen on taking, not with Fay. "There are at least two bandits in the forest."

He spoke to Fay, but it was Pete who replied with a cough and a spit of tobacco juice. "There's more'n two vagabonds out there. Your brother made a few enemies. Best to travel in the daylight." He turned and went inside, leaving the door open.

"Enemies?" Fay whispered up at Garrick, clutching at his wrist with her other hand.

Garrick's mind screamed at him to get this girl on a horse and hightail it out of there. If it weren't for the strangers in the woods, he might do just that. "You trust him enough to sleep here?"

"I don't know what other choice we have."

Garrick tried not to growl. It was looking as though Fay knew little to nothing about this man. But vagabonds were more a threat than Pete. The rough kind who traveled the roads were godless men who had done unspeakable things. "Better the devil you know than the devil you don't," Garrick murmured, leading Fay into the cabin.

Once inside, the warmth hit them and within minutes. Garrick's cheeks pricked to life, the cold turning into needles before surrendering to the cabin's heat. Fay spread her damp gloves on the floor near Pete's stove. Her fingers were so dainty compared to the rough, too large gloves. He glanced at her boots. Also too large and a hindrance to riding too, but better than the women's boots he'd removed from her feet a few nights ago. Was it only two days ago that she'd searched all over the county for her brother?

Pete stood at a table, mixing something in a bowl. "Hugh and the lady were here while I was in town on a supply run. Good thing too. They ate more than their share of my stores."

Fay breathed on her fingers, the tips pink except for her nails which were bluish white. Her fingers must hurt every bit as bad as his cheeks. He longed to go to her, to catch her hands in his own and rub warmth back into them. He balled his fists at his side and looked to Pete. "You said Hugh made enemies?"

Pete set the bowl down on the tabletop. "He was driving the coach alone, the fool. The trash came upon him. Hugh said there were three, and one died on account of Hugh shootin' him."

"He shot a man?" Fay's voice grew to a squawk as she moved closer to Pete.

Garrick came behind her and placed his hands on her shoulders, both for show and for comfort. He didn't know her well, but he'd never heard her voice reach that pitch. Her family really was everything to her. She leaned back slightly into Garrick's hands. That was the most acceptance he would get from this girl. "You think they're still after them?"

Pete barked a hard laugh. "I'm surprised he even hit one. Boy can't shoot worth beans. He should stick to trapping."

Fay drew a shaky breath. "Hugh's out there now, with those men?"

"Well, not *with* them. But that's why I nearly shot you two. Thought they might still be sniffing around the place." His gaze ran the length of Fay's body.

Garrick hooked his arm around the front of her shoulders, pulling her back up against his chest. She gripped his forearm like an anchor in the storm that was fear for her brother.

"You don't exactly look like a *girl* in that getup." Pete shook his head and muttered to himself. "Folks are getting odd these days."

Garrick bit his cheek to stop a smile. He leaned down and whispered into Fay's ear. "He's alive. Those men didn't say anything about killing a man, or even tracking him down. They're headed to Billings to sell whatever they stole. Hugh's headed home. We'll see him again soon."

Fay nodded, turning back to the fire. She swayed on her feet, and Garrick took the chair from the table where Pete was working and set it near the stove. Fay gave him a wobbly smile and sat down. "I don't know why I'm so weepy. He's safe." She laughed, but it was the shaky kind that did more to release anxiety than to convince anyone.

Garrick knelt at her feet and removed her boots, smiling at the memory of the last time he'd done this. When he slipped the battered leather off, he was surprised to find rags tied around her stockinged feet, making them bulkier, if not larger. He laughed and whispered, "How long did it take to get these on this morning?"

Fay colored and tucked her feet under the chair. She leaned close and spoke softly so Pete wouldn't hear. "I slept in them."

The clomp of boots preceded Pete's arrival at the stove. "Quit whispering." He passed the bowl to Fay. "A bit of batter for some cakes."

Fay took the bowl and looked at the lumpy mess. "Thank you, Pete."

He returned with a skillet and, without a word, set it on the flat top of the stove.

Garrick could almost read the man's mind. He lived alone, and over the past few days he'd had four guests eating from his coffers. He wasn't about to serve them a meal without making them work for it.

"I have a bit of money. Can we pay you for what we use?" Garrick patted at his vest pocket, realizing he'd left the money in his saddle bag.

Pete glared at Garrick. "I ain't a barbarian. I can be hospitable like anyone else in that stuffy old town. Keep your money."

Fay leaned forward so she could see Pete around Garrick's legs. "He's not from Dragonfly Creek."

Pete surveyed Garrick with a look that wasn't admiration, but also wasn't disgust.

Fay continued, "He's from Omaha. I work for his sister, who lives deeper in our valley."

Garrick didn't know why Fay was telling Pete more than he needed to know. Soon he was going to start asking things like when did they marry and what was Fay's favorite food.

Garrick cleared his throat. "I'm sure you mean to be a generous host, but I can imagine it ain't easy getting supplies out here. I'm happy to bring out some things when I accompany Hugh back here with your horse."

Fay clicked her tongue. "Yes. Is there anything else you need from our stuffy town?" She set the bowl onto her chair and walked past Garrick and Pete to get a tin of grease from the cupboard.

Pete's beard twitched. Fay might have almost gotten a smile from the hard old man.

"Your chickens still laying?" he asked.

Fay dabbed a bit of grease on the pan, and it melted and spread with a pop. She poured a bit of batter on top. "Not ours, but I bet I can find some. I hear the Griffiths let their chickens inside in the winter."

Pete shot Fay a look then laughed outright. "Never did like those Griffiths."

"Well"—Fay repeated the process, pouring another cake—"I hope you're not so stuck-up that you won't eat their eggs."

Pete harrumphed and lifted his coat off the hook by the door. "I'll get your mounts settled in the stable."

When the door clicked closed, Garrick turned to Fay. "I didn't see any stables."

"That's because you were too busy eyeing his rifle." She jerked her head toward the window. "It's small, and our horses won't be comfortable, but I think they can handle one night."

Garrick nodded. He didn't much care how comfortable the horses were. He was still twitchy about being in this house with the idea of a few desperate ruffians out in the woods. "Suppose we should get our story straight. About the wedding and all."

Fay waved him off. "Pete isn't going to ask about a romance." She cocked an eyebrow. "He'll likely keep you busy asking about the war."

"That's what I mean. If I mention the war, he'll know I've been gone, and then when would we have been able to get married?"

Fay smirked. "Perhaps we just got married, and this is our honeymoon."

"Fay." He growled. Her utter refusal to take him seriously was grating. *She* was a friend to Pete. It was Garrick's life at risk here.

Fay ladled another cake into the pan. "He isn't going to ask. If he does, we can just tell him it's not true. Now he knows you don't have a gun on me, he's not going to care."

Garrick took the blasted bowl from her hands so she would pay him attention. "We are *not* going to tell him any such thing. We'll keep this ruse up until we leave in the morning. It wasn't *your* heart he was aiming that rifle at."

Fay narrowed her eyes, but the side of her mouth

quirked. "I'm still considering telling him the truth in hopes of just such an outcome."

Garrick glared at her mock-innocent smile.

"Okay." She laughed. "He's not going to ask. It's enough that you're single and from a good family. Folks don't marry for much more than that out here."

He thought of Fay having no suitors. She hadn't said so, but he suspected she had the same inclination as her sister to not marry. Or maybe she only wanted to marry someone with gold like Aaron had. "Some wouldn't marry even for that."

Fay cut him with a look.

He wasn't even sure if he was talking about Eloise or Fay. Sometimes they got mixed up, even in his own mind. But the way Fay had held on to him under that pine tree, the way she'd curled her cold hand into a fist and let him warm her fingers...now *that* was different.

Something more than *good family* and *employer's brother* had sparked between him and Fay. He eyed her, attraction luring him closer. What he felt for her was nothing like the friendship he and Eloise had shared. A match had been struck today, and he wanted to set it under some dry tinder to watch the flames lick up the sides. In the absence of dry wood, he might be content to set himself on fire.

———

FAY WATCHED as Garrick removed his boots and socks, hanging them next to the rags he'd removed from her feet. Watching Garrick tend to her had stirred something inside her chest, and had it not been for Pete's watchful eye, she might have stopped Garrick from touching her altogether.

She could still remember his hands around her waist when he'd helped her from the saddle. The gallant way he'd stepped between her and Pete. Was it the soldier in him, committed to his vow to protect a citizen? But no, he'd wrapped his arm around her shoulders when she thought she might cry out at Hugh being in danger once again. She wouldn't rest easy until she saw her brother at home in their mama's kitchen, heaping his bowl with a large portion of dinner.

Garrick draped a quilt over her shoulders. "Your gloves were made for work, not warmth."

She glanced at them, hanging over the wooden drying rack, the holes facing up. She'd not thought to turn them down so nobody would see the holes. At home, there was nobody to mind the shabbiness of their belongings. Fay pulled the quilt tighter around her shoulders. "Gotta keep my hands soft." She didn't dare meet his eyes.

Most men were oblivious when it came to women. Why did Garrick have to be one of the few men who noticed things? Wet boots, worn out gloves. Even her own brother refused to acknowledge he had feelings for Edna. "Pete said Edna was with him. Her mother must be wearing a hole through her rug worrying."

Garrick flipped the cakes a little too early, but Fay was finally warming up in the cocoon of the quilt and she wasn't going to complain.

He crossed his arms, the spatula sticking into the air. "When we divvied up the routes, we figured if they hadn't made it to the train station, Mrs. Archer might not know Edna was coming at all. Seems she hadn't been planning to go home."

"No," Fay replied. She chewed her lip. One more question that remained unanswered. "I can't wait to be home."

Garrick straightened and clicked his heels once and held a flat hand at the edge of his brow in a military salute. "I'll escort you home on the morrow, ma'am."

Fay chuckled. "More like I'll lead *you* home. I still don't know what they were thinking, sending you out. You were more likely to get lost than to find anyone."

Garrick laughed, squatting to slide some cakes from the spatula onto a plate. "I had a map."

"I suppose you might have found your way back. Or perhaps you would have met with one of Hugh's attackers." Fay's heart gave a defiant thump at the thought of someone harming Garrick. Or perhaps it was merely the thought of Hugh having attackers to his name. "Let's leave at first light."

8

*W*armed and fed, Garrick and Fay spent the rest of the daylight hours earning their shelter. Garrick worked outside with Pete, chopping wood and tanning hides. They'd found a fresh catch on a line near the house, and Fay worked inside with a bit of the skinned rabbit simmering over the stove.

Pete's cupboards were filled with herbs, as many of them medicinal as for cooking. She dared only use the leaves with familiar scents, for fear she would poison them all. She cleaned cabin corners and tightened hinges, wondering how long Hugh and Edna had been here and what they'd done to pass the time during their stay. Pete had told her the shortest possible version of events, and she was dying to bend Edna's ear for the rest.

Had they finally realized their feelings for one another? Had they felt like a little family alone in this tiny cabin? Or had Hugh once more lied himself out of his feelings for Edna? Surely, it had been far more romantic than Fay's adventure was turning out to be. She wore men's clothes, a damp braid trailed down her back, and she was stuck with a man who was as near an enemy to her family as there ever was.

And yet. She straightened from her crouched position where she'd been cleaning behind a tall shelf. And yet he'd protected her. He'd said that was his intent with Eloise too. But it was different. He'd loved Eloise. With Fay, he surely felt only responsibility. Some sort of debt. Perhaps he regretted, after all, his interference in her family's affairs, and was intent upon making up for it.

The front door swung open, and Garrick stepped through, stopping short to see her kneeling on the floor, a dusty rag in her hands. A slow smile split his face. "Have you been dusting with that cloth or with your hair?" He walked over, and she stilled while he pulled a bit of spider webbing out of her braid.

Fay let out a shiver at the thought of that web housing one of the eight legged creatures. "I *thought* I was using only the rag." She couldn't help but check over each shoulder and hope they were clear.

Garrick removed his hat and hung it on Pete's peg. This house was interesting, meant only for one person. He had a single peg for his hat and another for his coat. One chair for the table. One plate and set of utensils. Even the bed was smaller than Fay's bed back home.

Garrick turned back to the room. "Smells mighty nice in here."

Fay laughed. She was no hand at cooking. Della did most of it at Aster Ridge, leaving the cleaning and tending children to Fay. "Rabbit is easy to stew. It's ready if you boys are."

Garrick glanced back at the door. "Pete said he's staying out for a while. He wasn't shy about telling me he was sick of company and wanted a bit of solitude."

Fay bit her lips together, but a laugh escaped anyhow. "Must be all that chatter you can never seem to quit."

"Me? Last I remember, you were the chatter girl."

"Well, that was a long time ago."

Silence fell between them as Fay spooned a large serving of stew into Pete's only bowl and another into a tin cup. She passed the bowl to Garrick.

He took it, his fingers grazing her own. "You've changed since I was here last."

Fay harrumphed. "Of course I have. I was just a little girl then."

"And now you're all grown up." The last word had an upward lilt.

She sensed a teasing note in his voice and narrowed her eyes. "You don't seem the same yourself." She pointed her fork at his tall frame leaning against the wall. "You're not a beanpole any longer."

Garrick laughed into the back of his hand. Swallowing down his food in a large gulp, he said, "It seems Milo has taken over that role. I opted for a more manly appearance."

Fay smiled at the mention of Milo. He was Willem and Lydia's young son, and he was growing so quickly his mama could hardly keep him in clothes that fit.

She glanced at Garrick again. He'd done well. Fay couldn't argue that. Whatever the army had done had changed Garrick's look, but also something else about him, and she couldn't quite identify it. Perhaps it was all part of growing up. Perhaps she looked as different to him as he did to her. People said she resembled Eloise. Was that why he sometimes looked at her for a beat too long? Or why he'd been keen to step between her and Pete?

Would there ever be a day she wasn't compared to

Eloise? She swallowed a bite and watched Garrick. "Do you think I look like Eloise?"

Garrick kept his nose in his bowl, and as the silence stretched, she wanted so badly to know both what he would say and why he hadn't said anything yet.

Fay set her cup down and cut a few slices off the loaf of bread. She'd made a batch of dough, and Pete would be able to put it in the oven tomorrow. This way they'd leave him with more bread than he'd had when they arrived. She couldn't speak to Garrick while looking at him, couldn't bear to watch him think of Eloise while he considered her. She focused on her work instead as she spoke.

"People say I look like her. Different, sure. But obviously sisters. She was well-liked in town. She had something about her. Something people couldn't help but adore. I don't have that quality."

If she had, Ginny Price might have remained her friend, instead of spreading lies and slandering Fay's name. Just because Hugh hadn't made an offer of marriage to Ginny's sister didn't mean Fay thought herself above everyone in town.

If anything, she'd felt below everyone her entire life. Always poor, living so far out of town as to miss any of the festivities and chances to make a best friend. That was, until all her siblings got old enough to go to town without Ma and Pa. But by then the lines had already been drawn where Fay was concerned. She was the sister to the man who had made Ginny's sister cry, and Ginny had made up her mind. The Morrises were the enemy.

For fear or friendship, the other girls had followed Ginny's lead. Even the boys. They dared not express any interest in Fay, for Ginny told everyone the Morrises thought themselves too good for anyone in their town. She used Hugh as the prime example and Eloise as another. Fay wasn't going to marry any of them, and yes, it was true that none of them were rich enough for her. But couldn't they understand? Her mother had married for love, and where had that gotten her?

A worthwhile trade wasn't enough. Neither was a farm and land. Fay needed a man with savings, perhaps an inheritance. Or the ability to ensure she would never have children of her own and could therefore work. She thought of Della and Lydia's children. Even Ivete and Mel's little babies. The thought of never having a child of her own pained her, but not as much as it would pain her to watch her children suffer. To live at the whims and mercy of mortality. No. Love just wasn't enough.

SHE DID LOOK a bit like Eloise. The same color eyes, though Fay's were a different shape with a subtle lift at the corners, and the same wide smile. But Fay's nose was slightly upturned and her jaw and cheek bones were more angular. Perhaps that was what had changed since he'd seen her last. She certainly hadn't yet become the beauty she was now. The thought that no man had gone down on his knee for her shocked him. He realized he'd never gotten his answer regarding her having a beau, interrupted as they'd been by a bullet piercing the air.

"You look like your sister. But you're distinctly you."

A bit of pink color shot through her face, and the sight warmed Garrick to the bone. Before today, he'd have never thought to bring a blush to her cheeks. But after having his hands on her waist, having held her hand as they entered this cabin and pulled a web out of her hair, he wanted nothing more than to make her blush. And laugh. And lean into him the way she'd done when she'd heard about Hugh being attacked.

He would never wish ill upon the man. They'd been friendly once, but just now he could do with this woman showing him a bit of weakness, even if it meant her brother might be in a smidge of danger. He wanted her to lean on him. Just a bit.

Fay sniffed and rolled her shoulder, like she too was thinking of his hands on her. And shaking it off. "Of course I'm not her twin, much as you and many others wish I was. But even if I were her twin in appearance, I'd be a sorry replacement for Eloise. I'm nothing like her."

Garrick's frown deepened with each word. "I'm sure nobody expects you to be a duplicate of Eloise."

"I've seen the way you look at me. You wish I was her."

Garrick coughed, inhaling a bit of soup in the process. "I don't... I never..." He might have compared the sisters a time or two—something that shrouded him in regret now —but he'd never wished Eloise to wipe away Fay entirely.

"It's fine. You're not the first man. They used to talk to me, trying to know her better. Then they talked to me to see if I was like her. Then they stopped talking altogether." Fay gave Garrick a curt nod. "You'll get there too." She glanced down at her bare feet. "I guess you should keep looking. The truth might dawn sooner that way."

Even as she said the words, Garrick could read her body, her posture. Her shoulders were stooped and her lips thinned into a knife-sharp line. Her knuckles shone tight and white through her delicate skin. She said she wanted him to keep looking and find her lacking, but she didn't mean it.

Pete came in well past nightfall. Garrick and Fay had endured working inside the cabin, accompanied by an endless silence where Garrick tried not to look at Fay for fear of what she thought he was thinking, and he didn't dare speak and risk hearing more harshness from her lips. She was most certainly not Eloise. Eloise was soft and caring. That was part of why he couldn't bear the idea of her forcing herself to marry that outlaw. A girl like Fay might have been able to handle marriage to such a man.

Garrick was still ashamed at his treatment of Eloise. He'd been an utter fool. Thinking she cared for him in ways she hadn't. Thinking himself a knight in shining armor to the damsel. Rather, he'd been the villain, and coming back had only reminded him of who he'd once been—a man too like his own father. A man who handled a woman like Eloise in an attempt to make her do what he wanted her to do. A man who inflicted pain to get his way.

Was he any different now? Or had he simply channeled that need into boxing fellow soldiers and fighting the enemy? Unlike Stimps, he hadn't hated the war. He'd enjoyed the physical stress of training. Enjoyed boxing for money and gambling it away again. Enjoyed the short battle and subsequent victory. The rush that came with the fear of defeat, and the joy that followed winning. He didn't even mind losing, because a tough opponent meant something to live for, to train harder for. He knew he would do better the next time.

Good men didn't like things like that. Good men liked... he didn't know what. But it wasn't violence. From every angle, he wasn't the hero.

Not until he'd stepped in front of Fay had he realized he even had the desire to try to be a hero once more. As luck would have it, it was with a woman who shared Eloise's blood.

Fay was right. He'd been comparing her to Eloise. But not in the way Fay had said. Not in hopes that Fay was somehow a younger version. He hoped she *wasn't* like Eloise. Hoped that when tested, she would stand up for herself. He glanced at her in her men's shirt, the neck entirely too big and revealing a bit of her collarbone. Her legs, covered in baggy men's trousers, rolled at the hem around skinny ankles. He had no doubt that her right hook was just as sure as whichever brother had worn those trousers last.

Fay was most certainly *not* Eloise. Fay was not a damsel, which was good, because Garrick had learned he was no knight.

9

*F*ay let out a breath of relief when Pete came through the door. Finally, someone to cut the tension.

The old mountain man glanced up, his gaze flitting between herself and Garrick. The large aquamarine stone set in the band around his hat caught the lantern light. No doubt he'd found it out here and set it himself. "Thought you two would be in bed already."

If they'd been speaking, they might have done so. Fay shot a look at Garrick. He met her gaze for the first time since she'd hit him with the truth like a slap to the face. She wasn't Eloise, and though he knew it, that truth coming from her mouth had stolen Garrick's ability to look at her at all.

He was looking at her now, worry plain on his face.

Pete served himself a portion of stew. "Smells nice." He sat in the chair, stretching his legs straight and crossing his boots at the ankles. "I told your man you two were to take the bed. I let the lady sleep in it last night. I suppose I ought to keep up the good behavior."

Fay's hands flung in front of her like fending off a rabid dog and not a mattress. "Oh, I don't need..." She gestured between herself and Garrick. "We have bedrolls. We don't need..."

Pete's gruff voice cut her off. "Nonsense. You made me dinner, and your man did a fair amount of work out there. More than your brother did with his lame arm."

A lump formed in Fay's throat. "What is wrong with Hugh's arm?" Pete hadn't mentioned any injuries. Only that their horse had been shot from under them. "Was Hugh shot too?"

Pete cocked his head at Fay as though she was dense. "Didn't I say?" He turned back to his stew, cutting into a potato with the side of his spoon. "Sure was, but his lady tended him well. She knows a smidge about medicines."

Edna knew medicine? That was surprising. Edna knew plenty about baking and even cooking. But there had been many things about the West that she'd had to learn. Compared to her, Fay was a hand at all things to do with a household—teaching Edna had been the one time Fay had actually felt adept at her daily chores.

Garrick stood at Fay's side, but he didn't touch her. It was proximity for Pete's sake, for the sake of the lie, not to comfort her. She had half a mind to tell Pete the truth and let him shoot Garrick if he wanted. But she'd made a promise. It was as if Garrick had known the shallow friendship formed this morning was bound to disintegrate and he would need to lean on her promise at some point. How had he known? *She* hadn't even known. For a time, she'd thought they'd found a real truce between them. Now her promise was landing her in a bed with this man. He'd probably close his eyes and pretend it was Eloise at his side.

If anyone heard what was about to happen, she could only imagine what the town would say about her next. Too good for all of them, yet she fell into bed with a soldier who had previously betrayed her family. No, it would not do.

Before long, Pete finished his dinner. Fay took his bowl and spoon and washed them for him. He rolled out his bedroll and tucked himself into it. Fay and Garrick met eyes once more. Thank goodness only one lamp remained lit, or both Garrick and Pete would have seen the bright blush that warmed the skin from her navel to the tips of her ears.

Garrick scratched at his jaw, just below his ear. Then he gestured with his head toward the bed. Fay let out a sigh and walked over. Garrick took her shoulders and whispered into her ear. "I can get my bedroll and sleep on the floor."

A decent idea. Fay cast a sideways look at Pete, who was watching them with beady eyes. Fay turned back to Garrick and faked a smile. She touched his cheek, the way she'd seen Mama do so many times to Pa's evening stubble. Garrick had more than a day's stubble, and she found it was both scratchy and soft at the same time. "Let's get to bed. I'm sure you're tired from all the work you did for Pete."

Understanding flashed in Garrick's eyes, and he led the way to the bed. Fay glanced at Pete, who had rolled over, apparently satisfied with their ruse. Though she was wearing men's clothing, she still wore a corset underneath for support. She grimaced at the thought of sleeping in the thing, but what else was appropriate in these circumstances?

Garrick removed his vest and untucked his shirt. The

way the loose fabric billowed made Fay think of the ship he must have taken to the tropical island where he'd fought. She couldn't recall the name, and she didn't dare ask. Not while Pete lay awake with one ear cocked. She shook her head. She barely knew this man, and yet she was following him to bed.

Garrick tucked himself inside and flipped the covers over on her side. It was a roguish invitation, and she wanted to smack him for it. She untucked her own shirt and tugged loose the ties on her corset, confident in her loose shirt's ability to provide her some modesty. She crawled into the bed, more than grateful for the breeches she wore instead of a bulky dress, or worse, a shift.

At least in attire she was equal to Garrick. She curled her toes, grateful she didn't have to sleep in boots. As she lay back, her arm and shoulder lay flush against Garrick's. She rolled onto her side and put her lips to his ear. "Nothing funny."

Garrick gave a little snort and nodded.

Fay rolled back. So long as they both lay perfectly still all night, she had nothing to fear.

GARRICK LAY ON HIS BACK, his heart beating a death march in his chest. How was he to lie next to this hot-tempered woman who had stirred feelings in him he could not dare acknowledge?

She wasn't Eloise, and she wasn't even sorry about it. Worse, neither was he.

Somehow, this revelation made sleeping next to her all the more inappropriate. What would her parents say?

What would Eloise say? Any one of them would gladly slit his throat.

If he'd been thinking, he would have made their beds on the floor, and they could have feigned sleep when Pete came inside. Why hadn't he thought?

He'd been caught up in Fay's proclamations about who she wasn't. The longer he had stewed on her words, the more he understood what went unsaid. In her long list of things she wasn't, she'd made no mention of the things she was, but he could see that clearly anyway. She was fiery and bold and brave and loving.

It was good he was leaving Aster Ridge after Christmas, heading to Texas and far away from Fay. He needed to get away from this family that had an uncanny ability to make him lose his mind. Perhaps he could find a nice girl in Texas who didn't stir every dangerous emotion within him. He would be the kind of husband every woman wanted—kind and gentle, fair and hardworking.

He would forget how his thoughts circled around being that man for Fay. He wouldn't be able to do that anyway, she brought out the worst in him. He'd raged at her as they made their way to the outcrop. He'd blurted all his conclusions, and Fay had hardly argued. Whether because he was right or because she wasn't the type to deign a response after being spoken to so harshly, he didn't know.

She was something, that he knew.

Now she was in bed with him. When she'd climbed in, she'd set her lips against his ear to warn him in harsh whispers not to do anything funny. Only in doing so, her lips had brushed his ear and hot breath had rolled across the side of his face. She'd not seemed to realize that her mere whisper had almost slaughtered his self-control.

He'd longed to pull the rest of her toward him. Was she so ignorant of her own appeal?

A few heartbeats later, a deep, rumbling snore came from Pete on the floor. Garrick laughed again, unsure how they were going to sleep at all, given the circumstances. They might have been better off setting out for Aster Ridge and risking an encounter with the bandits than waiting for a sleepless night to pass and traveling tired. After all, he was a sure shot, and during his time in the Rough Riders, had become more than adept with his fists. Surely he could manage a ruffian or two.

As he contemplated the intricacies of their journey home, Fay's voice drifted over, the quietest whisper, but since they were so close, he could hear it clearly. "What island did you go to?"

He blinked. Her mind certainly wasn't on the same thread as his own. "Cuba." He said the name, but it didn't hold the same excitement it once had. Battle was bloody and coarse. It was no adventure. Worse, they had left the island and he wasn't sure they'd done any good at all. Apparently, it was his fortune to try and fight battles for others and leave them off worse.

He could still remember the excitement of all the men on the ship headed there. The name of the island was so unfamiliar, yet uttered with such reverence. Theirs wasn't a normal army unit. Volunteers, all of them, many older, washed-up military or law enforcement. They were a true ragtag bunch of cowboys looking for a fight.

"Why were you fighting them?"

Garrick turned onto his side to better cut Pete's snores out of the conversation. In the dark, he could barely make out her profile. A small dot of moonlight reflected in her eye as she stared at the ceiling. "We didn't fight the

Cubans. We fought the Spanish. Cuba wanted to be free from the Spaniards, and they needed a bit of help."

"Like the French helped us get free from England?"

"More like your mama telling Hugh to stop picking on you." He thought of the small island, too small to build an army capable of defending themselves against the Spanish, almost like a silly young man trying to save a girl from marriage to the wrong man. Even then he'd known fighting was his gift...or curse. But perhaps, just like then, he could try to use it for good, in the service of others who needed him.

She gave a small hum that he might have taken as a laugh if he could have seen her smile. "And now they're free?"

That was the worst part. It seemed that the United States had taken over rule of Cuba. "I don't much know."

Silence. He racked his brain for a question, anything to make her talk to him more. To hear her scratchy voice next to him, whispering so as not to be heard by the man who was clearly sound asleep. If it had been anyone else, Garrick might have thought his quickness to fall asleep simply a ruse, but in his short time knowing Pete, it was clear Pete wasn't the type to feign anything.

Fay murmured, "I appreciate what you did for Eloise. It was poorly done, but men often bungle things like that."

Garrick chuckled. "Do we?" He smiled. "I behaved poorly. I'm sorry to think I cost your family any happiness. I guess I was only thinking of hers. And mine."

"You're sorry." Fay let out a huge sigh. "Why does he have to be sorry?" she asked the ceiling, and for a moment, he wondered if she would answer her own question.

She turned to look at him, her face obscured from the

moonlight, but he didn't need to see her face to know it was mere inches from his. He could feel the warmth of her breath against his mouth. He wanted badly to lean closer. To press his lips to hers and test her response.

Would she push him away and lecture him about who she wasn't? Or would she melt into him, the way she had when he'd helped her off her horse? Suddenly the smallest of gestures, the smallest of touches felt big. Too big.

Garrick rolled onto his back again, which, given the tight quarters, was less of a roll and more of a shuffling until he no longer rested on his side.

"I think Eloise was a bit like Cuba. She was never going to be free. If she hadn't married Aaron, what would have happened? If she'd run away with me, she'd still have been forced into a marriage."

"Run away?" Fay rolled to her side again, filling the distance he'd just gained. Only now she was in control of the space, and the idea of being at her mercy was delicious. Her voice came again, hot on his cheek. "You asked her to run away with you?"

"When I realized she'd gone through with the wedding, yes. I offered for her to come away with me. I don't know what I was thinking. Why I thought she was better off somewhere else. It wasn't a true offer. I knew what she would say. I guess I just needed to know she was doing what she wanted. That given an out, even a poor one, she would still make the same choice."

Fay brushed a lock of hair from her face. He didn't see it, glued as his eyes were to the black ceiling, but the movement of her arm was clear.

"I wonder if she ever really had a choice," she said. "You or Aaron. Marriage or not. Love or commitment.

Eloise sees things differently." Fay sighed. "I didn't help. I always let her carry the heavier load."

"You never answered me before. Do you plan to become an old maid, working at Della's forever, for the benefit of your family?"

Fay let out another low hum that fed something hungry between Garrick's ribs. "My plan? Well, I'm beginning to realize how foolish it is."

"Why?" Garrick flattened his palm over his stomach and shifted closer to Fay. He couldn't touch her, but the need to be closer was almost overwhelming, and this was as far as he would allow.

"As you know, Eloise was always the one with suitors. She wanted none of them. I, on the other hand, want them, and apparently they don't come to just anyone with the last name of Morris."

Garrick laughed. "You make it sound like a watering trough. Nobody is fit for everyone, not even Eloise, whom you seem to have placed on a pedestal."

"I'm not the only one who put her up there. You did too."

Garrick smiled. "You're right, I did. But I was young." He glanced at Fay. "How old are you?"

"Old enough to not make a foolish boy's mistakes."

His hand twitched. She probably *was* the age he'd been when he'd left. Yet she was far more mature. She'd gone off to rescue her elder brother rather than spend her days ruining other people's lives as Garrick had done.

"I did wrong by your family, and I'm going to see about making it up to them. To you."

Fay was silent for long enough he thought she'd fallen asleep. But then she said a single word.

"Maybe."

Her breath brushed across his neck, warm, and then slowly the warmth dissipated, chilled as it was stolen by the cabin air. This night was much the same, her voice close and warm. Yet when morning broke and they left for Aster Ridge, the cold would be upon them once more.

10

———

*G*arrick fell asleep dreaming of waking with Fay entangled in his arms, her hair spread on the pillow, and her vanilla and chamomile scent all around them. But the reality was much more sobering. He woke with a crick in his neck from having slept still as a corpse with his shoulders bunched around his ears.

She rose at the same time, rolling her head side to side as though her night had been rough too. Her hair was still in its braid, though loose pieces framed her face, highlighting her natural beauty. Pete was already out of the cabin, possessing the apparent stealth of a catamount.

Fay plucked a piece of clothing from the floor and hugged it like a precious memory. "I've never heard a man snore so loudly, and I have three brothers. It's no wonder he lives alone all the way out here."

Garrick grinned as he tucked his shirt into his trousers. "I didn't notice it much. I guess I'm used to barracks with snoring men."

Fay shook her head as though what he'd just

described was her absolute nightmare, but she kept the clothes clutched tightly to her chest.

Garrick squinted at it. "What have you got there?"

Fay spun around. "My personals. Can I have a bit of privacy?"

Garrick's face heated like he'd just stuck his head into Pete's black-bellied stove. He stepped into his boots, not bothering to lace them, and tugged his jacket off the wall on his way outside.

The crisp morning air did wonders for the blood warming his face. Why had he asked her? What had he been thinking? Yet he'd seen her crawl into bed last night. She'd not taken anything off. Perhaps in her sleeplessness she'd shed personals. The thought was too much to consider further, and he turned to the sound of a horse nickering.

Pete had Garrick's mount, Dusty, by the bridle, leading her toward the cabin. He tethered the animal to the post and patted her neck. "She's too big and eats too much."

Garrick grinned and nodded. It was true. But he also had the suspicion that this horse was why he'd been accepted into the Rough Riders at all. Many of the volunteers had far more experience with both horses and fighting. Garrick had only possessed a fine mount thanks to Bastien, which gave him the appearance of knowledge. "You said Hugh took your mount? When he returns, I'll be sure to send some feed along too."

"Nah, they're feeding my horse and heaven knows they can't afford to." Pete gestured with his chin toward the house. "You take good care of that one, you hear? Whatever it is that's wrong between you two, make it right."

Garrick kept his focus on his horse, not daring to look into Pete's too astute eyes. Apparently they hadn't performed their charade well enough. "I'll do my best to make sure she's happy."

As he spoke the words, his heart shifted in his chest, revealing a truth—he *did* want to make her happy. Once again, he was falling for a Morris girl, a girl who had no intention of returning his affection. A girl who would one day break his heart by giving her life away for the sake of her family, even if it meant denying her own heart.

She wasn't Eloise. No. But she was still a Morris.

———

FAY EXITED THE CABIN. Though the morning sun had barely risen, it glinted off the snow, and Fay had to blink into the brightness. Garrick and Pete stood near Garrick's horse, which was tethered to the hitching post.

She took a step toward the small barn. "I'll just go get Lady and we can be off."

Pete put up a hand. "I'll keep her until Hugh comes back with my mount."

Fay reared her head back on her shoulders. "Keep her?" She glanced at Garrick, who was slack-jawed and apparently just as surprised as she. "But I still have to get home."

"Your man has a fine mount here. More than large enough for the two of you." He strode past them and into the cabin with what Fay was almost certain was a smirk.

Fay followed on his heels. "Pete, we need our horse for the farm. We can't just leave it here."

"I'll take good care of her. Better even. Whoever trimmed her hooves last did a poor job of it."

"I'll have her hooves looked at." The words tumbled out, and she no longer cared about the charade or about keeping the desperation out of her voice. It was winter, and Hugh was apparently injured in some unknown way. Who knew how soon he would be able to get back here with Pete's horse?

"I need a horse too. This way we'll each have what we need until the weather allows us to trade back."

Of course he needed a horse. Fay closed her eyes and pulled a deep breath through her nose. Garrick came behind her and placed his hands on her shoulders, the additional pressure forcing the air back out and soothing her temper. She turned to face him, looking up into his gray eyes. "A whole day's ride double saddle." She shook her head. It was going to be misery. The discomfort as well as the additional need to rest the horse. They wouldn't be home until past nightfall.

Garrick wrapped his arms around her, and she tensed at such a forward action. But Pete must be watching them, so she jerkily laid her face against his chest, the spicy scent of him only worsening her anxiety. She'd already spent an entire night encompassed in that smell, not sleeping. Between the noise of Pete's snores and the inability to move without touching Garrick, Fay had barely slept a wink. Now she was going to have to dodge contact with Garrick for a full day. No chance to catch a bit of sleep in the saddle. Instead, pure misery.

Dusty was loaded high with both Garrick and Fay's packs. Garrick climbed into the saddle and reached out to pull her on. Both her legs were on one side of Dusty's neck, and to get her right leg over she had to lean into Garrick. Once again, she was grateful for the pants she wore. More than a few things would have been different if she'd been wearing skirts all this time. When she was positioned, she leaned forward, putting a proper amount of space between them. A paltry victory when his legs were still pressed against hers.

Pete handed her a cloth bundle. She peeked inside through a gap in the tied corners to find a stack of jerky and half a loaf of bread. "Thank you. For putting us up for the night and taking care of Hugh." She lifted the food. "And for this. Take care of yourself, Pete."

He gave her a single nod and turned. Garrick leaned closer, his breath tickling her ear as he took the reins. He kicked the horse forward, and they were off, swaying with each crunching step of the large mount.

Fay could understand Pete's need for a horse, but there was something about this situation that bothered her. They had barely set off into the thick woods that surrounded Pete's cabin when Fay said, "Did you know he was going to keep my horse?"

"I learned about it the same moment you did. Makes sense though. He's down a horse. A lone man out here needs a way to get around. I bet he was feeling mighty uncomfortable sending Hugh off with his only means of transportation."

"I feel mighty uncomfortable now."

Garrick's chest pressed against her back. "Does this help?"

Fay elbowed him. "Get off. We aren't husband and wife any longer."

Garrick laughed. "I think I liked it. We could join one of those traveling shows, be actors."

Fay didn't laugh. She wasn't traveling anywhere. Not just now, maybe not ever. Had Eloise felt this unsettled when she'd made her choice? Or had she been resigned to her future? Garrick could do anything he wanted. He could join the army, or the actors, or be a peddling tinker if he wanted. No family held him back. No precedent had been set that required he lay down his life for others.

"So, back to the army for you?"

"I was never in the army. I was with the Rough Riders. We were a volunteer bunch."

Fay's breath flew from her. "Volunteer? As in, not paid?" He was poorer than she'd thought.

Garrick chuckled. "Volunteer as in I could quit at any time."

Fay remembered the boxing he mentioned. "And you boxed for extra money?"

"Yup."

"Would you ever join the regular army?"

His arms tightened ever so slightly, then loosened again. "I don't know." Silence. She could hear every breath leave him, but the cold air stole it away before she felt it. "I shouldn't want to fight."

"Yet you chose to fight both your enemy and, in your free time, your comrades." It just didn't make sense. Who wanted to watch violence? Who wanted to *participate* in it?

He laughed again, and his chest brushed against her back. "You're right." His voice was laced with sadness, and the corners of Fay's mouth tugged downward. Why had he enjoyed it?

"Why not stay here?" she asked. "Work with Bastien. Heaven knows they need the help, and he's slow to hire anyone on."

"I'm too old to rely on him. I need to make my own way."

"Working *is* making your own way. Do you mean you want to *own* something of your own?"

"I don't know."

His reply rankled her. *He didn't know.* He had all the

freedom, and he didn't know what to do with it. "You could become a bandit. Plenty of fighting *and* money there."

He shifted his grip on the reins, his arm brushing hers and making her feel both trapped and secure. "Perhaps I could. When I'm rich, with a bounty on my head, I could come back and pay your family for your hand in marriage. Then we could run off to live in obscurity with Eloise and Aaron."

His voice was hard and his words painful. An ache caught in her throat and Fay gulped. "We didn't sell Eloise."

"It doesn't much matter now, does it?"

Fay drew her arms in, trying to make herself small. Trying to avoid touching him anywhere, but the saddle was too small, and no matter how she tucked her arms in, their legs would continue to touch unless Garrick scooted back. Apparently, he didn't have any qualms with the contact, and like any good soldier, he held his position.

His voice was softer when he next spoke. "What would you do? If you were me?"

"If I were you, a man? Or if I was me, Fay Morris, but with your freedom?"

Garrick fell into silence, and Fay wanted to turn around to read his countenance.

Finally he spoke, his words gentle, matching the still reverence of the sleepy snowy forest around them. "If you were you, but with freedom."

She'd never really thought of it. She would never truly have Garrick's freedom. She could never box for pay or live free in a barracks with a slew of rowdy men. What did women do who had the freedom to explore the world? They needed the safety of a family wherever they went. "I suppose I'd go find Eloise. See what adventures awaited in —there."

She'd almost said Oregon, and as much as she thought Garrick had changed from when he'd turned Aaron over to a bounty hunter, it wasn't Fay's bet to place. She wasn't going to be the one who told Garrick the whereabouts of Aaron Harder.

"Or maybe," she added, "I would stay here and see what life is like without the confines of..." It felt wrong to call her family a sort of prison. Her stomach flipped at the words she'd almost spoken.

Garrick's voice came soft and soothing, like he was trying to tame a wild mustang. "It's okay to want more than you have. No matter if what you have is really quite good. Just because you want a life outside of them doesn't mean you don't love them."

"Love is different for you. You can write letters and come for a visit to show your love to your sister. But I cannot leave my family. If I did, I could not write to them or visit them after having left them to destitution."

The crunch of hooves on snow was louder than ever in the silence of their unspoken words. Did Garrick finally understand? They hadn't sold Eloise. They'd failed her. The decision had been made long ago, when Pa's body had decided to live and yet fail him.

"I have half a mind to become a bandit and give all my earnings to your family until all of you are free."

Fay shook her head. "Stop it." He could speak these fanciful notions. But it was a wonder none of her brothers had gone and done just that. Easy money was too tempting, especially when the hard-earned kind was too easily spent.

"You're doing the same thing as her. Giving yourself to

them as a martyr. What if I did the same thing as him and set you free?"

Fay tensed. "Him" referred to Aaron. She was Eloise in this scenario, but it was different. For the first time since he'd returned, Fay felt certain Garrick didn't see Eloise when he looked at Fay. Perhaps at this close proximity he could no longer fool himself.

"If you want to become a bandit, go right ahead. But don't do it for me."

They approached a low branch, and Garrick reached ahead and broke it off before it reached Fay's face. He offered it to her, but she kept her hands on the horn.

His hand fell to his thigh, his fingers twirling the prickly bough like it was a flower to be placed in a bouquet. "Because you'd still not marry me?"

Marry him? Was this some backhanded proposal of marriage? Had their ruse convinced more than just Pete? "I'm not going to tell you to rob innocent folks, or to do it for anyone but yourself." Just as he admired the pine branch, he had mistaken her for something beautiful when everyone knew she was really a twig covered with sharp needles.

"Eloise didn't want to marry, but with you it's different. You want to marry, but"—he gave a bitter laugh—"you want someone rich."

Fay tensed. He was too close to her, and she could feel him looking at the back of her head. She had to get away from him. She caught the strap of leather reins stretched between Garrick's hands and the halter and pulled, stopping the horse. She swung her leg over Dusty's neck, ignoring the way she had to press into Garrick as she did so. Then she hopped down, her too large boots landing in the soft snow. The one benefit of riding double was that her boots wouldn't catch in the stirrups. It also meant the skin on the inside of her thighs was bound to be gone by the time they reached home. Once that happened, she'd be grateful enough to return to her skirts.

Garrick climbed off too, and walked to Fay's side. She resented the comfort his proximity brought, the same one that had shown itself when Pete was telling her about Hugh's injuries.

"What if I did stay here? Worked for Bastien. Bought a ranch for myself and became independent? What then? Would I be rich enough for you?"

No. He would still be reliant upon work. He would be exactly where her ma and pa had been when her pa got sick.

That dark laugh came again, a throaty reply to her silence. "So you won't take a hardworking man. Willem's guests have put ideas into your head. Haven't you learned from Ivete that money isn't everything?" He leaned back, staring at the gray blue sky.

Anger rose in her like a wind across the prairie, bending the blades of grass, then setting them right again. "It *is* everything. Ivete can only say those fanciful things because she is a Graham. She has her rich papa to run to if life ever deals her a poor hand." Fay shook her head and turned to face Garrick. "It's different for women. Marriage means children. It means mouths to feed. Once we're married, we can't better our circumstances." Her pa's words rang in her head. *A man gets one mistake in the forest; a woman gets none.* It was true outside the woods too. "It's only good sense to do what we can when we can. I cannot fix my pa. But I can use my position at Willem's ranch to find myself someone who can take care of him, of all of us. Forever."

Garrick looked down at her, shading her face from the sun. "What of love? Ivete might have a rich father, which means she might not understand what it's like to live without the security of gold. But you have parents in love. That's a different type of security that *you* have never lived without."

Love. She'd already thought through this a thousand times. Love could be built. It was something Fay could control. If her marriage didn't have enough, she could just give more. It was boundless. It didn't need to be split equally. If she found a man with enough money to solve her problems, she would love him dearly for all of her days.

Garrick's voice was soft, distant, as though it was a memory that spoke instead of the solid form in front of her. "Not having love is just the start of what could go wrong. Some marriages are downright awful. I don't suppose your pa ever hit your ma."

Fay instinctively leaned away, her heart in her throat. "Of course not." It wasn't as though Fay had been blind to this possibility. There were a few folks in town whom Fay had heard stories about. Women who failed to hide bruises, and men who failed to hide tempers.

"It's common where I'm from. Death was freedom for my mama."

Fay's anger turned fully to sadness. She'd heard little about his mother, only that she was with the angels. Fay glanced upward to the canopy of trees, covered in snow, just behind Dusty. White against brown. Pure and fresh resting along something old and worn. Suddenly she wanted very much to know more about Garrick. About his life before Aster Ridge. About what he was going to do with the rest of it. She didn't want him to be a bandit.

Most bandits didn't live long enough to run away to Oregon. Most of them were shot on sight by a bounty hunter or a trigger-happy sheriff who wasn't keen to let the law make up its mind.

No, she wanted him to build the life he'd described. To make something of his own, something honest, something here. But she couldn't say that, and she couldn't tell him to stay. He was thinking things he shouldn't think, and Fay knew better than to give him false hope. She glanced at his glove, the two fingers sewn off to match the hand inside. He was mortal, and she wouldn't blame him for it, but she wouldn't marry a man like him. She would stick to her plan. But she could say one thing.

"Don't become a bandit. Become someone to make your mama proud."

She turned and walked back to Dusty, plucking her reins off the snowy ground. She smirked to think Garrick had dropped them in his haste to follow her. His mama must already be proud of him. Strong and gallant. Fay would be proud to have such a son herself. She ignored the tempting pride that might come with being such a man's wife.

11

*G*arrick wanted to reach out, to take Fay's hand in his. But talk of his father had extinguished any romantic thoughts. He'd practically proposed. The closeness had allowed him to forget who he was. He'd come from the hardest of men, and when Garrick's temper had been tested, when Eloise refused to allow him to help her, he'd reacted like his father. With force, with hurt. Garrick wasn't good enough to marry Fay. He wasn't good enough to marry anyone.

He watched the snow crunch under Fay's men's boots. She had Dusty's reins in her hand.

"Are we going to walk the whole way, or have you forgiven me enough to ride?"

Fay shot him a glare, and he laughed. She smiled too. She was easy to fire up, but she was also forgiving. The more time he spent with her, the more time he wanted to spend at her side.

He climbed up and slid his foot from the stirrup so she could use it. His legs were much longer than hers, which meant the stirrups didn't get her high enough. He had to grip her under her arms to pull her up the rest of the way. She leaned into his chest, effectively stopping his heart, then leaned forward again, positioned with one leg on either side.

The tiny hairs at the bottom of her hairline fluttered with the icy breeze. He'd been freezing on the ride to Pete's, but now his blood pounded at a rate bound to wear out his heart. How had he never noticed her when he'd been at Aster Ridge a few years ago? She'd been young, but only a few years younger than him.

Stimps had a sweetheart he'd known since childhood. Fay could have been that for Garrick, if he hadn't been so starry-eyed for Eloise. He knew now, had known for quite some time, that Eloise had never been right for him. She was too gentle, too kind. Garrick had proven himself not to be trusted with a woman like her.

Did that mean there *was* a woman right for him? One who would fight back if he ever leaned toward his father's way of treating her? The thought churned in his belly. Fay had already said it. Women didn't have freedoms. If a woman's husband changed, she couldn't stop it. How could Garrick guarantee he wasn't that same man? The man he'd been running from ever since Eloise and Aaron's marriage? The man he'd been trying his best to train out of himself. Had joining the Rough Riders taught him control, or had it only made him better at violence?

As the day wore on, they talked less, and eventually Fay leaned into him and fell asleep. He practically chanted to himself as she slept. *Not for you.* But she intoxicated him. Not just the feel of her leaning into him, but the way she argued with him, the way she cared for her own, the way she acknowledged the unfairness in the world, yet still lived with a fierceness and—at least for everyone else—a smile.

He'd only been half-joking when he offered to become a bandit and have Fay for himself. He hadn't yet acknowledged the thought when he voiced it, but now it joined in the chant. *Not for you. Never for you.* No alternate reality existed where Fay could be his.

As they rode with her shoulders and back pressed against his chest, he dreamed of other lives where she was his. One where he had been raised by a better man, a rich man who had taught Garrick to be gentle with a woman and left him a fortune. But in that life, Della wouldn't have run off and married Bastien, and Garrick would never have met Fay.

Any way he spun it, he wouldn't have made it to this valley with this woman in his arms if his father hadn't been such an awful, belligerent man. As much as he hated the man, no child could deny the effect a parent had on their life. For good or ill, wherever the child was now, was in part due to their parents.

He couldn't change that. But he did have the power to control himself. To be the man he wanted to be, to one day find a woman who would take him as he was—a poor boy who would have to work hard for his future. He wanted to be angry with Fay, but he couldn't be, at least not when she slept, vulnerable, in his arms.

He did know one thing—he had to go, to leave Aster Ridge, or he would find himself more than a little in love with this woman. That was a bit of history he'd rather not act out again.

When they reached Dragonfly Creek, they earned more than a few curious glances. Garrick considered waking Fay, but he knew as soon as she wasn't sleeping, she'd lean away from him, might even hop off the horse altogether for propriety's sake. Garrick risked her reputation by allowing her to sleep on him in front of her townspeople.

He lowered his mouth to her ear. "Fay."

She gave a small jerk and straightened her back. Her head moved from side to side with the disorientation of waking up to have arrived at one's destination.

A young woman came out of the post office and watched as they drew near. When they were close enough, she smirked. "Morning, Fay. I have a letter for Aster Ridge. Will you take it to them?"

Garrick reined Dusty to a stop. The girl flashed Garrick a look through her lashes and a small smile, then focused on Fay once more. Fay nodded, and the girl disappeared into the post office.

Fay turned. "Will you give me a bit of space?" A large yawn overtook her, dulling the cut of her words.

Garrick scooted back on the saddle, but it only gave the semblance of space. "Didn't sleep well last night?"

"You should know. I'm sure my tossing and turning kept you awake too."

"I'd gladly pretend to be your husband if it meant I could sleep by your side again."

He knew he shouldn't tease her, but he couldn't seem to help it. Even though he knew he wasn't good enough, he still wanted her, wanted to flirt with her and make her smile.

Fay opened her mouth, but she snapped it shut again when the girl exited the office. She brandished a letter, holding it out so Fay had to lean down to reach. Garrick couldn't stop himself from hovering his hands around her waist in case she slipped off the saddle altogether. The girl didn't miss his action. Her gaze flicked between his hands, not quite touching Fay's waist, and him.

"You're Mrs. Graham's brother?"

Fay had the letter now, and she leaned back, closer to Garrick once more. His chest felt cool where she no longer leaned into him. He hated even that brief distance and wanted to wrap his arms around her completely. To pretend for just a little longer.

Instead, he answered the girl. "Yes, ma'am. Garrick Hampton." He touched his hat and nodded.

Fay apparently found her manners and turned slightly in her seat. "Garrick, this is Ginny Price."

The girl bobbed a curtsey, but her smile wasn't sweet like it had been before she'd gone into the office. Now, accompanied by the glint in her eye, it looked sinister.

Garrick gave her a nod. "Pleased to meet you. I must be getting Fay back to her family."

"Of course." The girl looked almost amused as they moved away.

When they were out of earshot, Garrick couldn't dispel the feeling he'd missed something. "That girl a friend of yours?"

"No." Fay's voice was hard. "No friends, remember?"

Garrick hardly knew how to reply, so he stayed silent. Eventually they were out of the town limits, and Fay loosened the rod that was her backbone.

He moved the reins to one hand and held his other hand out, palm up. "If you'll give me the letter, I'll put it in my pocket and take it to Della."

The paper was slightly crinkled from Fay's clenched fist. She smoothed the paper out on her leg and gave a little huff. "It's for Edna."

She passed it back and Garrick slid the envelope into his breast pocket. "Edna *is* your friend?"

Fay nodded. "Ginny used to be." She huffed. "A few years back, she decided my family was her enemy because her sister has had her eye on Hugh as long as I can remember."

"What's that got to do with you?"

"Girls are different. I wouldn't expect you to understand."

"Try me."

Fay remained silent for so long, Garrick gave up on a real answer. Light flakes began to fall around them. Each one glimmered in the sun setting further in the valley, not touched by the clouds hanging over their heads.

"I suppose I've given her a bit of ammunition."

Garrick laughed. "Ammunition? Now you're speaking my language."

Her shoulders lifted as she drew a deep breath. "She knows. Everyone knows. I'm not planning to marry anyone from town. There was a boy—"

Garrick's arms tightened around her, and he clenched his jaw as he forced his arms to relax. Of course there was a boy, probably a whole host of them, chasing after Fay. Maybe he'd been wrong about no man going on his knee for her. Perhaps she'd simply refused them.

"He ran off without proposing. Maybe I should've thanked her. She did me a favor because I didn't have to reject him. But I know she did more. After that, the other girls wouldn't talk to me. My refusal to marry any of the men in town offended them. Their brothers weren't good enough. Not even the men they'd chosen to wed were good enough." She sighed, and a small noise sounded in her throat. "I suppose I can't blame them for being offended."

The way she said *them* made Garrick wonder. Had everyone in that town turned against this woman? Sure, she could be prickly, but he'd seen the way she interacted with her family. She was sunlight on a cloudy day. Surely not every friend had been lost due to Fay's desperate attempt to secure a future for her family.

Soon, the Morris' house rose into sight.

Garrick jostled her between his arms. "We made better time." He laughed at how lost they'd been. He might have followed Fay to the ends of the earth if she'd let him. He laughed again, the sound rolling across the wide valley. It was a wonder how this place could feel like home when he'd been here such a short time.

Fay bumped him with her shoulder. "If I hadn't caught up to you, all of Aster Ridge might be out there now, looking for you."

He would have been fine using the map, but he chuckled anyhow. "You're not wrong."

He reined in Dusty at the hitching post, and they climbed off the horse and shook out their legs. He wanted to reach out to her, to pull her close once more. He wasn't yet ready to let her away from him. He knew once she went into that house, the closeness they'd shared during their brief adventure would disappear like fog in the morning. Soon there would be no sign of it. Not unless he or Fay chose to acknowledge it, and he knew, without a doubt, she never would. She'd made her position clear, and she might trust him enough to sleep on his chest, but she didn't trust that he could make a life for them, at least not a life to match the expectations she'd set.

Fay glanced at the house and back to Garrick. "Don't

say anything about the bandits. Mama's got enough to worry about these days."

Garrick nodded just as the front door opened, and out came Mrs. Morris, hugging Fay to her, then pushing her away to get a good look at her. "Are those Otto's old pants?"

Fay tugged at the garment. Garrick hid a smile as the two women spoke in a low murmur. He untied Fay's pack, setting her things on the ground while he buckled his things back in place.

Sure, he'd liked Fay dressed in her best the way she was on Sundays, but she still shone in an old handed down work shirt. He just hoped she kept that shine no matter who she married. There were good men who were also rich. Stimps attested to that. Perhaps she would have both love and money. He bit his cheek as he told himself he hoped she would find just that.

Fay extricated herself from her mother's grip. "I'll be in." She gently urged her mother toward the door.

Mrs. Morris glanced at Garrick and gave him a curt nod before disappearing inside.

Fay plucked her bedroll from the ground. Turning to look at Garrick, she said, "Hugh is inside if you want to see him. Mama says he's awake."

He shook his head. "You go have your reunion. I don't imagine your ma wants me in her house."

Fay clicked her tongue. "As far as she's concerned, your gallant efforts saved my life. If you want to, you're welcome to stay."

Garrick remembered Mrs. Morris's tight expression. He pushed the memory away and donned a smirk. "You didn't straighten her out? Tell her it was you who saved me from being lost to the forest?" He unwrapped Dusty's reins. "I better get back to Della." He climbed on his horse and turned it around.

Garrick wanted to stay. Boy, did he ever want to go in that house and plead them to forgive his foolish actions that had forced their eldest daughter away from them. But no, it didn't matter if they liked or disliked him. He'd made up his mind. He was going to get a good night's rest, kiss his sister and niece and nephew, then be off to join Stimps in Texas.

He had left this place before, and the reason still stood. There was nothing for him here. Only reliance on Bastien, and Garrick didn't want that. He wanted a life of his own, not borrowed land and borrowed women.

Garrick arrived at Della's home, and Bastien found him in the barn. "Thought I heard a commotion."

Garrick smiled at his brother-in-law. It was a wonder to think he'd once thought Bastien the enemy. It was a true testament to how a child would believe a father's words without question. He'd known their father had never treated Della fairly. Garrick should have trusted that any man Della chose would be better than their father.

Bastien assisted in unloading the pack and then the saddle. "Hugh's back."

"We heard." For all his teasing, Garrick was glad Fay had lost them in the forest. If she'd better known the location of Pete's cabin, they wouldn't have had to backtrack and would have met Hugh and Edna on the road. They would have stayed enemies and never had to pretend to like one another. He would never have learned that he wanted more than forgiveness from Fay.

"Stimps sent a wire. Said you met up with Fay. Did you drop her at home?"

Garrick nodded and shut the door to Dusty's stall. She still needed a full bucket of oats and plenty of water.

"I'm glad you're both safely returned." Bastien let out a sigh of relief that made Garrick respect the man even more. Fay wasn't merely a servant to him and Della. She was like family.

"She's tough and can handle herself surprisingly well." Garrick thought of her men's clothes and boots. Besides getting her toe caught and possibly being dragged by her horse, Fay would likely have handled the mission perfectly well on her own.

Bastien cocked a brow. "These women aren't like the ones in the city. That's the truth."

Garrick smiled. They certainly were something else. "I've learned my lesson when it comes to Morris women. They've no patience for a man like me."

Bastien smiled. "Your sister has been worried about you both. She'll be glad when you tell her Fay is home safe. Why don't you head inside and get warm? I'll finish here."

Garrick gladly accepted the offer. He went right to the fire and warmed his hands. Della came out from the dark hallway and slid an arm around his waist, leaning her head against his arm. "I'm glad you're back."

Did she mean from the mountains, or from the war? "I'm not staying."

She loosened her hold and looked up at him. No matter that she wasn't his mother's daughter, she still reminded him of her. It was in the way she moved, even the way she laughed. Blood wasn't the only element that shaped a person. "Not staying? Where will you go?"

"Not sure exactly. To Stimps' place in Texas to start. Then I don't know. Just far from here."

"Far from what? Or who?"

Garrick shot Della a look. How did she read him so well? Perhaps reading folks was a family trait. "Just... away."

"Is it the Morrises? Eloise?"

She wasn't wrong. Eloise was part of it, but it wasn't love for her that drove him away. It was affection for her sister. And acknowledgement of who he was.

"I treated Eloise badly." He wasn't sure how much of the truth had been conveyed to the rest of the ranch. He'd run away with no care for what he'd left behind. The mess he'd left Eloise, the work he'd left Otto. Then he'd gone and done even more damage, turning in Aaron. "I don't like the man I am here. I need a fresh start."

Della leaned into him again with the easy silence of siblings.

He wrapped an arm around her shoulders. "Thank you for taking me away from Omaha. From him."

"You're not him." Her words were quiet, and he wondered if she'd ever seen a bit of their father in herself.

His throat grew tight. Della and Bastien had fairly rescued him from that life, from their pa. Had literally saved his hand from amputation. But, perhaps like his fingers, a bit of him had already been lost, goodness and innocence gone before they could be sewn back on. Were curled fists and hatred all he was good for? Perhaps a life of violence was inevitable. Part of him the same way his father's blood ran in his veins.

12

*F*ay hugged her brother's neck, tears of relief spilling into her cheeks. "Pete kept my horse." She laughed as she pulled away. "I guess we missed you on the road. I didn't exactly remember how to find Pete's cabin, and we had to double back."

Hugh lifted one eyebrow. "I still can't believe you and Garrick traveled together."

Fay understood his confusion. Last Hugh knew, she was avoiding Garrick at all costs. "Well, he just happened to have the route where Pete's cabin was. And we both know Pete would have put a bullet in his chest as soon as he'd let him in the cabin."

"Fay!" Ma swatted the top of Fay's head. "Don't you speak like that."

"Sorry, Ma." Fay suppressed a smile, sharing a companionable look with Hugh.

"So, he kept Lady? Can't say I'm surprised. He was none too pleased to send Edna and me on his horse."

"Yes, well I had to ride double the whole way home with *Garrick Hampton*." She said the name with drama, but even as she did so, a tiny fist beat inside her chest, demanding justice. Garrick wasn't half as bad as she'd thought. She turned to their mother, who was sitting near the fire with her bare toes stretched close to the grate. "Ma, he's real sorry about turning in Aaron."

Ma huffed. "Is he? And is he sorry for kissing our Eloise when she was a married woman?"

Hugh straightened, and Fay's eyes nearly popped out of her head. "*Kissed* her?"

Ma nodded. "Tried to make more than a little trouble for her."

Betrayal sliced at Fay's chest. Both from Eloise and from Garrick. Fay had already mourned the loss of her sister and how she wasted Eloise's last weeks at home by being jealous and petty. But Garrick hadn't mentioned a kiss either. Why had he told her about asking Eloise to run away and left out the kiss? Perhaps Fay didn't quite know him the way she'd thought. A couple of days couldn't reveal everything about a person. Why had she wanted it to?

Fay shook off the confusing thoughts. "Where's Pa?"

Ma glanced down the hall. "In bed. That cold has settled in his chest."

Fay frowned. His inability to stand and walk meant his lungs were prone to these colds. He got at least one every winter, and they meant many nights of coughing and tinctures from the doctor. Money spent that they didn't have.

"And Lachlan? Is his spell over?"

"Nearly."

Hugh leaned his elbows on his knees. "Ma, we have to tell him about the medicine, about what Aaron left us and what it was for."

Mama shook her head.

Fay stood from her place next to Hugh. "Then what was it all for? He doesn't *need* to have these spells."

Hugh cleared his throat. "She's right. Edna figures she's got a friend in Chicago. Knows a bit about making pills, and Lachlan isn't the first man to have malaria."

Ma's mouth twisted in the way Fay knew meant they were wearing her down. Fay took her seat again. "Eloise is happy. Otto is too. She might have married Aaron for Lachlan's sake, but it was the best decision she ever made. A blessing even." Fay hated that she was repeating Garrick's thoughts, but they were true. Eloise and Otto were both better off in Oregon.

Hugh shifted with a wince. Fay ran her gaze the length of her brother. "You're hurt. Pete mentioned you might be."

"Shot, but it went through. I'm right as rain."

Fay nodded. "I can't wait to hear everything from Edna." She pinned Hugh with a look. "She wasn't shot too, was she?" Pete hadn't mentioned it, but he had been rather vague in general.

"Don't know if you'll be getting much from Edna. She might be headed home with her mother and Brandon."

Fay pulled her head back on her shoulders. *Mother?* That wasn't even the most confusing part. "Who is Brandon?" Wasn't Edna an only child? Her father had died before Edna had gained any siblings.

"He's her beau, I guess." Hugh's voice had that detached way to it, the one that meant he wasn't paying attention to their conversation, but was wrestling within himself.

Fay balked. "Her *beau*? Edna doesn't have a beau." But as Fay spoke the words, she realized that since Edna's arrival at Aster Ridge, she had stubbornly refused all of

Fay's attempts to find her a match. Fay had hoped it was because she was hiding feelings for Hugh, but... *Brandon*? Now Edna's refusal made sense.

Hugh raised his brows, his mouth pinched. Fay turned to watch the flames dance. She wouldn't believe it, was almost certain Edna didn't have a man in Chicago. Fay had never seen her post a letter besides the ones she sent to her mother.

"He's here?" As much as she wanted, she couldn't deny an actual person. Perhaps she wrote to him in the care of her mother. She'd save on postage that way.

"At the Grahams' right now." Hugh's voice held an edge of misery. They met eyes, and she could see a sadness there. His gaze shot to Ma and back, and Fay understood what he'd said in the language of siblings. *Not in front of Mama.*

Fay stood and stretched. "My back is killing me. Remind me never to ride double again." As she said this, she realized Hugh would have ridden double with Edna the whole way home. And now Edna's beau was here to bring her back to Chicago. A weight pressed on Fay's chest. Poor Hugh. He'd been trying to deny his feelings all this time, only to have whatever may have been kindled stamped out by a stranger.

Ma took herself to bed and Fay got herself a bowl of cold stew. Hugh stayed by the fire, his whittling tools in hand as he worked a new piece. It didn't resemble anything yet. Just the bark had been removed.

The two sat in silence—her with her stew, and him with his whittling. She didn't press. Hugh wasn't the type to be bullied into talking anyhow.

Fay had scraped her bowl clean when a soft tap came on the door. Fay and Hugh glanced at each other. Hugh stood and moved toward the door. Fay glanced down the hall and listened to hear if Mama was still awake. Her gaze snapped to the door when she heard the voice.

Garrick. "Della said they were going to bring you these in the morning, but I wasn't sure if you were intent on an early departure. There's plenty to keep here and take some to Pete's. I guess Edna's mama is a baker."

Hugh chuckled, accepting the basket of bread. "She is that."

Garrick's eyes flashed to Fay, who still sat at the hearth. Her position wasn't inviting, and she was doing her best not to lunge at him and beat at his chest. He'd *kissed* Eloise? Anger burned as hot as the fire at her back. Furious as she was, she could see the benefit of the revelation. She'd begun to feel things for Garrick that were best buried. With this new information, the logical side of her brain could take over, and she would remember why she was keeping this man far away from her heart.

Hugh said something, but Fay was too busy pretending there was still food in her bowl to hear his words. But when Garrick spoke, her ears perked up like some obnoxious dog wanting to lay at its master's feet and hear every word he muttered. "He's her fiancé now. Got engaged earlier today."

Fiancé? Were they talking about Edna and Brandon? Fay stood then, wanting to go to Hugh. He might be intent on denying feelings for Edna, but this would still be a blow.

"Good for her," Hugh said as he unloaded the basket. His voice sounded genuine, so much so that Fay froze, almost believing him. She stared at the back of his head, her chest tight. She wanted to whack him between the shoulders, but even more she wanted to wrap her arms around him, the way he had done for her that time she got her finger caught in the hinge of a trap. Funny how the older she got, the less he felt like her *big* brother. More and more, he was just her brother. Not bigger, just him.

She glanced at Garrick, and he looked away as though he didn't want to be caught staring. She watched him for just a moment longer. It wasn't often that he was too shy to meet her gaze. Of course now was the time he chose, now, when she wanted to glare frost at him and for him to feel every icicle in his chest.

MORNING CAME and Fay couldn't wait to get over to the Grahams. She wanted answers from Edna. She wanted to meet this Brandon fellow. She wanted to see Garrick. Wait, that last want didn't belong. Garrick didn't matter. She'd just spent more than enough time with him, and the truth was they'd argued for half of it. He wasn't someone she should *want* to encounter. He was someone to be *endured*. If she saw him, she would endure him.

She walked alone to the Grahams since Hugh was readying to head for Pete's, claiming a sore shoulder wasn't enough reason to leave a man in the woods without his horse.

On Sunday, Willem had explained how he insisted on paying Hugh for his time away and the time it would take to return Pete his horse, claiming Hugh had been injured in the line of duty. Fay grit her teeth with embarrassment. The Grahams were generous, that was to be sure, but she hated how her family had come to rely on their generosity.

She suspected Hugh's decision to leave right away had

less to do with his employer and more to do with Edna's engagement.

Just as the Grahams' house came into view, so did Garrick, bounding up the lane. Had he been watching for her? "Morning." His voice fell flat.

She glanced at the scowl marring his face. "Bad night?"

"Edna's man is still here."

Fay raised one eyebrow. "Are you jealous? Have you got a habit of falling for any woman working for a Graham?"

Garrick glared at her. "He was up late, clattering around the guesthouse."

"I thought you could sleep anywhere, even in a tent full of soldiers."

"Yes, well, in that case an early bedtime was prudent for all." He covered a yawn. Then ran his gaze along the length of her skirts. "I see you decided to change."

Fay flushed. At breakfast, her ma had explained why, exactly, it was inappropriate for a woman to show her legs in the manner Fay had done. She'd worn her brother's breeches before, when they were branding cattle, for example, but she had never thought about the reason for not wearing them off their land or around other folks.

And now she'd worn them through town, half of which she was sleeping on Garrick. Even when she'd been awake, she had still been riding double, in pants, with a man who she'd spent two days with. Mostly alone. She shuddered to think what might happen if anyone found out just how they'd spent their evening at Pete's. With a slow breath, she reminded herself that Pete had just come to town, so he wasn't likely to return any time soon. She should have sent a note with Hugh. It could have said:

Sorry, everything we told you was a lie. Please don't tell anyone.

Dishonestly yours,

Fay Morris

"It's best if you forget everything about the past few days. I think you've got enough to worry about with figuring out your future." As they drew nearer the house, Fay could see men loading items into Willem's wagon. Was Edna going to leave with her new fiancé without even saying goodbye?

Her heart gave a thump at the cruelty, but it wasn't allowed to wallow. Garrick cleared his throat and narrowed his gaze. "I don't think I could forget *everything* about the last few days."

Fay glared. Did he mean lying to Pete about being married? Or how she'd fallen asleep on him as they made their way home? If he'd had as little sleep as her, he'd have done the same. Or...? Her face burned. Did he mean sleeping in the same bed? Fay grabbed Garrick's wrist with both hands. She hated how the gesture looked too much like a prayer. "You said you wouldn't say a word," she hissed.

"I don't need to say anything to remember it." He closed his eyes, a small smile spreading his lips. Fay knew he was picturing something. She just didn't know what. She threw his hand away and quickened her pace toward the house.

Once she was on the other side of the wagon, Edna and a dark-haired man came into view on the side of the house. The man spat, then turned away and stalked toward the barn. As he rounded the corner, he kicked a fluffy gray barn cat.

Fay flinched at the cruelty, then glanced at Edna. She

did not wear the expression of a blushing bride-to-be. Fay looked back to Garrick and lowered her voice. "You better go tell your new friend to stop abusing the livestock before I murder him."

"Murder? Another secret I should keep for you?"

Fay grabbed the sleeve of his shirt and moved closer to him. "Stop. Everything I did was for your sake. I'm not going to be held hostage for protecting you."

His smile fell. "You're right. Only...what if I wanted to pretend a little longer?"

Fay dropped her hand and stepped back. Not because the idea was so preposterous, but because some silly, childish part of her wanted it too.

Garrick laughed. "I'll take care of him." Then he jerked his chin toward Edna. "You take care of her. Then I'm heading to your place to accompany Hugh to Pete's house. Nobody should be in those woods alone just now." Before he turned, he gave her a wink that made her stomach hit the soles of her ratty boots.

Fay took her time walking to the house, letting the icy wind cool her flushed cheeks. When she entered, Edna met her with a bright smile.

"Fay!" Edna pulled her in for a tight hug. "Garrick told us you were home, but I didn't expect you'd be in this morning." She bustled Fay into the kitchen, which smelled like some sort of bakery heaven.

"Mama, I want you to meet Fay." Edna turned to Fay. "This is my mama."

Mrs. Archer came to Edna's side, wiping her hands on her apron, which was made with an unfamiliar pattern. Fay smiled. To think! This woman was so dedicated to her work that she packed an apron when she left home.

She took one of Fay's hands in both of hers. Hers were

strong and callused, and Fay couldn't help but glance at Edna. Her friend must resemble her father's side. "I'm Agatha Archer. Pleased to make your acquaintance." She had an accent that, despite her soft tone, made every word sound like a harsh reprimand.

"Fay Morris." Fay couldn't help but smile into the woman's pale green eyes that matched Edna's in color. So they *were* related after all. She pressed Fay's palm, and Fay felt the sort of warmth Edna possessed from her mother too.

"Are you leaving so soon?" Fay asked.

Mrs. Archer smiled. "Not soon for me. Heaven only knows what will be waiting for me when I get back to the shop." Fay's gaze flicked to Edna. Her friend had mentioned the shop was her mother's second child. Fay got the impression it commanded their lives as much as they commanded its business. But Edna was looking at her mother with a sweet smile.

Fay remembered the argument she'd seen between Edna and the man, and the man's subsequent abuse of the feline. With a thick throat she asked, "Where is your fiancé?"

Edna's face darkened. "How did you—"

"Garrick came by last night with a basket of bread a mile high."

"He's not my fiancé."

Fay gave a slow nod, trying to read Edna's face. "Awfully nice of him to come here and make sure you're doin' all right."

"He had hoped, but I refused." Edna raised her chin, as though summoning the same courage she used to deal with that awful man. Then she touched Fay's elbow. "How is Hugh?"

Fay eyed her friend, failing in her attempts to stifle her curiosity. "On his way to Pete's with a basket a mile high. Does Della have *any* flour left?"

Agatha cleared her throat. "I bake when I'm worried, and Edna was gone for too long."

Fay grinned. "I hope you're not too wrung out to teach me a few things. I'd rather learn from the master than her apprentice." Fay bumped Edna with her hip.

Edna didn't smile. "Hugh's off to Pete's already? Did he tell you a bullet went through him? I did a poor job patching him up. He might've gotten blood poisoning if Pete hadn't returned when he did."

Fay cocked her head and gave Edna a coy smile. "He might have died a happy man in your care."

Edna's cheeks turned pink, and she returned to her mother's side, slicing bread. Fay watched the back of her head for a moment. So she knew Hugh liked her. What did she think of that? Fay wanted desperately to ask her, but she couldn't. Not with Mrs. Archer right there.

Fay came to Edna's side. "What can I do to help?"

"Not much. The heap Garrick brought was only some of it. We have more than we need. I'm just making a bread pudding for later."

The sound of someone entering through the front door made all the women turn. A tall man with dark features came inside. Brandon. The cat kicker. This close, he wasn't bad on the eyes, but she was proud to note that he didn't have Hugh's wide shoulders.

"Bastien says the wagon is ready." His accent matched the Grahams' Chicago lilt. Fay pegged him as born and raised in the city and by parents who possessed the same lilt. Not immigrants like Edna's parents.

"That's me." Mrs. Archer tugged loose her apron

strings and rolled it tightly. She paused and looked at Edna with an audible swallow. "You're sure about staying?"

Edna nodded, though her face said she was anything but certain.

The two embraced, and Brandon exited the house without so much as a word to Edna. Engaged, they definitely were not.

13

The week passed quickly, with everyone working hard to catch up from the days lost in Hugh and Edna's disappearance. Though Edna hadn't actually been engaged, and she proved her commitment by both staying at Aster Ridge and helping to procure affordable medicine for Lachlan, Hugh was still grumpy and doing his best to ignore her.

"We're late," he grumbled as Fay climbed into the wagon in her Sunday best. She met Lachlan's eyes, and they both sighed. Hugh had given her strict instructions not to meddle, but her big brother needed a bit of help, otherwise they'd all be dealing with angry Hugh for who knew how much longer.

When they arrived at the church house, Fay bustled the Grahams and her own family inside, which was no easy task. Thankfully, Garrick had hold of both his niece and nephew's hands and seemed keen to do as Fay beckoned.

Hugh tried to find his spot on the pew, but Fay snagged him, spouting nonsense about Edna and how he needed to apologize for the way he'd spoken to her earlier in the week. He'd heard it all before, and with a grumble he walked to the pew. Fay ran ahead and sat down first, ensuring he was the last on the row, with only one seat left for Edna.

All this matchmaking meant she had little time to note the stares pinned to Garrick. Fresh meat was scarce in Dragonfly Creek, and Garrick was both handsome and well connected. If he decided against moving his life to Texas, he would have any number of options here. She glanced around. Every woman in the church, married or not, stared at him.

The only one who didn't was Ginny Price, who stared directly at Fay.

Fay turned away, suppressing the urge to shudder. She wasn't in school any longer. Ginny had no power over her anymore. Fay could go to town when she wished. They were adults now. Surely, others were growing too wise to believe the other girl's cruel words.

When the sermon ended, Fay tried her best to stay close to Hugh as he followed Edna out of the church. The throng of people separated them, and when she was out on the lawn, she could see Hugh taking long strides toward Edna. She gave a squeak of delight and watched as he reached her. The pair stood close, speaking words she would pay good money to hear. She sighed. Hopefully, her brother wouldn't bungle everything in his usual way.

She turned to search for her mama and Lachlan, only to bump into Garrick. She stepped back, quirking her brow. "Can I help you, Mr. Hampton?"

He laughed at her stiff behavior. "Just watching whatever you're up to."

Fay couldn't stop her gaze from flicking toward Hugh and Edna.

Garrick crossed his arms over his broad chest, and a small smile lifted the corners of his mouth. "He loves her." Garrick's voice echoed deep, cutting into her hopeful thoughts.

"I know." Her heart was so hopeful, she didn't care to scold Garrick for assuming he knew her brother better than she.

When Hugh pulled Edna to the horse and out of sight, Fay turned and looked up at Garrick. "They're good for one another."

Garrick nodded.

Fay felt a pang of want for love, for someone who was perfect for her the way Edna was perfect for Hugh.

Violet came and took Garrick's hand. "Mama says it's time to leave."

He hefted her into his arms and said, "We must obey your mother always."

With a wink toward Fay, he strode away. A wink. Such a simple gesture, yet to Fay's exposed heart, it hit like a bullseye and made everything swell with possibility.

EDNA JOINED their wagon on the drive home, her hand entwined with Hugh's. Fay heard murmured words of marriage and living situations before she slid to the front of the wagon to give them ample space to discuss their engagement.

Whatever joy Fay harbored over Hugh's success was quickly smothered the moment Fay entered her room to change out of her Sunday clothes. Mama followed hot on her heels and closed the door behind her.

"There's been talk."

Fay turned. "What?"

"Talk. Of you and Garrick Hampton."

She said his last name like there were a thousand Garricks in the world and she had to specify which one they were discussing. Fay didn't know many men, but she knew he was different from all the ones she'd ever met. There was only one Garrick.

"What are they saying?" Irritation replaced the happiness she'd felt only moments ago. The hypocrisy it took for folks to use a worship service to gossip made her want to spit.

"That you are ruined, and Garrick has no intention to make you an offer."

Fay stepped backward, far from the words, the lies. "Mama, I'm not ruined. We were gone only a few days." She glued her feet to the floor and pinned her mama with a stare. "Days spent searching for Hugh."

"You were wrong to go. You knew it, which was why you snuck off. I should have never given you rein to search for him. I should have known you'd have your head and take off without a care for propriety." Mama shook her head in disappointment. "When will you learn to quit being so impulsive?" The words hit Fay like a knife to the heart. It was that same foolish impulsive trait that had her calling lies to Pete in the forest, that landed her in bed with Garrick in the first place.

But Mama wasn't done. "You are not a man. You're traipsing through town in trousers, sharing a saddle with a man, the catch of the town to boot. Of course folks are talking. The maids are jealous, the mamas are intrigued, and the men, well, who knows what they think of you now?"

"Mama, it doesn't matter what they think. It's not as though they had a high opinion of me before."

"Yes, well, they were never correct before, were they?"

Her words stung like the time a young Eloise snapped Fay with a wet towel. Fay took another step back. Her bed pressed against the back of her legs. "They aren't right, Mama. I went to find Hugh. Nothing, nobody, could have prevented me from searching."

Mama surveyed her, her mother's eye assessing the truth in Fay's words. "You best hope Pete comes to town soon and confirms all you say. For right now, there is nothing to be done."

Mama's comment did nothing to soothe Fay's worries. Pete coming to town would do the opposite of assuaging the rumors. All this did was make the goal of finding a husband all the more pressing. Though she didn't intend to marry anyone from Dragonfly Creek, the man she did marry might ask about her in town. She would just have to pray that the word of the folks in Aster Ridge would be enough for any man who took an interest.

She prayed none of this got around to Garrick's ears. He might be an impressive boxer, but she had no idea how well he bluffed.

14

————

*G*arrick pushed inside Della's house. The children were all abed, and the home held a quiet stillness, like it had been tucked in too. He hung his hat and coat.

Della sat near the dying embers of the fire, watching him. He would miss her when he left, but he couldn't keep pretending. This was what families did. They grew up and lived separate lives.

She stood. "Would you like a drink?"

Garrick shook his head. Too many times he watched his pa stumble around, stupid with drink. And that was the best of nights. He'd also seen fellow soldiers sobbing into their cups. He wasn't sure which one was worse, and he didn't want to be either.

"Sit." She gestured to the chair on the other side of the fireplace.

He did, running his hands through his hair, which had grown long since he'd left the Rough Riders.

Della hardly met his eye, and he watched her, tugging

132

at the cuffs of her shirtsleeves. "I'll write." He tried, unsure what it was that was bothering her.

"I was in town today." She was looking at him with the strangest expression.

Garrick nodded, waiting.

"There's been talk of you and Fay."

He jolted. *Talk?* "What do you mean?"

"I mean, if what they say is true, you can't leave. You need to take responsibility for your actions."

"My actions?" he parroted, knowing he wasn't contributing. But he'd missed something in Della's words. He was meant to know something he didn't.

"With Fay. You need to make an honest woman out of her."

"Hon—what are folks saying?"

"That you two shared a bed and"—Della's face twisted in anger—"that you'd never propose because you're too good for Fay Morris."

Garrick gripped the arms of the chair. His carnal instinct roared within him, begging to be let loose, to find whoever was spreading the rumors and stop them from hurting Fay. "I'm not too good for anyone. They want me to *marry* her?"

"If what they say is true, I want you to marry her too."

Garrick blustered. How? Why? Who? But a memory clicked in his mind. "Was it Ginny Price?"

Della cocked her head. With confusion or interest, he couldn't tell.

Garrick swore under his breath. "Fay has had some dealings with the girl, says she is intent on ruining Fay's happiness." He tried to picture Ginny's face, to recall if he'd seen her at the chapel. He'd been too caught up in

Fay sharing his saddle that he'd hardly noticed the girl's features.

"Well, at this time, it is you who can solve her unhappiness."

"Della, she won't marry me. I'm the reason her sister is living under a rock somewhere in exile. She may not have killed me while we were looking for Hugh, but she hasn't forgiven me enough to marry me."

"Did you two share a bed?"

Garrick gulped. Maybe he should have accepted Della's offer and had something to drink that was stronger than his own dry throat.

Della gave a stiff nod. "That's answer enough. Bastien said he'll float you the money you need to get yourself started."

"Float? I don't need money." He winced at the assumption. This was precisely why he wanted to get away. Nobody here saw him as a man—always the little brother. The dependent. The troublemaker.

"You do if you're going to stick around here."

Garrick closed his eyes. It seemed no matter what he said, Della was having the conversation she wished.

"It is not me you need to convince." He looked at his sister, hoping she would understand his next words. "Fay will not marry me."

"She will. Her reputation is in shambles. As far as I know, she wasn't fighting off suitors before you came around and blackened her name."

"Pete was there. We may have shared a bed, but nothing happened, nothing *could* have happened." Even if Fay hadn't hated him, even if she'd loved him, they wouldn't have been able to do anything with Pete sleeping so near and keeping a watchful eye.

"Rumor says you told him you were wed."

Garrick's breath blasted out of him. "Who told them all this? Has Pete come to town spitting more words than he spoke to me in all the hours I was staying at his house?"

"Ginny says she heard it from you and Fay. When you stopped for the post."

Garrick closed his eyes, pinching the bridge of his nose. They'd done this to themselves. He released a slow breath, letting his frustration with the situation ebb. Nothing mattered, except... "Fay will not marry me. She's waiting to marry a rich buck, one of Willem's guests."

"She doesn't have much choice."

That situation was all too familiar—a Morris girl having no choice but to marry a man she had no love for.

"No," he said.

Della's face hardened. "Garrick, you *will* make her an offer. I'll not have my brother coming to town and ruining a girl's reputation just to turn tail. I know Pa didn't teach you much in the way of honor, but—"

"He taught me plenty about how to handle a woman. Trust me when I tell you Fay is better off ruined than saddled to me."

Della's face softened. "You're not Pa. I've never seen you hit a woman."

No, he'd never hit a woman, but he'd been rough with Eloise, and her life was forever changed because of his careless actions. "Is that the mark of a good man? One who *doesn't* beat his wife?"

Della leaned forward and put her hand over his. "You are a good man. If I didn't believe that, I wouldn't be asking you to stay."

Garrick lifted a brow. "This isn't some awful way to

force me to stick around?" Even as he said it, he knew it wasn't true. With the details Della knew, Ginny truly must have heard Fay and Garrick teasing one another outside the post office. He shook his head. They'd been so reckless.

He sighed. "Shall I go tonight?" He could picture her parents just as he'd left them the night he had helped deliver their Christmas feast. It seemed unfair that Mr. Morris wouldn't be in the position to pummel Garrick for ruining his little girl's reputation. "Her parents might be the ones to say no before Fay even has a chance to reject me."

"Go tomorrow while Fay is here. Speak with her pa first. He's a reasonable man."

Garrick sighed and nodded. Della stood and ran her hand over his head as she passed, then moved down the hall, leaving him alone.

He stared at Bastien's curio of spirits. It wasn't merely the appearance of stupidity or pitifulness that kept him away from drink; he also didn't drink the stuff because that was what made his father the meanest. Garrick wasn't about to fuel his greatest fear.

He was right that the Morrises, Fay included, would say no to whatever he proposed. But what frightened him the most was if they said yes.

THE MORNING DAWNED dull and gloomy. The sun took its time burning away the clouds, and it hadn't yet completed the job when Fay and Hugh came down the path. Garrick watched Fay smiling and talking with her brother. They parted ways at the fork in the path, Fay for the house, Hugh to the stables where Garrick waited.

He kept to the shadows, wondering if he should talk to Hugh about what was coming. In the end, his cowardice won out. That, and the idea that if Fay or her parents rejected Garrick's offer, her brothers might never know what had transpired. Folks in town would have to be fools to blab gossip to her brothers, large as they both were. At least those two could continue thinking on their sister without the least shred of disappointment.

Hugh stepped into the dim interior of the stables and grinned at Garrick. "Fay said you were leaving. Wasn't sure when."

Garrick forced a return smile. "That's not exactly decided yet."

"Well, it's been good having you here for a bit."

Garrick tried for a laugh. Hugh might be punching him in the nose very soon, but Garrick would take the compliment. "Thanks." He gestured to the stalls he'd already cleaned. "I have something to do this morning, so I got an early start."

Hugh nodded and took the spade from Garrick's hand. "I'll finish up."

Garrick walked away, the tension in his shoulders not the least bit eased by leaving his work behind. Afraid as he was, he'd much rather muck a thousand stalls than face the foe before him.

Fay's pa would never accept Garrick's proposal. Not unless Della spoke true, and Fay had truly been diminished in the eyes of both the town and her family. Garrick's heart broke at the prospect.

He'd been so careless, forcing her to promise to lie. He'd thought only of himself, of the barrel pointed at his chest. But Fay was right—a woman faced different enemies than the ones a man faced. These thoughts chased him across the prairie, so the trek to the Morris household felt like it had only taken one ragged breath.

Garrick stared at the door and, straightening his shoulders, strode forward with purpose. He rapped on the door and waited as footsteps drew near.

Mrs. Morris opened the door and blinked in surprise at Garrick. He pulled his hat off his head. "Morning, ma'am."

She crossed her arms and leaned against the door-frame, her glare colder than the wind at his back. "What brings you to our door, Mr. Hampton?"

"I wished to speak with yourself and Mr. Morris, if you have a minute."

She lifted her chin slightly. Apparently her manners were strong enough to eclipse her hatred of him. "Mr. Morris hasn't been well."

Garrick's brows twitched. He'd been in his chair the other night. "It's rather urgent."

"This about what folks are saying in town?"

Garrick's heart sank. He'd hoped the Morris's infrequent trips to town meant they hadn't been subject to embarrassment due to his misdeeds.

"It is, ma'am."

"Come in then." Mrs. Morris stepped back and held the door open.

Once Garrick was through the door, Mrs. Morris closed the door to the icy wind. "He's in the bedroom."

Garrick followed her down the dark hallway and into a small room. Mr. Morris lay on his back, his body limp but his eyes sharp. He didn't speak, merely followed Garrick's movements with his eyes. Mrs. Morris took the only chair, which sat in the corner. She lifted a bit of mending from the chest of drawers and squinted at it, then her fingers began to work deftly.

Even in Cuba, with bullets raining around him, he'd not felt so alone. At least there he'd had comrades in the same situation. He cleared his throat. "You might have heard." He swallowed the thickness in his throat. "I fear my adventure with your daughter has cast doubt on her reputation. I wish to first assure you that there is no reason for you to doubt her chastity. Your friend Pete was there—"

Mrs. Morris cut in. "And he thought you two were wed." She didn't take her eyes from her mending as she spoke.

Garrick sighed. How did everyone have the right of it so quickly? He wasn't used to small town gossip. Or perhaps he'd merely never had to mind it until now. "Yes, well, that was my idea. Fay merely agreed in an attempt to keep me safe."

"From Pete," Mr. Morris confirmed.

Garrick nodded. The reason behind their actions was quickly crumbling, like poorly set mortar. He leveled Mr. Morris with a look. "I intend to marry her and quash any false rumors."

"You will do no such thing." Mrs. Morris dropped her hands in her lap.

"Ida," Mr. Morris warned. Then he coughed, a single hoarse bark that turned into a fit of coughing.

Mrs. Morris flashed an angry look and said, "Help him to sit up."

Garrick caught Mr. Morris under the arms and hefted him forward. His weight reminded him too much of the feel of a dead comrade over his shoulder, and Garrick was glad when Mr. Morris finally stopped coughing and Garrick was able to lay him back again.

Was it possible Garrick had fooled himself into believing he *wanted* a life at war? If he never held a dying comrade's hand again, it would be too soon. He wasn't built for fighting. Doing well at something did not make it his future. He still had a choice, and he chose to stay here, to protect Fay's reputation in whatever way he could.

Mr. Morris's breathing was wheezy, but his eyes were strong once more as they pierced Garrick. "You did not like our Eloise marrying Aaron."

Garrick shook his head. "I did not, sir."

"Why?"

"She was too good for the likes of him."

"And you are good enough for my other daughter?"

Garrick's heart stuttered. "No."

The room grew thick with a painful silence. Garrick had never felt more ashamed in his life. "I'm sorry about Eloise. I'm sorry to once more be the cause of trouble for your family."

"You are a soldier?" Mr. Morris continued, undeterred by Garrick's weak apologies.

"Yes, sir."

"Do you plan to quit that life? Do you have any way to care for Fay?"

Mrs. Morris made a squeak from her corner, but Garrick had eyes only for Mr. Morris. Was it possible this man *wasn't* completely opposed to the idea of Garrick wedding his daughter?

"I don't want to be a soldier." The sentence, finally spoken aloud, rang with a truth that was a song to Garrick's heart. "I have a bit saved. Bastien will lend me whatever else I need to start my life."

When Della had offered it, Garrick had flinched at the idea, but now that he was in this moment, he realized a man needed means to provide for anyone in his care. He was comforted by the fact that finances weren't a taboo topic in the Morris household. Fay meant to marry for just this reason. "Fay told me of her intentions to secure a monetary match for herself. I may not have much, but you can be assured if anything ever happened to me, she would be provided for and loved by Della, more than she already is... which is a great deal."

Garrick forced himself not to smile. Speaking of a union with Fay allowed him to dream of a life with her. A life like Della and Bastien's, with a home and a farm and, one day, children. A place that felt like home because it was his and not merely because it held all the attributes he wanted most in life. "I will love her, sir." His words were quiet, too vulnerable to be spoken with anything except reverence. It was only once he'd said them that he realized they should have been his starting words.

Mr. Morris surveyed Garrick with watery eyes and slow, whistling breaths. Finally, he said, "I'll give you the same deal I gave Aaron Harder. You have my consent, but it is your responsibility to convince her."

Garrick's hand jerked at his sides. He pushed away any thoughts of his similarity to Aaron and focused instead on the fact that Mr. Morris wasn't forbidding the match. "Thank you very much, sir." Garrick glanced at Mrs. Morris. Hers was not the approval Garrick needed, but he'd very much like to have it as well. "I *will* be good to her."

Despite being shorter than him, and seated, Mrs. Morris still managed, miraculously, to look down her nose at Garrick. "She's not our Eloise. Fay is quite different from her sister."

"It is not Eloise I wish to marry."

After pinning him with a long look, Mrs. Morris nodded and returned her attention to her mending. Garrick took it as a dismissal and backed out of the doorway, showing himself to the front door. Once outside, the biting wind buffeted his face. Only then did he realize his flesh burned with every emotion that had just thrashed him.

He bounded down the steps, not the least bit concerned with the next and possibly most difficult task: convincing Fay.

15

*F*ay felt Della watching her throughout the day. Whenever Fay would meet her employer's eye, Della would just smile and get back to work. Fay's cheeks would flush. No doubt Mama wasn't the only one to hear about the rumors in town. It was inevitable everyone else in Aster Ridge would hear about it too, her brothers included. She gulped.

When the men came in for lunch, even Garrick avoided her gaze. Was it only yesterday she was concerned he'd be leaving? Now he couldn't leave soon enough for her liking. Or perhaps he could stay and do something to ruin Ginny Price's reputation. Soldiers were known to do such things.

The moment she had the thought, she chastised herself for it. Not for wicked Ginny's sake, but for Garrick. He wasn't some pawn to be used. Nevertheless, the sooner he left, the sooner folks would stop speculating about their relationship.

He'd been too coveted at the Christmas dance. The women her age must have been put out to think Fay had her claws in him. She didn't dare tell them even *he* wasn't rich enough for her. There was nothing Fay could say to quell the rumors. Like any rumor, it had to run its course. The only thing that could help it along would be if something far juicier happened to draw everyone's attention away from Fay.

Unfortunately, the most exciting thing was Hugh and Edna's wedding, and that event only drew attention to the family. Some of the rumormongers even suggested their marriage was due to Edna having a baby on the way, for why would Hugh refuse Catherine all these years, only to up and marry Edna?

Finally, Della left to lay down with little Joshua, who had taken to climbing from his cot during nap time. Fay tidied the kitchen, then, just to feel the rare winter sun on her face, she went out to check the coop for eggs.

She was crossing the windswept lawn when a voice reached her. She twisted, unsure of the source. Garrick jogged toward her. She swallowed, waiting. Had he heard the rumors? Della and Lydia had been in town yesterday, but she couldn't be sure if any of the men had gone along. Perhaps Garrick had driven them.

"I was just headed in," he said. "I thought you might have a moment while the children were quiet."

She squared her shoulders. He most definitely knew. "I have time." The wind whipped her hair out of her plait and into her face. She brushed it away in vain.

"Can we step inside?"

Fay looked at the house. Her body tensed, preparing for whatever was to come. She nodded and started back.

She stepped inside, and when Garrick shut the door, she crossed her arms and raised her brows.

He waved a hand. "Could we have a seat?"

She didn't want to go further into the house. It was illogical, she knew, but her feet refused to retreat. Instead, she sat on the old church pew that served as a bench for those readying to leave the house.

A look of disappointment rolled across Garrick's face, and he sat too. He leaned his elbows on his knees and picked at his nails. "Della told me we've been discovered."

Discovered? Fay swallowed down her denial. Garrick was the one person she shouldn't have to defend herself to.

"I spoke with your pa."

Pa? Understanding stacked in her mind like playing cards shuffling together. He'd heard the rumors. Then he'd gone to ask for her hand. And he was here now, which meant Pa had given his approval. Why wouldn't he? Garrick was a sight more appropriate a husband than Aaron had been, and Pa had said yes then too.

Fay raised a hand, palm toward him in a stopping gesture. "Don't. You don't need to do any of this."

"Fay, I—"

"No. It was just Ginny up to her old ways, spreading falsehoods." Fay shook her head. It might have been Hugh and Edna's engagement that pressed Ginny into starting up her cruelty once more.

"I believe she heard us speaking outside the post office."

Fay froze, remembering. They'd whispered, and Ginny had been inside gathering the mail set for Aster Ridge. Hadn't she? "No. She's crafty, and just because she might have gotten a few things right—"

"She has it *all* right. Shared bed, fake husband. They all saw us ride into town with you asleep on my chest."

"I was *tired*."

Garrick raised his hands in surrender. "I'm not faulting you for it. But you must have looked a comfortable sight. Comfortable like a woman who had already slept in my arms."

Fay huffed. She wanted to spit, wanted to scream. She glanced at the door, wishing they'd stayed outside so she could do everything she wished without fear of waking the children.

He continued, his deep voice pulling her back from her dark thoughts. "Edna and Hugh getting married only lends credence to the idea. They think, in Pete's absence, his bed was used for all sorts of fornication."

Fay shook her head. "Fools who have nothing else to do with themselves."

"I mean to make an honest woman out of you." He reached out.

Fay drew her hand away and when it wasn't enough, she stood, taking two quick steps backward. "No, Garrick. There is no need for you to do this. I'm not marrying you. I don't care what they think. I never have."

"But your prospects—"

"I don't want any of them anyhow." She prayed the men who visited Willem's ranch would require only the recommendation of the folks in this valley when they asked after Fay's reputation.

"You're still set on marrying rich?" He spoke with such frankness. No censure darkened his words, and he leaned forward, bracing his elbows on his knees and hanging his head. He didn't look or sound like a man who faulted her, who judged her. He looked like a man... disappointed. But not necessarily with her.

If her life had been different, if her family had been self-sufficient, if Eloise had married for love and not made an enemy out of Garrick, might this man before her still have proposed one day?

She flicked her head, shaking off the dreamy notion. "I am." As she spoke the words, she realized she'd been faltering. She'd had an adventure with Garrick, and it had changed a small part of her. After spending mere days with Garrick, something stirred that she'd never felt after spending her entire life near the boys in town. She feared love wouldn't be so easily conjured with whatever man she chose. Nor was it easily snuffed out when the wrong man came along. But now that she recognized it, she prayed she could shut that fear away and bind it tight.

"You feel nothing for me?"

The earnestness in his eyes sliced at her heart. She'd only ever been honest with Garrick. There was no reason he should have come here expecting anything except the answer she gave him.

"I feel friendship," she said. "Perhaps the folks in town are right that we got closer than appropriate. But I have an idea of what will force me to marry, and it was never going to be the cruelty of Ginny Price."

Garrick nodded. "The last thing I want is to force you into marriage."

"You'd be the worst kind of hypocrite." An image of the last time she saw Eloise flitted around in her mind. She'd barely gotten to say goodbye as her sister had rushed to leave town.

Garrick lapsed into silence, lost in thoughts Fay could only imagine. Were they the same as hers? Did his remorse run deep enough that he truly understood all he'd done to her family? She couldn't resent him as she'd done before. She understood him now, his reasons, even his foolishness.

"I thank you for offering," she said. "You are a good man."

His brows squeezed together. "Della said the same. I don't think that has the same meaning out here as it does to me."

It was Fay's turn to give him a quizzical look.

The side of his mouth lifted in a sad smile. "Good man." He sighed. "I'm no such thing." Standing, he wiped his palms on his pants, and they left a bit of darkness in their wake. Sweat. He'd been nervous, probably worried that he would be saddled to Fay all his days. He'd told her once how disagreeable she was. Plopping his hat on, he gave Fay a nod before exiting the home.

She glanced around the space, an entry she'd walked through hundreds of times. But it would never be the same for her. Their adventure had changed more than she ever could have anticipated.

When Edna and Lydia returned from town, they laid their wares on the tabletop. Their lighthearted laughter was just the distraction Fay needed, and her shoulders relaxed as they told her about how Edna had haggled with the shop owner on the price of flour. Among their wares was a bolt of fine fabric in a lovely green-blue, a gift from Willem and Lydia's family. Fay ran her fingers along the material with appreciation. "The color suits you." She grinned at Edna and her sage green eyes, like she was born to match this prairie.

Lydia's eyes sparkled. "Doesn't it? We'll need to get started right away if you want *any* embellishments."

Edna laughed. "I told you, I don't need anything special."

Fay and Lydia scoffed, then laughed at their synchronized thoughts.

Soon they had the doors bolted and the curtains closed. Edna stood in the front room atop a crate, her arms splayed out like a scarecrow, while Lydia ran the measuring tape along her frame. Fay watched, not nearly as handy with a needle as Lydia was. She would be put to use as Lydia's assistant.

Before long, Fay had to pull herself away from the project and get started on dinner. As she worked, she listened to the hum of eager talking between Edna and Lydia. Amidst the excitement, Fay had done a fine job of putting Garrick's unnecessary proposal out of her mind, but as she stood in the kitchen she felt too near that entryway, too near what had transpired only hours ago.

Soon he would be entering the house along with the other men, expecting his dinner. How could she face him after refusing him? Not that his proposal had been true. He wouldn't be heartbroken, only embarrassed that a girl with as little means as Fay would refuse a man who rightfully might have suited her. After all, though not a Graham by blood and lacking their inheritance, he was Della's own brother. Surely, he would do well in life once he settled down and put his mind to it. Perhaps if he had been ten years older, ten years into his life, his proposal would have been something she could have accepted.

So why did that idea turn her mouth down in a pout? She didn't want to say yes to him for money. If she couldn't do so for Garrick, would she be able to do so when it truly counted? Or would her feelings grow for any man she seriously considered?

Now that she'd refused him, perhaps he would be on his way down to his friend in Texas. His need to stay had vanished with her refusal. He said so himself—he had no intention to live on Bastien's charity. He wanted to be his own man. Such a dream. One her brothers had too. Perhaps one day she would see all her siblings happily living the lives of their dreams. Perhaps Garrick would find his peace as well.

Della joined her in the kitchen, and together they finished preparing dinner. Fay was cleaning when she heard the front door and the thud of boots. Garrick's voice floated into the kitchen, followed by Bastien's.

They came around the corner, and Fay kept her eyes on the dish she was scrubbing. She was a servant, and there was no need for her to verbally greet her employers every time they entered a room. Most masters would surely prefer a worker who kept her eyes down and her mouth shut. She channeled that attribute as she polished off one dish after another.

Finally, the kitchen was clean, and Fay tried to catch Della's eye. She had to march into the sitting room before Della finally looked up from entertaining little Joshua. "Oh, Fay. Leaving so soon?" Della shot Garrick a pointed look.

Fay didn't dare look at him to see his response. For all she could tell, he wasn't even looking at his sister.

"Unless you'd like me to stay."

Della waved away Fay's offer. "Of course not. See you in the morning."

Fay smiled and spun on her heel. As she moved away, she heard the murmur of a whisper and quickened her pace. She tugged her shawl off the hook and put it on as she marched toward the stables in search of Hugh.

She found him mucking a stall. He glanced over his shoulder. "I have a bit more to do."

Fay passed a hand over her head and along her braid. The winter days were shorter, and the sun had already set.

She wasn't keen to walk home alone. Instead, she perched on a barrel and waited.

As Hugh worked, Fay spoke. "Edna has a bit of fine cloth for her dress. They started on it today."

Hugh gave a *hm* that was both acknowledgement and somehow meant to assist in hefting a large scoop of soiled hay off the ground.

"How did you know you loved her?"

He stopped, cutting her with a suspicious glare. "It's not too different from the way you love her. She's kind and strong. Selfless and joyous." A dreamy smile graced his mouth. "I knew I didn't want to live without her. And more, I wanted her with me always."

Fay wanted Garrick to *leave*. Once he did, the rumors would fade into nothing. Her parents would no longer be embarrassed. Eventually, Pete would make a trip to town, and Fay could beg his help in reversing the damage done. So long as he didn't confirm it first. She should have sent that note with Hugh when he'd swapped horses.

"How was Pete when you returned his mount?"

"He was Pete." Hugh's voice held an exasperated edge.

"I only ask because, well, perhaps we should visit him more often."

Hugh stopped his work and leaned on the handle of his tall spade. "I plan to."

"Good. I'd like to join you. On Saturday?"

Hugh lowered one brow. "I've got plenty to do preparing for my wedding. 'Tis not the time to be using daylight to visit a friend I saw just last week."

Fay sighed. Hopefully Pete wouldn't have need to visit town, since he had only just returned from a supply run.

Hugh finished his work, and they walked home. The

moon was bright, its light reflecting on the snowy surfaces.

When they entered the house, they were met by Pa's raspy cough echoing deeper in the home. Fay frowned at Hugh. Lachlan stood from his seat by the fireplace and helped serve them supper. They all worked so easily around one another. Every one of them had a part to play, and yet, when Eloise had left, they'd been fine. And again when Otto went. Perhaps Fay had been wrong about being needed. Perhaps a person was only needed if they wanted to be.

All three of them sat at the table. Pa's coughing was punctuated by the sound of something clattering to the floor in the bedroom. Lachlan glanced down the hallway, then back at Hugh and Fay. "It's never been this bad."

Hugh shook his head. "Remember when Otto chipped a tooth coughing?"

Lachlan gave them a grim nod. "At least we can be glad Pa is too weak to hurt himself."

"What do we do?" Fay's voice was quiet. If her brothers couldn't help, how could she?

"Pray." Lachlan's voice was grim.

Fay nodded. She believed in faith, but she also believed in works. "What about that poultice we got a few years back? It was bad then too."

Lachlan nodded. "Might be worth a trip to Billings."

Billings. Fay hadn't remembered they'd had to go so far for it. "What about the apothecary in Worthington that makes Lachlan's medicine?"

Hugh huffed. "I've missed too much work. And Lachlan has enough to catch up on himself. A half day spent going to Worthington and back...? Let's wait to see how bad it gets."

Fay's brothers leaned their heads together, solving what problems they could and unburdening the rest upon the other. Fay's chest pinched with longing for her sister. She wanted a woman to lay her burdens upon.

Mama bustled down the hall. "Glad you made it. Have you had supper?"

"Yes, ma'am." Fay gave a single nod.

"Good." Ma's hands worked fast tidying the kitchen. Fay stood and helped, but most of the work had been done before Fay even got home. She put a hand on Mama's forearm. "Lachlan says it's never been this bad."

Mama's gaze swept to Fay's, and she held it for a moment, as though deciding what to say. Finally, she shook her head. "I'm sure it has."

Fay's throat shriveled. "What do we do?"

"We're doing it." She straightened the towel. Trying to appear busy, no doubt. "I've spent today caring for him. I do this every winter."

"Mama, it's only the start of the year. There's a lot of winter left."

Mama's eyes snagged on Fay's, and for a moment, she saw a weakness, a desperation in them. "We'll do our best. It's always been enough."

Fay nodded. Mama was right. They hadn't lost someone yet. There was no reason they should start now.

Nevertheless, could Pa hold on long enough for Fay to find herself a match? Was this a single bad winter, or did it foretell a weakness in Pa? She straightened her shoulders. A new batch of guests was due to arrive in one week.

The following week would be Edna and Hugh's wedding. Then another batch of guests. As Willem's gentlemen ranch collected clients, Fay's chances grew at finding someone for herself. Perhaps she need not be so particular. If she applied pressure, surely she would find someone suitable. Perhaps she could even move to Chicago, and Pa could go to one of the fancy hospitals Della had said was making miraculous strides in medicine.

Even as she hoped for such an occurrence, she couldn't quite imagine what she could offer such a man. Why would he choose her, a wild country girl with a half-ruined reputation? Any of those city men were more likely to string her along, hoping to take his pleasure and ruin her completely.

She padded to her room and removed her dress. She would have to be smart, witty. She pulled her hair up and surveyed herself in the mirror. She might not have Eloise's beauty, but she wasn't easily ignored either. Earlier that day, she'd looked through the book of patterns Lydia had bought in town. The sketched women wore their hair differently. Fay's long braid had never been stylish, but she wasn't a young girl now. She would be sure to pull her hair up more than only Sundays. She moved her knot of hair this way and that, trying to replicate the images she'd seen.

A soft tap on her door was followed by Mama.

"Did Garrick speak with you?"

Fay nodded, not the least bit irritated with both her folks for granting their permission. But she could hardly say so with Papa abed.

"Did you accept his offer?"

"No, Mama. I told you this morning, I'm not ruined. He had no need to make any such offer."

"He seemed keen on the idea."

Fay looked at her mama sidelong. "I think you and

Papa are blinded by our own love for one another. That man was prepared to fulfill a *duty*."

"Are you not consigned to duty yourself?"

"Yes, and Garrick is not what I had in mind. He has nothing to his name save a very large horse and a bit of money earned boxing."

Mama reeled her head back, her eyes bulging.

Fay smirked. Her comment had hit exactly where she'd wanted it to. "You do not know the man you allowed to make me an offer today." The last of her words came out bitter, and her smug smile fell.

A crease formed between Mama's brows.

The urge to apologize flickered in Fay's heart, but her pride stamped it down. She was right. Her parents were apparently so keen to see their children married off they allowed any offer presented. Thank goodness Fay didn't live in the past, when a woman's consent wasn't even needed.

Just because life had turned out well for Eloise, didn't mean what had happened wasn't an anomaly. Fay and Garrick were like oil and vinegar. They could be shaken and forced to combine, but once the liquid settled, they would separate again, each respecting the line that stood between them.

"I suppose you are right, but it's not as though your pa handed you over to him. Garrick still needed to gain your approval. Are you sure about refusing him?"

"It's done. I did not need a night to think on it."

Ma nodded, her eyes darting about the room. "Well, that's that settled then." She stood. "Get some sleep, darling."

Pa coughed in the other room, and Fay wondered how much sleep Mama was getting herself. Fay had thought

Ma's eyes looked worried, but now she saw it was fatigue marring her usually pleasant face. "No, Mama, I want to tuck *you* into this bed. I'll tend Pa for a few hours while you get a bit of uninterrupted rest."

Mama shook her head.

But Fay pressed her back. "Just a bit won't hurt. I promise to wake you if anything is amiss."

Ma sighed, and a surge of protective love swelled in Fay's chest as she pulled the covers back and tucked the quilt around her ma's shoulders.

She took the lantern and carried it into her parents' bedroom. Pa lay with his eyes closed, his breathing ragged. He looked like any other man while he slept.

The chair squeaked as she sat down, and Pa's eyes fluttered open. He smiled, his one dimple winking as he did so.

"How are you feeling?" Fay knelt closer to the bed, resting her arms atop it.

He closed his eyes and nodded. "Well enough. Did that boy, Garrick... did he speak to you?"

Fay swallowed. "Yes, Pa. He did."

Pa nodded again. "He will take care of you."

She thought of all her parents had done for them, of all the things every parent does. But her pa was special. Because of his disability, he had been around far more than other fathers. Fay learned to read at his knee, cried into his shoulder when Ginny's words cut too deeply and again when Eloise left.

Fay leaned forward and cupped the top of her pa's bald head. "I've been taken care of my whole life. What I want is to take care of *you*."

Fay had no memories of her pa on his own two feet. She'd been a babe when the polio came. She did, however, know these colds. The one last year had also been the worst they'd seen. The others might not be making the connection, but Fay was. Pa was getting worse, and if they wanted their family to remain together, something had to change, starting with the expensive poultice. They had the funds now that Edna had discovered a cheaper treatment for Lachlan.

"With that new recipe for Lachlan's medicine, we have extra money to get you a poultice from Billings. Hugh and Lachlan could pick it up next week when they go collect Willem's guests."

Pa shook his head, but then he started coughing, as though his body was begging for what his mind wouldn't give him. Fay helped him lift his head and shoulders so he could get a decent breath of air.

"Pa, this one is at least as bad as last year. What if it gets worse?"

He shook his head still as she laid him back down. "I get these every year, you know that. We can't go spending all our money on a little cold."

Soon his breathing turned deeper. He was asleep.

Fay couldn't lie to herself. This cold was already worse than the others. What was the point of money if they weren't going to use it to keep them alive?

With silent movements, Fay crawled under the bed and located the saddlebag Aaron had given Mama when he and Eloise had left for Oregon. Pulling a handful of coins out, she hefted the weighty metal in her palm. They could start with the poultice from Worthington, and if that didn't do the job, Hugh could get some from the apothecary in Billings when he went. Fay knew just who could afford to spend a day riding to Worthington and back. The question was if she dared to beg it of him.

16

*G*arrick woke with misery in his heart. The only thing that propelled him from his bed was the thought that if he waited too long, he would have to face Fay's cold shoulder once more at breakfast.

He readied for the day and did his best not to focus on the pain of her rejection. He'd known what her answer would be before he asked. Apparently, there was one rogue sliver of his mind that had hoped, and it was that part that mourned now. He entered the kitchen with quiet anticipation, and when he found it blessedly empty, he fed himself a few slices of bread. Then he saddled Dusty and went for a hard ride.

He and his comrades had done this often, raced one another on horseback. Some would even set up targets and shoot while they raced, but Garrick had never excelled in that game. He wasn't as practiced a rider as most of them. His fine horse was only his due to Bastien's generosity. Besides that, Garrick possessed a heart desperate to prove its worth to the world.

Garrick proved himself best with his feet on the

ground and his fists protecting his face. The lack of two fingers may have made his right fist smaller, but when curled, it was no worse as a weapon. The memory of the way Pa used his own fists surged within Garrick. Still, after so many years away from the man, Garrick would never escape the dark memories of his childhood.

He kicked his horse harder, and Dusty, used to the game, pounded her hooves faster. The icy wind pained Garrick's face, but he embraced it. He remembered being younger, seeing Della be taken away from their home by her first husband, a cruel man. Only a young boy himself, Garrick had been helpless to stop the cycle. Hatred raged in his chest at the memory.

He pictured the look on the nurse's face when she had told him his pa refused to pay for the medicine necessary to stop the infection spreading up his arm. Garrick had no funds of his own. All his pay from the factory had gone to Pa's pockets, which had apparently been sewn shut. Helpless once more.

Finally, he recalled Eloise telling him she had no choice but to marry Aaron. Apparently the only thing worse than being helpless was to watch another suffer in helplessness and be unable to assist.

Now Fay had lost her reputation due to Garrick's association. Never before had he been the *cause* of the issue. The good news was that Garrick had grown used to being unable to help. He should have been able to swallow the bitter soup down instead of attempting to beat it away with every thundering pound of his horse's hoof.

Fay had blessedly said no. But what if she'd said yes? He shuddered to think. He chewed the reason. It was too raw for him to yet explain. He would love nothing more for Fay to be his, to smile for him, to entertain his kisses, to bear his children. But the idea of being hers gave him pause. For her to suffer his moods, to suffer his poverty. How could he prove to himself that he was enough for her? Perhaps if he could convince himself, he could convince her too.

He slowed his horse as this thought weaved its way through him. First, he'd have to scrape himself off the bottom of the barrel. He'd speak with Bastien, ask for a loan to get himself a farm. He'd buy a goat off the Milneses and a milk cow from Willem. Spring would be here soon enough, and he'd plant a garden. He'd create the home Fay deserved, and he would wait, promising her his love until she recognized it for the offer it was. Not one to save her from ruin, but one to bring them both the happiness of a husband and wife who needed and loved one another.

With his mind cooled, he returned to the stables and settled Dusty in her stall. Garrick worked alongside Hugh as though he wasn't causing their family any strife. When they'd completed the bulk of the chores, he found Bastien in the corral, training a young horse. Garrick watched from the side until Bastien led the horse back to its stall.

Garrick followed his brother-in-law, his stomach twisting with the words he planned to speak.

When Bastien smiled at Garrick, he stepped forward, removing his hat. "Della mentioned you might be willing to lend me a bit of money to buy my own place and get set up."

Bastien lifted a canteen from the wall and took a long drink. He wiped his mouth with the back of his hand and nodded. "I'm glad you're thinking about staying. Della will be right pleased." He screwed the lid back on and hung the canteen on the nail. "It will be a loan, you hear? You'll pay me back, and whatever you build will be yours and not mine. What are you imagining?"

"I thought to live off the land, mostly. Garden, hunt, and raise a bit of cattle to make up the rest. I have a bit of my own saved, but not enough to buy a plot."

Bastien nodded. "Many folks make a life out of what you described. How much do you need?"

Garrick shrugged. "I don't rightly know. First, I need to find a bit of land for sale."

Bastien pointed vaguely. "There's a bit for sale the next valley over. A wide plot, but they might sell you a portion. Wright is their name. See what you think of it."

Garrick nodded, excitement making his breathing increase. "I'll go look today."

With a firm handshake, he took his leave. Saddling Dusty for the second time that day, he set off in the direction Bastien had pointed. *Wright.* Perhaps this family would be willing to sell, and perhaps Garrick could make a life for himself. Perhaps if he stayed close, he could convince Fay.

FAY HAD JUST FINISHED her workday and was waiting near the stable for Hugh. The sound of stamping hooves drew her eye. Garrick rode up, a wide smile on his face.

Pa had been better this morning, up and smiling, but Fay still had the weight of the gold hanging in her pocket, waiting for her to beg Garrick to spend it.

He dismounted with all the grace of a catamount and led his horse right up to Fay.

"I'm buying a bit of land just north of here."

Her brows clashed together. "What land?"

"The Wrights'. They're selling all of it, and he agreed to give me the southernmost portion. Ten acres."

She shook away his answer. She'd asked the wrong question. "Why?"

"Well, I told you I didn't want to live on Bastien's dime my whole life. I figure I better get started." He leaned down and worked the buckle of the saddle.

"I thought you were going south to Texas?" Rumors in Dragonfly Creek would never cease if word got out that Garrick intended to buy land. First, the rumors would be that he was marrying Fay, then the truth would come out that they weren't engaged, and the rumors would truly fly. She could almost hear their words now. *Not even her employer's brother would suffice for stuck-up Fay.*

"Not Texas. There's plenty of opportunity for me right here in Montana."

Fay narrowed her eyes. Where had this new optimism come from?

He lifted the saddle off Dusty and walked it into the stable.

Fay followed. "There are the same opportunities there always were. What's changed?"

He set the saddle on the rack and walked past her once more. Fay pivoted, but had only made it a few steps before he started back with Dusty's reins in hand.

"Things are a bit different now," he said. He stuck Dusty in her stall. With deft fingers, he unbuckled the halter and slid it down Dusty's nose.

"What's different?" Fay watched his every movement like he was a mountain lion and her the deer, trying to sense if the cat was hungry or just passing through.

"Well, I suppose I have a bit of a mess I'd like to see

cleaned up. But, also, if I'm going to make my life anywhere, I'd like it to be with family."

Fay's heart teetered at his words. Della had missed Garrick while he'd been gone. Fay had listened with only a half-sympathetic ear, since that man was the reason she'd lost her sister and best friend. But seeing Della now, with her brother returned, nearly broke Fay's heart. His niece and nephew loved him too. He belonged here with his family.

"Della must be pleased." The words were painful to speak. Fay wasn't used to being this generous regarding others' feelings.

Garrick gave a rueful laugh. "She demanded I stay, demanded I propose marriage to you."

Fay's head jerked like she'd been slapped. "I'm not marrying you." Her words were flat and slow. Had she missed something?

"Oh, I know. But I'm hoping to convince you."

Fay's mouth popped open to accommodate the rush of air that left her lungs. She hadn't found words before Hugh came in from the other end of the stable. "Ready, sis?"

Hugh, teasing as always, was an unchanged tether she desperately needed with Garrick's confusing proclamations of… she wasn't sure what it was, but she knew for certain it wasn't love. Nor was it courtship. She'd watched plenty of boys court Eloise, and they'd spent time with the family, spent time on the porch, and taken walks together. That was romance.

Fay slammed the door of her mind on whatever loomed in the entrance to her heart and slid her gaze to Hugh. "I'm ready."

She turned away from Garrick, too stunned to say anything more to him.

When they were nearly halfway home, she finally found her words. "Garrick proposed marriage to me."

Hugh spun to look at her, his eyebrows low. The brim of his hat shaded his eyes from the moonlight. "Marriage?"

"It's duty only. Della made him because there are rumors in town about him and me spending two nights together on the road."

Hugh scoffed. "Folks could say the same about me and Edna."

Fay cocked her head. Did he really not know? "They do."

His eyes widened. "What?"

Fay gave a disappointed sniff. "It is not *your* reputation in question, so I suppose there is no need for anyone to speak to you about such things."

"But Edna's?"

"Yes. If you two have a baby right off, there will be talk about it being conceived prior to your nuptials."

Hugh glared at the path they walked. "Does Edna know?"

"Most certainly."

"She's not said anything."

"I suppose it will settle. Soon she'll be part of the makeup of this little valley, and it won't much matter when your children are conceived."

"Still." Hugh was not nearly as settled with this new knowledge.

The crunch of rocks and old snow filled the quiet while Hugh walked in shocked silence. Finally he said,

"And they think you and Garrick…" He glanced at Fay's flat stomach. "That you might be with child?"

"I guess." Fay shook her head at the ridiculousness. Her brother had been missing. Would she really have stopped to…? She cut off the wicked thought. She didn't want to think about it. Just the idea that folks suspected it of her was enough.

"And Garrick wants to marry you?"

"No." Fay was clear on at least that one part of all this. "He felt obligated to offer it, but I refused him."

Their home came into view, their mama's shadow moving around in the illuminated kitchen.

"Was that what he was asking you when I came into the stable?"

Fay shook her head. "He is buying a parcel from the Wrights."

Hugh stopped in the yard. "I thought… not Texas?"

"Apparently not."

"Why?"

Garrick's words rang in her head. To convince her. Had she really heard that? Or was her head still spinning from all the revelations? "You'll have to ask him."

Hugh surveyed her for a long moment, his eyes even darting to her stomach in the process.

Fay wanted to growl, but she kept her voice civil. "I'm not with child."

Hugh shook his head. "I never said—"

"You didn't need to. But I expect you to tell that to anyone who insinuates otherwise."

Hugh started for the house again. "I would have done so anyway."

Fay followed in his wake, the way she used to when she'd

help him along his trap lines. When the snow piled high, she would step in his footsteps as he held branches and cleared the path. There was no snow to clear this night, but Fay knew just the same that if she needed protecting, both Hugh and Lachlan would be up to the task. Otto, too, if he were still here.

When they entered the house, Fay found herself swimming in damp air. The interior was hot, warming her face and, within minutes, dampness spread under her armpits. "Mama, it's blazing in here."

Mama turned, her face a mixture of fear and pain. "Your Pa has taken a turn."

"What?" Fay glanced down the hall. She heard no coughing, and suddenly she would give anything to hear it, to spend another sleepless night kept awake incessantly by the sound of her Pa's hacking cough.

Mama lifted a plate piled high with supper and passed it to Hugh. "I need one of you to make a trip to Worthington tomorrow. The apothecary should have something to remedy this."

Lachlan's footsteps sounded down the hall, and his voice wavered with weariness. "Mama, I said I'll go."

"Son, you're barely recovered."

Lachlan's gaze slid to Fay's. "I'm well enough."

"I'll go," Fay volunteered. "Edna can do my work." With desperate greed, she realized bringing Edna into the family was going to give them one more slice of pay.

"You cannot go. Not when your brother was just set upon by bandits." Mama pinned Hugh with a stern look. "You will go."

Hugh nodded.

Fay groaned. "Mama, Hugh just got back. He's working late every night because he's behind on his work. I can go. I was fine going to get Hugh." Her mind protested the lie, but those bandits were headed east to Billings. She'd be fine.

Mama used two hot pads to lift a steaming pot from the stove. She started down the hall, casting over her shoulder, "We aren't going to test fate twice, child."

Fay huffed and entered the kitchen, dishing herself a plate. She sat at the table across from Hugh.

He watched mama go, then shifted his gaze to meet Fay's. "She's right. It ain't safe out there for a man. Worse for a lady."

"I'd take the pistol."

Hugh fixed her with a narrow stare. "Don't go getting ideas. Mama's got enough on her mind. She has no need to worry about you too."

Fay released a slow breath. Hugh was right. "I'll behave. What about you?" Of course Bastien wouldn't begrudge him the time, but... "How long will Bastien keep paying you for work that ain't getting done?" She glanced down the hall, making sure Mama hadn't heard her slang.

Hugh's mouth flattened into a straight line. He felt it too. She could tell. The Grahams' kindness had begun to feel less like hospitality and more like charity. "Perhaps your man is looking for a way to win you over..."

"Win...? Hugh, I told you. Garrick only offered because his sister required it."

"He's still buying the land, ain't he?"

Fay stuffed a forkful of dinner into her mouth and shrugged.

"I've seen the way he watches you. Ever since you returned"—he cocked his head and narrowed his eyes—"and before."

Fay shot him a startled look.

Hugh's mouth lifted in a smug grin. "Yep, he looked at you before you two had your escapade."

"He did not." Fay's words rang hollow. She'd been so intent on *not* looking at Garrick, she couldn't speak to where nor how his eyes had focused upon anything. But if he'd been looking at her, it had been because she resembled Eloise and nothing else. Despite her attempt to quell the emotion brought on by this knowledge, it still stung.

17

The pale morning light accompanied Fay and Hugh as they traversed the path to the Graham homestead. Hugh led Lady behind them, intending to leave as soon as he'd spoken to Bastien. It was a formality, borne of respect. There was no doubt in Fay's mind Bastien would allow Hugh to take the day.

When they arrived, they found Garrick leading his own horse from the stables. He tipped his hat and said, "Morning," then cast a confused look over the horse behind Hugh. "Is Lady here to have her hooves tended?"

He looked to Fay with dancing eyes, but her heart weighed too heavy to appreciate his jest.

Hugh passed the reins to Fay. "I'm heading to Worthington today." He turned and strode toward the house to find Bastien.

When the door clicked behind Hugh, Garrick turned to Fay with a quizzical look.

She led Lady to the hitching post. "Papa needs medicine, and he needs it today." She looped the reins, tightening them with more force than necessary.

"Is he much worse?"

Fay's throat tightened. She could only nod her reply.

"I'll accompany Hugh."

Fay's heart tumbled around in her chest. Part of her wanted to refuse, but the pragmatic part reached into her apron pocket. She pressed her fingers against the cold metal of the gold she'd taken from under her parents' bed, still in her pocket, waiting to be needed. But Mama had given Hugh money, so Fay could keep this in her pocket until she was able to put it back without getting caught.

She could be bold. She could beg Garrick to help her family, even though she'd refused his offer of marriage.

Luckily, Hugh returned before Garrick noticed her flush.

Garrick stepped forward and once again offered to accompany Hugh, but her brother shook his head. "Sounds like you've got a bit of property to tend to. Worthington isn't so far. If Lady has the speed, I'll be back long before supper."

Garrick walked his horse to Hugh. "Dusty had a good breakfast. She'll have the strength." He held his horse's reins aloft, and Hugh stared for a beat before accepting them.

Hugh climbed up, and with a glance to Fay and a word of gratitude to Garrick, he tipped his hat and was off down the valley.

Fay stared after him, sending a prayer of safety and swiftness.

"Will the medicine be enough?"

Fay spun, having forgotten Garrick as worry tumbled about in her mind. "I don't know." She stroked Lady's rump. "Thank you for lending Dusty. She's faster than Lady."

Garrick stepped closer, toying with the limp end of Lady's reins. "You have only to ask, and I'd give you anything."

Fay's heart lurched. "If I knew what to ask for, I would." She looked down at her boots, at the lighter spot above each big toe that would soon wear into a hole. They needed so much. If she asked, she wouldn't know where to start. What she did know was that the asking would never end.

"Can I take Lady back to Lachlan?"

Fay met his gaze. "Don't you need her to tend to your property?"

Garrick shook his head. "I'm doing Hugh's work today."

"You don't–"

Garrick stepped closer, and Fay's words froze in her throat as she skittered back a step. Useless trying to escape. The breeze carried his cinnamon scent to her, and the distance she tried for did nothing.

He took another step, closing the ground she'd just gained. He tilted his head and surveyed her with that uncanny ability to read his opponent. Except, just now, he felt more like a comrade. "I want to help."

Fay nodded, her throat thick. "I have to get inside." She turned and, after a few steps, cast a look over her shoulder. "Thank you for lending your mount."

She twisted back to face the house, unwilling to wait for a reply.

The morning passed without fanfare, or perhaps Fay's mind was too full to notice anything except her chores. In the afternoon, the ladies worked on Edna's dress. With a gaping yawn, Lydia announced she needed a nap and left Edna and Fay to finish the hem.

Fay watched her go, then leaned close to Edna. "Do you think she's carrying a boy or a girl?"

Edna smiled at the fabric in her hands. "I hope a boy, and I hope he looks like a blend of Milo and Willem. He'll steal all the ladies' hearts."

Fay chuckled. "What do you want first?"

Edna sighed. "As a little girl, I always wanted a big brother. So maybe a boy first."

Fay snorted. "I've brothers aplenty. They're not all that great."

Edna nudged her.

"How many do you want?" Fay asked.

Edna blushed. "As many as Hugh will give me."

Fay considered the money required to raise an infant to adulthood. She had hardly considered the question herself. All she'd known was that when she married rich, she'd have the funds to care well for her children. She'd never stopped to consider how many she wanted.

"Well, the town says you and I both have one coming. I suppose you'll be the one to satisfy their curiosity one way or the other."

Edna sniffed. "I want one, that's sure, but I might choose abstinence for a bit just to prove them wrong."

Fay laughed. "Poor Hugh."

Edna laughed too. "I heard Garrick made you an offer?"

"You did?"

"Heard him speaking rather sternly to Della. Promising her that you'd refused, and he'd done his best to convince you."

Fay narrowed her eyes. "That sounds like a conversation you weren't meant to hear."

Edna lifted a shoulder and let it fall. "When they're speaking just outside my room, I can't help but hear."

Fay pushed her needle into the sea blue fabric, down and up, imagining the conversation between Garrick and Della. He'd done his best, all right. He was still doing his best. When would he give her up? Were his efforts only so he could tell Della he'd done everything he could? Did Fay dare tell Della she didn't want her brother's hand in marriage? If she used Eloise as an excuse, Della might be convinced. But the thing that had made Fay so hate Garrick no longer mattered, and it felt unfair to use it against him now.

"I hear he's bought a bit of land," Edna said, flicking a glance from the side of her eyes.

Fay drew in a deep breath. "You're meant to be preparing for guests in a few days. How do you have so much time to eavesdrop?"

"Lydia does most of the eavesdropping, and the bunkhouse needed a good cleaning yesterday."

Fay smiled as she pictured the two women cleaning and gossiping. It was a thing Eloise and Fay used to do. It was what women in Dragonfly Creek had been doing, passing speculations from one to another. Only, here in Aster Ridge, Fay was beloved, and anything spoken about her didn't possess an edge as jagged as an open can of green beans.

Fay drew a shaky breath and cursed her weakness. "He's bought land. I guess he decided not to go to Texas."

"I can imagine why." Edna looked up from her sewing and smirked.

Fay plopped her hands into her lap and stared down at the pool of fabric. "I've given him no reason to believe I will change my mind."

Edna shifted, and Fay could feel her friend's gaze. Finally, Fay looked up, and Edna spoke. "I meant the beauty of this valley that so transfixed me. I understand how it could catch his eye too."

"Oh." Fay felt as small as a mouse. "Yes, he does have good reason to stay."

Though all of Edna's reasons were sound, Fay knew in her gut they weren't correct. Garrick had all those reasons a week ago, and he'd still been planning to leave. The only thing that had changed was the slander of Fay's reputation. He'd stayed because of that. It was the reason he'd bought a bit of the Wrights' land. The only reason.

───────────

ON THE DAY the guests arrived, Garrick couldn't stop himself from gathering with the crowd outside the bunkhouse. Willem and Hugh had gone together to Billings on their mounts, and those horses trailed behind them now as Hugh drove the six-team coach Willem had bought to replace the one that had been lost when Hugh and Edna were set upon by bandits. Garrick hadn't expected it to be ready so soon, but all the things that money could accomplish never ceased to amaze him.

As the men piled out of the new coach, Garrick surveyed each one. A few were as old as his father, but the rest were as young as the Graham brothers. One of them was more than decent looking. Garrick couldn't stop his gaze from shooting to Fay. Was she eyeing this same batch of guests, deciding which heart she should charm her way into?

His glance only reached the hem of her skirt before he stopped and turned away. Instead, he walked to the barn, not strong enough to watch her throw herself at some rich Chicago man.

He tried telling himself he was staying for Della, for Violet and Joshua and any other little nieces and nephews that might come along. He was staying because out here he had family support, he had Bastien willing to lend him the coin if times got tough. He had all the Graham brothers to offer advice and, for the first time in his life, he was a beloved member of a family.

There might be opportunity in Texas, but there wasn't family.

As he entered the barn, the familiar warmth enveloped him. He wanted to ride Dusty over to the plot of land he'd just purchased. More, he wanted to build something on it. Even a basic structure. Somewhere he could keep away from Fay. If proving to her that he had stability and a future here in Aster Ridge wasn't enough, he would have to find contentment without her approval.

He entered the house for dinner and found it oddly quiet for a structure that was the center for everything in this valley. When he rounded the corner, he found not the hum of platters being assembled, nor even the aftermath of dirty dishes being cleaned. Instead, the table was set for five and Della was sliding Joshua into his seat. Fay worked quietly at the sink and he resisted the urge to let his gaze linger. Instead, he took his spot between his niece and nephew and tousled Violet's hair in greeting.

He glanced at Della as she sat in her own seat. "I didn't realize all the work would be done in Willem's house now."

Della smiled. "I'm glad to have it moved. To have my kitchen back and just be feeding my family instead of a slew of gentlemen."

"Are they all very rich?"

Della gave a slight shrug. "I don't rightly know. Willem doesn't let them come for free, and I suppose most of them haven't enough work to keep them busy back home. I'd say they must be well enough off."

Garrick glued his gaze to Della's face, refusing to allow it to travel to Fay. "His house is far from the bunkhouse though. Does he plan to build another, closer to his place?"

Della chuckled. "The men haven't complained yet. Perhaps Willem is selling cold food as part of the experience."

As though she resented that fact, Fay placed a hot plate on the table and Garrick's traitorous eyes met hers. She dropped her gaze as quick as a snake strike, but she'd looked at him. Had she been looking at him before? Did she harbor any affection for him?

Della turned and called to Bastien over her shoulder, and soon the family was gathered. Feeding two young children was a distractible task, and before the meal was through Garrick looked up to find Fay had gone.

Bastien's voice cut into Garrick's longing. "We're rounding up the pregnant heifers tomorrow. Christian will be here to look each of them over. He's going to need someone in there with him, helping soothe the beasts. You willing?"

Garrick shrugged. "I'm happy to give it a try." He'd not dealt too much with animals, but he was also interested in getting to know Christian a bit better. He was a Graham by blood, if not by name, and he and his wife lived on a bit of property bought from the Morrises. He'd met them his first Sunday in town, and had seen them each week, but they had a new baby and mostly kept to themselves.

Bastien nodded. "Hugh and I will round them up. Perhaps Willem and a few guests will join."

Morning came and Garrick found himself wringing his hands as he and Christian waited for the cows to come down the valley. Now that he was with Christian, he didn't have the courage to press him about his life and what had made him stay in Aster Ridge.

A bellow came from outside, and Garrick straightened, watching the heifers come down the path. He smiled at their use of the road. Smart creatures. Hugh was at the gate, funneling the beasts inside, but Garrick led one from the corral to the stable where Christian was set up with gloves and an instrument around his neck. They'd only just started on the first cow when Garrick heard boots shuffling behind him. It was the young and handsome guest.

His face was tense with awkwardness as he said, "I'm no good at riding horses, but I lived on a farm most my life. I've worked with animals."

Christian waved the man over. "What's your name, son?"

His throat bobbed. "Martin Kelley, sir."

"Glad to have you." Christian tugged a glove on and lifted the cow's tail.

Garrick's stomach tumbled, and he looked away. "I'll go get another cow."

He heard muffled laughter as he left the barn, but he hardly cared. How was it that Garrick could handle a battlefield, yet the workings of a cow turned his stomach?

As he brought the next one in, he decided to stay, to force himself to watch. He planned to have a farm of his own one day. If a man as posh as Martin could handle this, Garrick would too.

And he was right. After a time, the work became methodical. With over fifty cows and heifers to tend, they worked up until lunchtime.

Fay came out, her arms crossed against the wind. She cleared her throat, her eyes on Christian. When he paused and glanced over, she said, "Della is wondering whether you'd like a tray out here, or if you'd rather come inside for lunch."

Christian glanced at Garrick and Martin, then back to Fay. "Am I eating alone?"

"I believe Mr. Kelley will eat in the bunkhouse with the men."

Christian nodded. "I'll eat with the rest."

Fay bobbed her head and spun on her heel.

Martin looked after her long enough that Garrick wanted to knock him in the jaw. Martin jangled the oats he was feeding to the cow. "The women out here are mighty pretty."

Christian laughed through his nose. "I think it's all the wildness. They have a freedom here women in the city will never know."

Garrick glanced at Christian. "That's rather poetic."

He smiled. "Society has rules. Structure. I'm not saying it's wrong. Perhaps a city needs all that. But out here, most days are spent without anyone's eyes, anyone's opinion. It allows a woman, or a man, to think for himself. To sort out his own beliefs before enduring the opinion of others."

Martin's voice was wistful. "I have a mind to find me a girl and bring her out here."

Even though he'd suggested finding his own girl, Garrick's jaw twitched at the thought of this man being near Fay. "Not everyone is fit for the West."

Martin surveyed Garrick for a moment. "Is that what happened to your fingers?"

Anger surged in Garrick, and he wanted to pummel the man. To kick his fine behind until the man begged Willem for a ride back to the train station.

Christian slapped the rump of the cow. "This one's done. Let's get cleaned up and head to the bunkhouse to see what they've got for us."

The charged moment had passed, but Garrick's fingertips tingled at how quickly his mind had turned to violence. How was he ever to change what Fay thought of him if he continued to be the same man? But what was he to do? Let this man, or any of the guests who came to visit, close to Fay and risk losing her entirely? As his mind pinged with indecision, his instincts took over. He knew better than to let an opponent at his back. He let Martin pass first, and then he followed the two men out to the pump to wash their hands. Perhaps a good scrubbing could rid his fists of their urge to hit.

18

Fay's favorite place was a full kitchen. She'd missed this more than she'd realized since Eloise had left. Both daughters and their mama in the kitchen, canning vegetables in the fall, bumping hips and elbows in the too-tight space.

Della's kitchen was larger, and that meant more women were needed to make it feel full. Aster Ridge was anything but short on women. Mel had come over with her new baby, and Fay felt herself drawn to the tiny cherub. She happily traded her assignment peeling potatoes for holding little Ariella. Ivete and Thomas were there too, but as usual, Ivete was more comfortable on her horse and was out helping to wrangle the cows, with her new baby cocooned against her chest.

Since everyone, even the guests, were taking part in the gathering and checking of livestock, Edna and Lydia made one large meal to feed everyone. The house smelled of the meat pies in the oven, and Fay watched as Mel added too much sugar to the sweet pie she was making. Fay leaned close to the baby in her arms. "Your mama is making a good go of it, isn't she?" At least it wasn't too much salt.

The infant slept on, undisturbed by Fay's quiet musings.

Lydia sidled over, her stomach still flat, though she was expecting a babe of her own soon. "How is your pa doing?"

Fay gave a solemn nod. "Same. We're hoping the medicine Hugh got in Billings will pull him out of the worst part."

"The Worthington herbs didn't help?"

Fay shrugged. "It's hard to tell what is working. Maybe he would be worse if it weren't for that tincture."

Lydia twisted her mouth. "I hope Hugh knows he can take time to do whatever your family needs. We can make up the work, but we can't bring your pa back."

Fays' throat grew thick, and though the women in the kitchen laughed with one another and their bond filled a hole in Fay's life, she felt none of their merriment.

Lydia sucked in a breath, as though just remembering something. "Edna said you have your eye on one of our guests."

Fay's cheeks burned. "I think he is handsome. That is all."

"Is it? I was under the impression that you hoped to secure yourself a match with one of these gentlemen. Will you at least wait until the dance to decide whether or not he's the one?"

Ariella let out a wail. Thank goodness for the distraction. Mel rushed over, as new mothers always do, and Fay was all too happy to offer up the child. Unfortunately, Lydia held her ground, and once the transfer was complete, she raised her brows expectantly. Worse, Mel now hovered nearby. "Are you looking for someone with even more money? How much will satisfy you?"

The words might have been harsh coming from someone who didn't love Fay as Lydia did.

Mel patted Ariella's rump, rocking from side to side. "I know I won't be the first to tell you money doesn't solve all problems."

"I know," Fay parroted. It was what these ladies wanted to hear. And it was true. Meeting the Grahams, practically joining their sweeping family, it was easy to forget the dangers that accompanied too much wealth, the feelings of entitlement and privilege that caught like a scraggly bush on a dress made of too-fine fabric, digging deep and refusing to surrender its hold until the garment no longer resembled what it had once been. But she also saw what good they did with it. And more, she saw security.

A smile played on Lydia's mouth. "I heard Garrick rather botched his proposal."

Fay narrowed her eyes. "You hear everything."

Lydia shot Fay a coy smile. "My children bring me half the news. Milo is just beginning to understand all he's hearing. The secret is most of the adults don't realize it yet."

Fay grinned. Milo, at twelve years old, was forever chasing after being a man. "It won't be much longer. Is he taller than you yet?"

"Almost." Lydia laughed.

"Fay," Della called from the other side of the counter. "Will you go see if Christian wants to take his meal in here with us ladies or out in the bunkhouse?"

Fay bobbed her agreement and set off for the stable. She heard muffled talking and was able to find the large stall they were using to check the cows. As she spoke, she could hardly keep her feet from turning and running back to the house. Garrick and Martin were both there, and by the sour look Garrick passed between her and Martin, he had surely realized that Martin was precisely the type of man Fay had been waiting for.

As soon as Christian had given his answer regarding lunch, she spun on her heel and returned to the safety of the kitchen and all the women who, though they might tease her regarding her pickiness, all understood. A woman gets no mistakes in the forest that is marriage.

ALL THE MEN were too filthy to come inside any of the houses, so they crowded into the bunkhouse, and by the time Fay and Edna entered with the food, it was like joining a pack of hungry wolves. They waited patiently for the food to be set down and the women to back away, but then they dove at the table, even the Grahams clambering for their portion. The only two who remained against the wall were Garrick and Martin.

Fay gulped, and she didn't miss how Edna had stilled at her side. A soft hand gripped her arm and Edna tugged. "Enjoy the meal, boys." She pulled Fay out the door, and the two ran back to Della's house. When they stepped through the door, Edna unwrapped her shawl from her shoulders and hung it on a peg. "I thought you were going to drop your jaw as well."

Fay's laugh sounded more like a whimper. "I can't say I wouldn't have."

Edna led the way into the kitchen. "I can't wait to

watch them at the dance. This will be as good as any theater in the city."

Fay shot her friend a mock-glare. "You're about to be family. You should be invested in whoever I choose to pursue."

"Oh, I'm invested." But by the grin on her face, Fay could tell Edna still meant Fay as entertainment.

As she worked by Lydia's side, she wanted to tell her the truth—Fay's real problem was indecision or, rather, an unexpected change of heart. She didn't want Martin, who was exactly the type of man she'd always wanted. But her pa wasn't better. They had a saddlebag full of Aaron's gold under the bed, but it seemed all the money in the world couldn't cure her father's cough, couldn't heal his legs. Sure, it would provide a better life for her family, but it wasn't the ultimate solution.

She pictured Garrick's pained face, the way he watched her and Martin like a hawk on a fencepost. The closeness they'd shared when looking for Hugh was a tie she wasn't sure would ever break. He didn't love her, but she wondered if a part of him would always care a little about her. Perhaps a small bit of him would also forever be wounded at her refusal. Would he be pained to see her accept someone else? For that would mean she was finally satisfied, and it wasn't with him.

GARRICK STEPPED out of the guesthouse, ready for the dance. The Grahams held a dance for every group of men who visited the gentlemen ranch. They usually hosted these dances at the pavilion on the Grahams' property, but the winter weather meant they were all traveling to the grange in Dragonfly Creek for the festivities. Garrick wasn't certain he wanted to go, but the thought of Martin having every dance with Fay made his stomach turn and left him with little choice in the matter.

Della exited her house with Joshua on her hip. "Are you riding with us?"

Garrick shook his head. "I'll ride Dusty in case I need to head home early."

Della gave him a sly grin. "I know you're not worried about getting to bed on time."

He hoisted Violet into the wagon bed. Della came to his side and placed Joshua inside too. He offered his hand to help her in, but she tapped his chest. "Don't you have a tie?"

He shook his head. "Wasn't standard issue in the Rough Riders."

"Well, it is standard at a dance... if you want to look respectable." She stepped backward. "I'll get you one of Bastien's."

Bastien came outside and cocked his head at hearing his name, but Della walked right past him and into the house. When he reached Garrick, he said, "What is she getting of mine?"

"A tie. She says I need to look respectable."

"You do if you want to draw the attention of a certain Morris girl."

Morris girl. Bastien's word choice reminded Garrick this wasn't the first Morris he had been enamored with. Maybe it had been a mistake to spend all his money, and a bit of Bastien's, to start a farm. What if his affection for Fay was just as fleeting as what he'd felt for Eloise? Maybe this valley, with its happy marriages and open space, had done the opposite of clear his head. Instead, it had stuffed it full of dreamy notions.

Except his time on the road with Fay had planted a seed, and every time he saw her, he felt that seed grow just the smallest bit. It wasn't because she watered it, that was for sure. It was more of a scraggly weed that grew in gravel, without the apparent need for nourishment. But Fay was different from Eloise, different from all the women out here.

Just as Fay and him were different from each other. He wanted Fay to be his tether, to remind him what he could use his strength for, to make sure she didn't swoon over some rich boy who could offer her everything she thought she wanted.

As they rode through the valley, they stopped at Christian and Mel's home to load up with more passengers. Next, they passed the Morris's home to find their empty wagon out front. Bastien turned into the drive, and Fay came out to greet them.

"I was just coming to get the wagon ready. Hugh and Lachlan worked overlong today and are only just clean and ready."

Garrick couldn't help but notice she wore her one Sunday dress, and she'd taken more care with her hair. It wasn't covered with a hat, nor did it hang down her back in its usual simple braid. She'd piled it high on her head in coils and wraps that made her look older and more elegant, different from her usual self. He hated it. Not because it looked bad, but because it looked too good. He pressed his lips and looked away.

Hugh exited the house, as though to prove Fay's point. His hair curled damp at the nape of his neck, underneath the brim of his hat.

Bastien called out, "You're welcome to climb in. Willem and Lydia are already there with Edna and the guests, so we've got plenty of room."

Hugh nodded. "It'd save us time." He turned back and poked his head inside the house. "Lachlan, the Grahams are giving us a ride. You comin'?"

He walked by Fay and jostled her with his elbow. "See, we weren't running late. Just in time, I'd say."

Lachlan exited and everyone climbed into the wagon. Bastien was right. They had the space. But now the wagon was quite full. Thomas and Ivete had caught up and rode their mounts along with Garrick. He made sure he kept on Fay's side when Bastien urged the horses forward again.

"You look mighty nice today, Ms. Morris," Garrick said.

Fay looked at him sidelong, her mouth unmoving. Then her gaze flicked to his neck. "Your tie is undone."

He hadn't quite tied it before letting it hang. He'd planned to have Della tie it when they arrived. He'd tugged it so each side was the right length, then did his best to tie a knot in the thing. It looked bad—he knew that without looking—but he hadn't worn a tie more than a handful of times in his life and had never mastered the larger, fancier knots.

It didn't much matter. Fay had seen Garrick at his worst, with little sleep, or when he'd turned into a bear protecting her from Pete's threats upon their arrival. She'd not been impressed then. One nicely knotted tie wasn't going to change any of that. If she hadn't already seen it, he might have been tempted to remove the thing and the foolish hopes that came with it.

When they arrived in town, dusk had set, and Garrick made sure he arrived first at the end of the wagon to help the women down. When it came Fay's turn, she hesitated. She was the last in the wagon, and Garrick tried to ignore the suspicion that she'd waited, hoping he would be taken away by one of the other members of the family. But even young Violet hadn't stayed to hold his hand.

Instead of taking his hand, Fay leaned over the side, looking for a step.

Garrick bit his cheek. "There's nothing on this side. You'd have to climb onto the bench to find a step." Something he was certain she knew and had forgotten in her desperation to stay away from him. He couldn't help but smirk at the thought.

Her chest rose and fell, a sigh to her disgruntled expression.

Garrick couldn't help his smile. "Would you like me to fetch Bastien to help you down? Or perhaps you would prefer Martin?"

Her eyes flashed to him and, angry as she might be, he was glad to see something other than pity on her face. She'd wounded him with her refusal of marriage, but the worst part was that she knew it.

How could he explain that her refusal was the next best thing? That it meant if she ever accepted him, he would know without a doubt that it was because she loved him, and not because her family needed him.

She made as if to sit on the edge, but he stepped nearer, freezing her in a half-crouched position.

"You'll ruin your dress," he warned.

Rather than wait any longer, he reached up and took advantage of her lowered waist. Gripping it, he pulled her down and set her on the ground. He'd done so several times while she was wearing trousers and those ridiculously large men's boots. It was foolish for her to be so resistant to it now.

Before he released her, he tugged her close. "I don't need your pity."

He forced himself to remove his hands, wiping them on his pants to remove the ghost of her warmth. Her face was stricken by some strong emotion, lips parted, but then her eyebrows pinched together into an expression of confusion. Good. An emotion he *could* handle.

She raised her hands, and his breath stilled as he tried to interpret her intention. She tugged at his tie, pulling out his hastily arranged knot. Then she retied the knot and cinched it close to his throat.

He gave a small cough as her fist pressed on his Adam's Apple. She used the tie to pull him down, closer. As she leaned in, her chin tilted up as far as it would go. Her voice fell low between them as she said, "I don't pity you."

Before he'd regained his ability to breathe, she left in a whirl of skirts. He loosened the knot, sucking in the cold winter air, but it did nothing to clear the heat of her breath on his skin.

The murmur of the townspeople reached him before he entered the building, and he thought of all the men in there who would want to dance with Fay. He'd planned to ask her for the first dance, but he'd forgotten with all the choking and muttered proclamations.

Instead, he stepped inside and found Willem. With that man, there was always something that needed doing. He could keep himself busy while he summoned the courage to ask Fay for a dance and hoped she didn't try to strangle him again. He hadn't yet decided if such an emotion would serve his purposes or cause her to reject him the entire evening.

———

FAY WAS STILL FUMING from her interaction with Garrick. He'd been trying to anger her, that much she knew. She just wasn't sure why. *Pity?* She didn't pity him. She hated him. With his giant horse and its shifting gait that forced them to touch. If they had removed the saddle, they probably could have ridden all the way home from Pete's without so much as brushing against one another.

The townspeople were right. She'd allowed him too much leniency. She glanced around, trying to locate him in the crowd. He hadn't stuck around to pester her within the walls of the grange, but as soon as she noticed he was busy, loneliness swamped her. Edna was her companion here. And Lydia. Both were busy accepting goods for the tables from the folks of Dragonfly Creek.

She swallowed, entertaining the idea of walking over and joining them, but that was where Garrick had gone. As she watched, it seemed Edna and Lydia weren't as busy as they usually were. All the young ladies went right to Garrick to deliver their goods, though some of them even had to pass by Edna to do so. Fay watched with a disinterested gaze as the young women tossed their heads and smiled for him. Even Ginny lingered longer than necessary.

She had been the one to spread the rumors. If she had any interest in Garrick, she would have done well to keep her lips from spitting dust. Fay took a calming breath and startled when someone lifted her hand.

Martin.

She smiled, genuinely warmed by his attention.

"May I beg the first dance?" He kissed her knuckles.

Fay smiled and drew her hand away. Such posturing. "Yes, Martin. I'd be happy to."

He led her with a gentle hand to the center of the dance floor. As if they'd been waiting, the musicians started their first song. He took a step toward her, and as the rules went, Fay took a step backward. She'd never excelled at dancing, but as they moved together, she discovered Martin was quite honestly the best dancer she'd ever been paired with. His arms were strong and sure, guiding her, holding her. Though he'd only paid her scant attention this week, she was validated in her commitment to find a man like him, different from all the men she'd ever known.

When their dance ended, Martin escorted Fay off the dance floor and, to her horror, led them right for Garrick. Lydia stood at his side, and when Martin released his hold on Fay, he offered his arm to Lydia. She took it with a warm smile, leaving Fay and Garrick alone except for each other, heat simmering between them.

"I was going to ask you to dance," he said, staring out at the crowd.

"I'm glad you didn't."

Garrick shot her a look, but she kept her eyes on Martin and Lydia.

He jawed for a moment and Fay hid a smile at having bested him.

But Garrick sniffed and said, "Afraid your city boy would run off if he saw you dancing with me?"

Fay skittered her gaze along the other dancers, catching sight of Ginny. At first, Fay thought Ginny was watching her, but then the focus of her stare became clear.

She was watching Garrick. Fay didn't have to look at him to see what Ginny saw. An image of him could easily be conjured in her mind—tall and broad, dark hair, that one rogue lock falling onto his forehead.

"I'm afraid the women of Dragonfly Creek would be disappointed to see me in your arms. Word is you're looking for a wife to fill that house you're building."

Garrick stepped closer, and Fay couldn't help her attention from sliding to him. He lowered his voice. "I'm not building a house."

"Have you decided to leave?" Fay's voice sounded light. Hopefully, it conveyed disinterest. "I knew you had no reason to stay."

"I'm not—"

The song ended, and Garrick pressed his lips shut as the dancers filled the sides, pressing closer to them.

Fay couldn't even be glad for the irritation in Garrick's voice, because in addition to Martin and Lydia heading their way, Ginny Price also stalked toward them, a hungry feline.

Fay snapped her gaze to Garrick, and she hoped her face didn't betray her desperation. The reason for such desperation perplexed Fay. If she didn't want Garrick, Ginny should be welcome to him. Except their old feud burned hot, even as adults, and seeing Ginny with Garrick, imagining her becoming any part of Aster Ridge, filled Fay with such anger, she felt bold enough to step closer to Garrick. "Is your leaving the reason why you haven't asked me to dance?"

It didn't matter that the whole of Dragonfly Creek would be watching them, licking their chops and whispering behind hands. She'd rather they have it wrong about her and Garrick than for there to be any truth to an affection between him and Ginny.

Shock marred his face, and his lips parted as she waited for him to catch up to her sudden change of heart. She held his gaze, but in her periphery, Ginny moved ever closer now. A few more steps, and she'd have her claws in him for sure.

"Dance with me." His words were breathless, like the kind spoken after a hard ride or a dip in the lake.

She slipped her fingers into his, and though she noticed Ginny freeze, Fay didn't take her eyes from the man who held her hand.

They stopped, and he slid a warm palm from her waist to wrap around her back. She swallowed at his touch. Nothing more than he'd done on their adventure, but now he touched her in full sight of anyone interested enough to look. It wasn't a touch to prevent her falling from the saddle or to fool Pete. It was because he'd breathlessly asked her to dance.

The music started, a lighthearted song with a trilling fiddle melody. But Garrick didn't launch them into the dance with heels stomping the way the other couples were doing. He didn't even step toward her like Martin had done. Rather, he stared into her eyes with an intensity that had her taking a step backward. He splayed his fingers along her back and pulled her back to him so there was barely a handbreadth between them. Using their clasped hands, he kept that same distance, and she followed his steps, a slow push and pull.

He hadn't broken eye contact, and their intense staring was bound to draw attention, especially since their tempo didn't match the rest of the dancers. Her dance with Martin had been everything she'd ever thought she wanted in a partner—predictable, polished, comfortable. Dancing with Garrick was the exact opposite. He moved her in a way she'd never moved before, and to a rhythm of Garrick's choosing. It was raw and powerful, and Fay had no trouble keeping up.

As Garrick danced their bodies toward the back of the hall, they gained space, and soon they'd left the other dancers moving in time to the music behind. Fay and Garrick danced at the back with the little children, none of whom were dancing. Those same children she'd once been jealous of. But she wasn't a child any longer. In the arms of a man like Garrick, it was impossible to feel like anything but a woman.

"I'm not leaving." His voice was a deep rumble she could feel in the hand that rested on his shoulder.

She wanted to ask why, but her throat was stuck. His attention, the way he stared into her eyes, made her body clench up like she was traveling through woods with a cougar in the trees.

When she didn't reply, he went on. "I'm going to build a house when the earth thaws, and I'm going to need a wife."

Though Fay had no intention of being that wife, the thought of him with another woman, perhaps one who was in this very room, caused a swipe of jealousy to rip through her, the claws tearing flesh. She stiffened and planted her feet. Refusing to be led by him any longer. Refusing to allow her mind to spin fairytales that could only be fiction.

The song stopped, and Fay relished the opportunity to take her hands away from him. "There will be plenty of women in Dragonfly Creek who would make a fine wife."

The words were poison on her tongue and threatened to choke her.

She stepped back and turned away from him, walking as fast as she could without drawing attention. Dancing with Garrick might feel right, but dancing with Martin was the right thing to do for her family. And that's the only thing that ever mattered.

19

$\mathcal{B}$y the time the gentlemen guests were loading up their things for their departure from Aster Ridge, Garrick had had more than enough of that man charming Fay. She gave her smiles too easily and Garrick wanted to lash out like a bad dog and bite the man's wrist.

As Hugh and Lachlan pulled the wagon away from the house, Garrick let out an audible breath.

A snicker came from behind, and Garrick glanced over his shoulder to see Fay and Edna, their heads together as they returned to the house. They were probably just talking excitedly about Edna's wedding. It was to be in one week, after all. No. That wasn't true. They had to be talking of the men who had just left. Of one man in particular.

Garrick closed his eyes against the onslaught of emotions. For all he'd criticized Aaron for accepting Eloise's need of him, Garrick longed to do the same. He wished Fay needed him. Perhaps that would be enough until the love came.

Rather than follow the women inside, Garrick saddled

Dusty and rode for his land. There was still nothing to do except look over what belonged to him. Perhaps picturing the things he had would grant a slice of comfort.

Or perhaps it would only serve to show him that nothing would matter if Fay didn't come home with him every night but instead went home to her family, or worse, to a husband who wasn't him.

As much as he wanted to get started on his homestead, the earth was too frozen for any work to be done. Even pulling sagebrush would have to wait until spring.

As he stared at the land, he could imagine where he would build the house and the barn. Without Fay, there was no rush to build a home. He would construct a barn first so he could start buying livestock. He'd live in a tent himself. He'd done so for nearly a year when he was with the Rough Riders. He was anything but above tent living.

He climbed back on Dusty and rode for Aster Ridge. As he dipped into the valley, he saw Willem in the distance, working on his barn. Instead of heading to Della's, he went to Willem's home. He'd been wise enough to set the corner posts before the frost, and he'd been slowly working on the frame over the last few months.

He came out of the framed structure to greet Garrick as he climbed off his mount.

Willem smiled wide as he clapped Garrick on the back. "Come to help me?"

Garrick nodded, happy to help. "I thought you meant for your guests to do this."

Willem laughed, the boom echoing down the hill and into the valley. "They didn't love the cold. Perhaps I should have built my ranch out in California."

Garrick smiled to think of the men, especially Martin, tucked into a cozy coach and headed back to where they belonged. "Some men aren't cut out for the West." Not that he'd proved to be anything special himself, but he hoped to one day prove he was fit for this wild territory. He pulled worn work gloves from his saddle bag. "Let's get these trusses set."

They started working, Willem up on a ladder and Garrick on the ground passing the truss and holding it in place with a rope.

Willem kept his eyes on his work as he spoke. "Lydia said a few girls in town have been asking about you."

Garrick sniffed. He had eyes only for one girl.

"They're keen to know why you're staying."

"Does a man need a reason to set down roots?"

Willem pursed his lips. "I figure he doesn't."

Garrick nodded, glad for one person he didn't have to explain himself to.

But then Willem spoke again. "It's only they are hoping you want a wife to fill the home you're building."

"The ground is frozen. I'm not building anything until spring." Garrick could picture the girls, discussing this with Lydia, pressing her for answers. The vague image of that post office girl, Ginny Price, flooded his vision. He clenched his jaw. Was she one of the girls after him? He'd like to learn which girls had spoken to Lydia and tell that Ginny he wouldn't consider her even if it meant he spent his life as a bachelor.

Garrick passed another truss to Willem.

As the frame exchanged hands, Willem said, "They won't want a winter wedding anyhow. Spring flowers and all that. I suppose Fay has no intention of setting those girls straight?"

Garrick handled the rope, his muscles tensing as he held the frame while Willem secured it in place. "No," was all he could muster. His heart clenched, every bit as tight and weary as his arms.

"Did she say why?"

Garrick glared at Willem. "You're as bad a gossip as the ladies are."

Willem laughed and Garrick's heart couldn't help but feel just a bit lighter. If only he could command the carefree attitude Willem possessed.

"Did you know I had to win Lydia over? She wasn't keen on marrying me. I was too young and immature for her tastes."

Garrick laughed, but Willem's straight mouth said he wasn't jesting.

"Truly?" Garrick asked.

"Had to convince her I was the right one." He raised a brow and laughed at himself. "Had to convince myself too."

Garrick eyed the man—rich, young, and handsome. "I can't imagine it was too hard to convince her." He passed up another truss.

"A woman wants to know she's wanted above everything else."

Garrick couldn't meet Willem's eye. He wanted Fay all right, more than he'd ever wanted anything. But he was certain that didn't change anything for Fay. He was still the last person she'd marry.

Willem grunted as he tugged the rope, lifting the heavy frame. "Does she know you love her?"

Garrick opened his mouth to deny it, but the heat brightening his cheeks surely gave him away. He did love her. He wasn't sure when it had turned from wanting to loving, but sure enough, it had changed.

He heaved a deep sigh. "I've proposed marriage. I'm not sure what else I can do to convince her I'm in love."

Willem paused and pinned Garrick with a stare. "Della demanded you propose to save Fay's reputation. It wasn't the most romantic proposal."

Garrick held the rope, but he wanted to throw his hands in the air. "She'll hardly look me in the eye. How am I supposed to make anything *romantic*?"

Willem turned back to his work and left Garrick to answer the question himself. His friend was right. Garrick hadn't been clear that he'd loved Fay. He'd not known it when he proposed. Even now, his pride wanted him to say he only wanted her because she wouldn't have him. But he was no cat playing with a mouse. If anything, Fay was the cat, and she was as likely to crush him with her paw as she was to pull him in and keep him as a meal.

"Try again, my friend," Willem said. "Take whatever she'll give you until she gives you everything."

After the trusses were laid, Willem invited Garrick inside for supper, but Garrick hadn't seen Fay all day, and he knew she'd be serving supper at Della's house.

As he rode back, he considered romance. Unlike the city, there were no hothouse flowers Garrick could spend too much money on. Nor were there chocolates to buy or ribbons to offer. And, truly, he wasn't sure if any of those things would tempt Fay. What he wanted to get her was a new pair of boots or a new hat that didn't hang around her head, shouting to the whole world that she was wearing someone else's cast offs.

Just as Willem had suggested, Garrick would take anything and hope for love to come. He would do whatever it took to win her.

FAY WALKED HOME in the late evening light. She hadn't stayed to serve dinner. The winter solstice had sent the sun to sleep long before the men had come in for their evening meal. She'd prepped enough, though, and Della could manage the rest by herself.

As she walked along, the dead grass rose stiff from the ground, sharp blades in the sharper evening air. But spring soon would soften the ground, allowing flowers to pepper the valley. It was her favorite season. She cinched her fleece shawl tighter around her and walked faster to avoid the winter chill.

When she finally reached her home, she was met with silence. Her heart lifted to think Papa was finally healing. And soon Lachlan would no longer be on the list of her family who needed tending. A wave of gratitude rolled through her for Edna's thoughtfulness and her Chicago connections. Fay entered the kitchen to find dinner only partly prepared.

"Mama." She called into the house. It wasn't normal for Mama to leave a meal half-done or the kitchen a mess, but perhaps with her brothers gone to chauffeur the guests back to the train station in Billings...

"Down here," Mama called back.

Her words were more a greeting than anything else, as Fay was already on her way down the hall. She'd known where her mama was: tending her pa, as she'd been doing every day for all of Fay's life.

Fay entered the room, and Ma's drawn face was like a magnet, pulling Fay closer in a rush. With a hand on her mama's shoulder, Fay squinted into the woman's tired eyes. "You need to rest."

Mama shook her head, her eyes darting to Pa. Fay followed her gaze, and her heart dropped to the floor. He lay pale and gaunt from the weight he'd lost over the last month. His eyes were closed. Was he asleep?

"He won't eat," Mama whispered, never taking her gaze from his form.

Fay straightened her back. "Della gave us a ham bone. I'll make a bit of bone broth. He loves that." As she stood, she remembered she'd left the bone in Della's ice box. Her eyes darted out the window. A line of dusky light still stood out over the top of the ridge. She would go get it.

Mama gave a sad nod, but didn't spare a glance for Fay.

Fay left the room, feeling like she was leaving her mother to grieve rather than to make a bit of broth.

A sob tried to claw its way up her throat, nearly choking her as she held it down, channeling her emotions into pumping water to fill the pot. She returned to the house, placing it on the stovetop. By the time it grew hot, she'd be back from Della's with the bone in hand. She pulled herbs from the cupboard through tear-blurred eyes.

Soon, Mama called her back again. When Fay entered the room, Mama gestured her closer. "Do you think he feels warm?"

The room was as stuffy as it had ever been. As Fay stepped closer, she thought anyone would feel hot in this room.

But as she placed the back of her hand to her Pa's forehead, the air was sucked from her lungs. She pulled in a fresh breath, but just as soon it whooshed out again. She glanced at Ma's worried eyes and nodded. "He's fevered, Mama. How long?"

Mama twisted her mouth. "Maybe all day. I was hoping it was just me. Or the room." Ma's tentative diagnoses was all Fay needed to understand that sense and logic had abandoned her mama.

Fay shook her head. "We need to call for the doc."

Ma shook her head violently. "I won't. Last time the leeches drained your father so much he didn't wake for a whole day."

Fay looked at her pa's pale face. He didn't look like he was going to wake up any time soon. What if he didn't wake up ever?

Her mind tried working through the smothering heat to find another solution. Ma was right. The doctors never did much, and they charged outrageous fees. They'd used both the medicines from Worthington and Billings, and neither one had been enough. She wanted to stamp her foot at the injustice. First Lachlan and his spell caused by sheer stubbornness. Even healthy Hugh had a hole torn through him. Thankfully, Pete had treated that wound well enough. Her heart lifted at the thought of Pete, with his cupboard full of mountain remedies.

"I'll go get Pete."

"Pumpkin," Mama whispered. Fay's gaze shot to meet her mama's. That nickname hadn't been used since Fay was a little girl. Why would her mama be using it now? There was no need to comfort her over a scraped knee or a cruel word from Ginny.

She didn't need to be comforted. She needed to act. Fay straightened, swallowing down the fear that had lodged in the back of her throat, threatening to choke her.

"He's our last chance. I'll take Papa's pistol."

But Ma stood and caught Fay's arms just below the

elbow. Fay took her mother's arms at the same spot, and they locked eyes as their arms were interlaced.

"Pumpkin. Don't go. Stay with him."

Fay's eyes filled with tears, blurring the vision of a too-ragged Mama. "You need sleep."

"Fay." Mama's voice was firmer now, and she gripped Fay's arms with the same change in ferocity. "I'll not have all my children gone when—" Her voice cracked.

Fay shook her head, tugging weakly against her mama's hold. "He's not dying. I'll go get Pete."

A knock on the front door rang through the house, yet it was as far away as an echo from another life. One where her family wasn't constantly hanging over the precipice of sickness and death.

Slow steps carried Fay to the door, and she pulled it open to find Garrick on the other side.

In one blink he stepped inside and held her face in his icy hands. "What's wrong?"

A canvas bag was looped over his wrist, and it swung between them. The smell of ham drifted up, and she knew at once why he was here. Fay didn't have the energy to speak. She merely glanced down the hallway.

"Your pa?" He released one hand's hold on her, kicked the door closed, and set the hambone on the floor before taking her arm once more.

Fay blinked, and she hoped it was enough. Away from Mama and the need to convince her Pa wasn't dying, Fay didn't have the energy to convince herself. If Pa could just wait until tomorrow. Hugh and Lachlan would be home, Fay would have returned from getting Pete, and Pete would heal Pa from whatever consumed him from the inside, whatever it was he needed to cough out. Yet even as Fay thought it, she realized Pa hadn't been coughing tonight. He wasn't strong enough. Suddenly she understood Ma's fear.

"I have to go get Pete." Fay's words were a whisper, but Garrick's attention locked on her. He'd heard. She could tell by the change in his features.

A determination rolled across his face. "I'll go."

Fay wanted to argue, but relief rolled through her like a swift current. As much as she'd argued with her ma, she wanted to stay back. To be with Pa. If this was his final night, she'd not want to spend it chasing a false hope. Pete might not even be home, and Fay would have wasted her chance to say goodbye to her pa.

Garrick patted at his pockets, as though missing something. "Is there anything else you need?"

Fay shook her head. There was a chance she didn't even need Pete, that like the tinctures from town, there was nothing he could do for Pa. But they had to try, and Fay's heart told her Garrick didn't mind, that he would never hold this fool's errand against her.

Unlike Aaron, he wouldn't demand she marry him for his services, nor would he be bitter toward her for her refusal. Her heart twanged at the thought of any hurt she may have caused him.

When he turned to go, Fay caught his wrist. With her other hand, she cupped his cold fingers. Glancing around the room, she spotted the drying rack, bare of anything since both her brothers had gone and taken their spare gloves with them.

"You need gloves and a cap for your ears."

"I have gloves in my jacket."

Fay tugged him further into the house. She cast around desperately, searching for something to give him, some token to keep him warm on this journey that should have been hers.

She remembered a bit of wool fabric she'd set aside, intended for pockets in her next dress. "Wait here." She released his hand and clutched her skirts high as she rushed into her room and dug through the chest at the foot of her bed.

She found the strip of wool and carried it into the entry. "For your ears." She lifted it and Garrick ducked to allow her access. She set it just above his brows, covering his ears. Walking around his back, she tied it at the base of his head. She tucked the remaining fabric down the back of his collar, and he spun to face her.

The dark strip crossed so low over his brows turned his gray eyes even paler. She ignored the concern swaying in those stormy pools and ran her gaze down his frame. "Sometimes Hugh rides with a blanket over his shoulders."

Garrick sandwiched her hands between his.

She glanced at them, unaware that she'd been wringing hers. With a gulp, she met his steady gaze.

"I'll not be cold," he said. "Let me go, and I will return to you as swiftly as Dusty has ever carried me."

Fay's heart wanted to leap out of her chest and tuck itself into Garrick's vest pocket, close to his heart. This man, who had every reason to deny her as harshly as she'd denied his proposal. She swayed, the gold coins bumping against her thigh. She hadn't ever used them, hadn't asked Garrick, but she had no doubt he would have helped. This man, who had been silently serving her family these weeks, helping Hugh with work, lending his horse when needed, even offering his future to save her reputation. Who had tried telling her it was want and not just duty, only she hadn't been prepared to listen. Fay gave a soundless nod and Garrick released her hand. Once he turned away, a coldness touched Fay's chest.

She stepped closer. "Wait."

Garrick turned, not impatient, but his eyes searched her face, no doubt wondering what else she could do to keep him from his mission.

"I'll marry you." The words surprised even her, for just because her heart wanted this man didn't mean her mind had reached the same conclusion. But here was that impulsive behavior her mama had warned her about. Apparently, her mouth and heart were on one horse and her mind on another.

His lips twitched, but her declaration had rendered him speechless, just as it had her. She pushed on his shoulder. With only the briefest of hesitations, he allowed her to scoot him out the door and into the black night. When she closed it, she leaned against the thick wood and took a shuddering breath.

She was desperate, that was true. More desperate than Eloise had been. Garrick had less to offer than Aaron did, but this was what she got for waiting until death prowled in their yard.

Death hadn't taken her papa yet. The man was fierce, and one bad night, or even month, wasn't enough to defeat him.

Fay returned to the room and took his too-hot hand in hers. "Papa, Garrick has gone to fetch Pete. You hold on. Your sons will want to say goodbye. Don't you be a coward and go without telling them goodbye. They've done too much for you. You wait."

Her voice shook, but she hoped it only added vigor to her words. Fay mirrored her mama's position, with her arms folded on the mattress and her head lying atop her forearms. They each held one of Papa's hands and listened to his ragged breathing. The full moon rose, casting shadows about the room, but the space still held a darkness that pressed on Fay's chest.

Hurry, Garrick. She called to him in her mind. And, for the first time, her mind and her heart were speaking the same message.

20

In spite of Pete having a head full of gray hair, he had no trouble keeping up with Garrick's pace. They reached the Morris' home just as the sun was painting a pale yellow sky above the mountains.

Pete lifted his saddlebag onto his shoulder and pressed his way into the house. "Ida," he called with the familiarity of an old friend.

"Back here."

Garrick followed Pete inside, anxious to see whether they'd made it in time. Pete had gathered a few things at his cabin, and Garrick had tapped his boot with impatience. Had they made it back soon enough?

All he'd thought about on the ride was Fay's offer, her sacrifice.

Help my father, and I'll marry you.

He didn't want her sacrifice. He wanted her love. He supposed, in a family like this, the two felt permanently entwined, but Garrick didn't want a family like this. He wanted love, given freely, without benefits and consequences weighed first. He wouldn't deny this family loved one another, but it was the hopelessness of their love that made him uncomfortable.

Yet, now that he was here, all his concerns had fled, and the only thing he wanted to know was whether Mr. Morris was alive and if Pete could save him.

Garrick followed Pete into the bedroom and watched Fay throw herself into Pete's arms. Her palms flattened against his back, and she pressed him close. Garrick's throat grew thick at the fear that must have been consuming her all night.

Pete returned the embrace, then set her firmly aside and put his things at Mr. Morris's side. "Grant, now, this is no fair. I was enjoying a bit of solitude and now your daughter is no doubt going to press a bit of under-salted beans into my hands, and I'll have to eat her cooking for the next few days."

Mr. Morris didn't laugh. He didn't even raise an eyelid.

Garrick reached out and pulled on Fay's wrist with gentle fingers, tucking her close to him. She leaned her head against his shoulder and gripped his jacket in her fist. Mrs. Morris was kneeling on the other side of the bed like she was readying to say her prayers. Perhaps she'd not stopped praying all night.

Pete shifted his saddlebag and dug around inside. Glancing at Fay, he said, "I'll need a bit of boiled water. And strips of fabric."

Fay stepped away, leaving Garrick cold. He shook off the sensation. She wasn't meant to comfort him. That was his calling just now. He followed her swift footsteps and found her head-deep in the cupboard. She reappeared with a large pot of water.

Too large. It wouldn't boil before next week. "Maybe a smaller one to start, then we can get this one started."

She gave a vigorous nod, and when she wavered with where to set the pot down, Garrick took it from her hands. Setting it on the counter, he gripped her arms just below her shoulders. "Fay, Pete is here now. He'll do all he can."

She nodded. Garrick had never seen her so wordless.

"A small pot," he reminded.

She glanced up at the rack along the wall. A small pot hung alongside others.

Garrick lifted it from the hook and walked to the door. Before exiting, he said, "I'll fill it up. You get the fire going."

As he stepped outside, the rush of cold wind, though it had buffeted him all day, was a welcome reprieve from the stuffy heat of the Morris household. Had they arrived in time? Pete wasn't a saint who could cure a man taking his last breath. For all Garrick knew, he was just an old man who knew a bit about herbs.

Garrick strode to the pump and filled the pot, not caring how the water sloshed beyond the dish's opening and over his boots.

He returned to find Fay with her arms crossed as she stared into the flames. He set the pot of water on the grate and stood at her side, watching the orange dance over the wood that sat atop old ashes. "Pete brought medicines with him. Herbs and containers."

Fay's mouth twitched, and Garrick knew that was all the emotion she had in her. Experience had taught her that medicine wasn't enough to generate hope.

"Your brothers will be home tonight. Your pa will hold on for them. He'll wait."

Fay gave a single nod, which could have been mistaken for somebody falling asleep in church. He sat on the hearth and gestured for her to do the same. She did, sitting closer to him than he'd expected. His manners surged, and he longed to give her more space, but instead he took her hand, interlacing their fingers. Hers were cold, and he wondered if her heart was too injured and scarred to beat life into the rest of her.

"Have you eaten today?" he asked.

She drew a deeper breath and sighed.

If he'd been at Della's, he would have known just where to find a bit of bread and cheese. Just now, he didn't want to release his hold on Fay, and not only for his sake.

Her face dipped and she leaned closer to him, like a cat seeking for a place to rub its furry head. Garrick scooted closer and let her rest on him. With his free hand, he cupped her head, and when her shoulders started to shake, his heart broke into a million tiny pieces.

He let go of her hand then and wrapped both arms around her shoulders, holding them tight. He didn't want to stop her sobs. He wanted to absorb them, because this room already felt too full of sadness. Any more and it might cave in completely.

Pete entered the room and took a short look at the two of them. Fay hadn't noticed, and Garrick was beyond caring what the man thought. Did he still think them married? Or had he discovered the truth?

He placed his saddlebag on the tabletop and rummaged through the inside. Fay lifted her head at Pete's appearance, but let it fall back against Garrick's shoulder.

With a sniff she said, "Let me make you some supper."

"No," Garrick murmured into her hair. "You let us know when this water is ready. I'll feed Pete."

With one last squeeze, he released his hold and slowly moved away. She looked up at him with what could only be described as longing. Garrick blinked hard, clearing away the hope from his mind. He was tired and hungry. If there was even a hint of longing, it was solely for a bit of comfort. When her brothers returned, they would give her the love she needed. Her family had always been everything to her, and they were who she needed just now.

Garrick dug around the cupboards, glad when Fay didn't instruct him from her place near the fire, though surely she noticed his struggle. He made three plates of cheese and bread with sliced apples on the side, and filled a pitcher from the pump. Taking a plate to Fay and Pete first, he hesitated to take one to Mrs. Morris. Following Pete into that room was one thing, but taking himself there was another. He was nothing to this family. An acquaintance, an irritant, a devil. But he was all they had just now.

With renewed purpose, he entered the room and gave Mrs. Morris a small smile. "A bit of food."

She nodded and took the plate he offered. "Thank you, son."

"Is there anything I can do?"

She shook her head. "You've done more than enough already."

But it wasn't enough. Pete was in there grinding herbs, Fay was so exhausted she was ready to fall into the fire, and he seemed good only for slicing bread and smearing butter.

"Can the Grahams do anything?"

Mrs. Morris shook her head, then pursed her lips, as though refusing to say what she was thinking. One look at Mr. Morris told Garrick she was thinking there wasn't aught to be done, that her husband was on a trajectory and nothing would change his course.

Mr. Morris's chest rose and fell only slightly, his body clinging to each breath, refusing to let all of it slip away.

Garrick went to the side Fay had been on and dropped to his knees by the man's head. His cheeks were sunken, the white scruff catching the morning light. "Your sons will be home soon. Your dear, rugged friend is in the kitchen making you a remedy. Just a little longer, sir."

His breathing remained the same. Had Mr. Morris even heard his words? When he stood, Mrs. Morris reached out a hand. Garrick took her fingertips and pressed them tight.

"There's one thing you can do." Her eyes seemed as hollow as Mr. Morris' cheeks.

He would refuse nothing to a woman so despondent. "Anything."

"Take care of Fay. She's lost so much. I don't know if she can lose her pa without gaining something first."

Garrick nodded, though unsure what he could give her. He could release her from her words, but he was going to do so anyway, as soon as it was appropriate to discuss. He'd been too shocked to deny it before he'd left, but now there was no doubt in his mind. When Willem had said to take whatever she would give him, he surely didn't mean a promise given out of fatigue and desperation.

He left the room and returned to find Fay leaning against the rock mantle, her eyes closed.

He approached Pete and whispered, "What do you need? Della might have a bit of ingredients if you're missing any."

Pete gave the briefest glance at Fay. "Take care of your girl."

She's not mine to care for. The denial was on his lips, but he stopped the words before they were uttered.

There was no one else to care for her, just when she'd never needed help so badly in her life. Bags under her eyes, her hair loose around her face—such a contrast to the fiery way she normally appeared. Glaring at him or laughing with Edna.

Edna. That was who Fay needed right now. "I'll take our horses to the Grahams' barn. They've better feed."

Pete hardly nodded, intent as he was on his work.

Garrick cast a look at Fay. He wanted to lay her in her bed and tuck her under the covers. Let her sleep away this horrid day. Instead he knelt at her feet. "Fay, my darling." His heart stuttered at the nickname that slipped from his lips. Again he was letting himself believe the ruse. "I'm going to get Edna. She'll know what to do."

She opened her eyes, red and weighed down with weariness. She lifted a hand and brushed his jaw with her fingertips. "Thank you."

Garrick placed a hand over hers, holding her palm to his face, pressing it closer. If only she needed him like this more. He could work with *needed*. He could turn that into love. Releasing her, he stood and strode from the house.

21

Fay woke before the sun to the blessed sound of her pa coughing. He'd made it through the night when she'd thought he wouldn't even live through yesterday. She rose, careful not to wake Edna, who had slept soundly at her side. She had come the night before and couldn't bear to leave.

Fay walked through the quiet house, checking in on Hugh and Lachlan, who had returned late last night and were now asleep in their bed, each near enough to the edge that if she were to shout and startle them, they'd both fall out.

She smiled to think Otto used to fit in there too. It hadn't been fair when Eloise had left and given Fay her own bed, but Mama had insisted a woman needed her own space. Soon Hugh would be off, and Fay and Lachlan would be the only ones left.

Except she'd offered her hand to Garrick. And she'd meant it. All her holding out meant nothing if she didn't have someone she could count on. Garrick was that person. He was everything a woman should want in a husband. Everything she wanted in a husband—at least when she was only factoring in her own wants and not the needs of her family. But the other night had proved they needed him too.

For a moment, as she leaned against the doorframe to her brothers' bedroom, she imagined her life with Garrick. As though the image had been stacking up in her mind one brick at a time, only she just now opened the window to take a look. She saw a small house unlike any of the houses she'd been in. A unique space filled with love, much the way this house was. Garrick was there. She couldn't see him, but he was part of the vision the way one felt the sun on their skin, even with closed eyes.

She entered her parents' room to find Pete had made a pallet on the floor. Mama slept in the bed next to Papa. His breathing was still ragged, every breath scraping past his throat as he drew it in and let it out again. She stood and watched him for a moment, refusing to picture a life without him in it.

"He's doing better." Pete's hoarse voice came from behind her. Fay whipped around to find Pete had risen onto an elbow and was watching her.

She strode to him and knelt at his side. "Truly?"

Pete nodded. "Your ma says you've a bit of bone broth. Get it warming. If I can wake him, he'll need to eat."

Fay gave a vigorous nod and bustled into the kitchen. She pulled the pot of broth from the icebox and hooked it over the fire. She poked at the embers and added a new log, watching as the orange spots grew from a small glow to a steady flame that brushed the bottom of the pot.

Pete's footsteps sounded before he came around the corner. He held his hands out to the flames. "You're not married to that boy."

Fay shook her head.

"Hugh told me he was gettin' hitched at the end of this week. Didn't say it was to be a double wedding."

The sudden reality of her offer hit her like a sweeping wind, buffeting her and threatening to knock her down. Would Garrick want to be married right away? Was she even ready to be married?

She hardly knew the man. They hadn't taken all the normal steps before marriage. Those included conversation on the lawn outside of the church and dinners spent with her family. Flowers given and him begging permission from her pa.

Well, she had to admit he'd gained her parents' permission. And she remembered the pine bough broken off and offered up like a courtship flower. They'd even stood on the chapel lawn and watched Hugh and Edna's romance bloom. Perhaps they knew one another as well as any other engaged couple.

She drew in a calming breath, focusing on the things she did know. One thing, he would be a good husband to her. Another, they were well matched, or at least evenly matched. An image of her and Garrick in a boxing ring brought a small smile. Maybe the things she did know were reason enough to marry a man. Surely it would have been enough for Pete and her parents' generation.

But Pete expected more than a timid smile; he wanted an answer. Fay cleared her throat. "It won't be a double wedding. Garrick and I will have our own ceremony." Perhaps a hasty one like Eloise had done with Aaron. Just Mama, Della, and the preacher.

Pete walked to the table and crushed a bit of dry leaves into his hand. Rubbing his palms together, he let the pieces drop into a cup. Then he took the small pot Garrick had found yesterday and left to fill it with water from the pump. As she watched him through the window, the first sliver of light cracked over the ridge. When he returned, she continued watching the sunlight grow, and when it rose high enough, she put on her boots.

Pete glanced at her with a raised brow.

Fay rose to her full height and spoke with what she thought was conviction. "I'm going to speak with my fiancé."

As she neared Della's home and the guesthouse where Garrick was sleeping, Fay looked at the wealth that the Grahams had. At the large stable filled with horses and good feed. A fine house, well-kept and tidy. Perhaps she'd been a fool to reject his first proposal. Perhaps he could still give her everything she needed. He might not be rich, but he would have plenty, and that was enough.

She walked to the door of the guesthouse and gave it a sound rap. She stood with the wind at her back, shoulders hunched against the cold. Footfalls sounded from inside, moving closer. Then the door opened, and Garrick winced as the wind blew at his face and ruffled his hair. A ghost of a smile tugged at her mouth as she recalled the first time she'd woken him from sleep. He'd been barefoot that time too. Fay pushed her way inside and gestured for him to close the door.

He did, running a hand over his face to cover a wide yawn. "How is your pa?"

Fay gave a single nod. "He's..." *Better* wasn't the right word. *Healed* either. "Pete's taking good care."

Garrick nodded and cast about the room. The fire didn't even have embers, and she could only see half of his face, illuminated by the scant morning light filtering through the windows.

His hair was mussed from sleep. Fay stepped closer, the want to brush it away from his face almost overcoming her propriety. At the last moment, she gulped and crossed her arms.

Garrick didn't miss her actions, his gaze following the path of her hand as it reached out, then retreated.

"D'you need anything?" He still watched her closely.

Fay shook her head. He wasn't wrong to ask this. After all, she'd only ever come to him when she needed something.

"I meant what I said, about marrying you. I want to."

He blinked at her, then used the tips of his fingers to rub the sleep from his eyes. "Fay, I won't hold you to it. You were scared, and I would have gone without your offer. You know that, right?"

He had already been on his way, and she'd not doubted he would have gone as quickly as he could. She hadn't offered herself in exchange. She'd offered herself in gratitude. But also in need. Need for someone hale and healthy to go get Pete. Someone who could be just hers, and nobody else's. Someone whose arms would hold her together when she thought she was going to crumble like a day-old biscuit.

"I know."

A smirk lifted the side of his mouth. "So long as we don't joke about it at the post office, nobody need know. I won't say anything. It will be like it was never said."

Desperation clawed up her throat. He was annulling the engagement. "I said it, and I meant every bit of it."

Garrick shook his head. "No. I won't take advantage."

Hurt sliced at Fay, but anger followed quickly behind. "Did you change your mind? Decide my family would be too much of a burden for you?"

"What? No." Garrick reached out.

Fay stepped backward. "Then it's me. You've decided all your words over the past week were false, or perhaps you enjoy the hunt, and now that you have me snared, you'd rather let me loose."

"Fay."

The sunlight was brightening. A rooster crowed, and she could picture it standing tall and proud on the pitched roof of the coop. Della would wake soon, and it would be no good for a tousled Fay to be found leaving Garrick's house in the early morning. There were enough rumors already.

"I stand by what I said at your proposal. You have no need to marry me. My reputation is not ruined, and you owe me nothing." Turning, she strode to the door, but just as she tugged it open, it slammed closed again. One glance up told her Garrick's meaty hand was splayed against the top, holding it shut.

She twirled and craned her neck to stare up at him. Anger coursed through her, a steady, beating drum. With his arm above her and his body so close, she had only to slide sideways to be away from him, but she stayed, rooted in determination. He was the one refusing her. He should be the one to put distance between them.

His chest rose and fell with each breath, and just when Fay thought she couldn't wait any longer, he said, "You're right. I botched the proposal."

Fay rolled her eyes to the open side, a space to slip through if she wanted to escape his towering presence. His fingers grazed her jaw, pulling her back to face him. Heat singed her skin where he touched her, and she met his gaze once more with an angry set to her mouth.

"I proposed because Della told me I must—"

Fay looked away again, and Garrick caught her chin, surer this time. He dipped his head to the side, capturing her gaze completely. "I didn't want to because I knew I didn't stand a chance. You didn't want a man like me. I knew any proposal I made would be rejected. I was proud."

Was. As though he wasn't currently too proud to accept her offer. She couldn't meet his stare, and her gaze fell from his eyes to his mouth. Somehow his lips were the more decent option at the moment.

"I was not wrong. You rejected me before I even finished the words." His touch on her face softened and fell away. "I cannot blame you. The trouble I've brought upon your family. Forcing Eloise away, then Otto following. I offer no solutions, only separation and loneliness."

There it was again, the wrong reason for her to refuse him. Her gaze trailed down to the collar of his shirt, open and exposing his chest. The shirt billowed, untucked, and his feet were bare beneath his trousers.

"As shameful as it might be, I would not have proposed had I not wanted to marry you. Della does not have such a hold over me to make me marry a girl I do not love."

Love? The word shocked her more than the cold wind that carried her here. She longed to meet his eyes, to grip his shirt and pull him close. With his body surrounding her, his scent assailed her nose, and she was taken back to when they'd rode double on Dusty home. She wanted to lean into him again, feel the promise of his chest against her. Thank goodness for the solid door at her back, rooting her in her place.

"You think I am not in my right mind, with Pa so sick?"

Garrick nodded, though his face was pinched enough that she knew agreeing caused him discomfort.

"Then we'll wait."

Garrick cocked his head. "What do you mean?"

"I mean if I'm not in my right mind to say yes, then maybe I'm not in my right mind to say no either. Let's keep things as they are now."

Garrick's brows rose high, wrinkling his forehead. "Engaged?"

Fay nodded, trying not to let her desperation show.

Garrick's gaze took in her expression, and she doubted her ability to hide her every emotion.

She cleared her throat. "Like you said, so long as we don't go loose-lipping in town, there's no fear of other folks knowing. I will be able to change my mind when Pa is better."

Garrick's chest rose and fell with a resigned sigh. "I'd rather you be changing your mind to a 'yes' when this is all over."

"But I've already given you my yes." Fay knew they were talking in circles, that she was applying unfair pressure on this man who had ridden all over the state yesterday and whom she'd woken from a well-deserved sleep.

She stared at his throat, watched it bob as he swallowed, considered. The stubble tempting her to touch it. She lifted one hand and grazed a finger from his jaw to the hollow below his throat. He let out a deep sigh, leaning into her touch, his head falling when she stopped. She caught his face now, slid her palm up the scratchy scruff until her fingers tucked behind his ear. The words hung at the back of her throat, barely keeping back. *Kiss me.*

He wouldn't meet her eyes, and she tired of waiting. Tired of keeping the whole world at a distance for a goal she couldn't control. Her marrying rich only meant comfort. It did not guarantee her family would be any healthier, or even any happier.

She lifted her other hand, gripping his shirt and pulling. His arm that held the door closed was locked at the elbow, so her efforts only served to pull her own body closer to him, to remove that solid block of wood from her back, the only tether holding her in place. She expected him to lean into her, but he stiffened. She slid her hand back down the side of his face and hooked her first finger under his chin. Finally, he lifted his eyes to look at her.

"Kiss me," she whispered. Her stomach didn't tumble, her cheeks didn't heat. Though her mind screamed that this was a brazen request, Fay knew no shame. He wanted this. Hadn't he bought land over the hill? Hadn't he planned to woo her? Hadn't he just said he loved her? He was just too afraid to ask, and Fay wasn't shy.

She raised up on her toes, but still he didn't comply. She tugged his shirt so their bodies collided, and finally, *finally*, he lifted his other arm and hooked it around her waist, squeezing her close. But just as the heat from his muscular arm seeped through her layers and rested on her skin, he released her. Garrick dropped the hand that held the door shut and took a step backward.

The moment it was gone, Fay realized that arm was what was rooting her into place. Not the wooden door, but his hand above her head. Challenging her. Claiming her. Demanding she stay put until she understood. But she didn't understand. Not when he brushed her hands from where they clung to his clothes.

And most definitely not when he said, "You should go."

Heat burned through her now. She could almost hear it like a fire on a windy day, surging and dampening, snapping at the rejection.

It was just like him to be all in, demanding and pressuring her, then in a blink change his mind and let her loose.

Garrick didn't know what he wanted. He wasn't sure about his life when he first returned to Aster Ridge, and now he wasn't sure about her either. Fay didn't meet his eyes as she opened the door, her heart crying out when he didn't move to stop her.

Fay slipped out before he could convince himself to deny their engagement once more.

22

*G*arrick stumbled away from the door, collapsing with a huff into the chair by the empty fireplace. He'd nearly caved, nearly pulled her into his arms and told her he didn't care if he was taking advantage. *Take whatever she's willing to give.* Willem's words ran through his head. A mantra. An excuse. He'd done his best to push them away when she'd been in his house, pinned to the wall, but now that she was gone it was safe to consider them.

Here was the fact. Fay was more desperate than ever. If he didn't take her now, she was going to sell herself to the highest bidder.

As soon as he formed the thought, he withdrew, knowing it wasn't accurate or fair. Surely she wouldn't marry just *any* rich man. Otherwise she would have found somebody by now. What was it she waited for? What did she want in a man, besides money, that she hadn't yet found in the many guests who had come to this valley?

What was it she had seen in *him* to make her change her mind? Did she see it still? Or had he ruined whatever traction he'd gained by refusing her now? She must be embarrassed. Garrick knew well what it felt like to have a proposal refused, but surely, given a bit of time, she would understand his reasons. Perhaps she would even feel gratitude toward him.

Once dressed, he went to the barn to milk the goats. It was usually Edna's job, but Edna was still at the Morrises. When he entered the main house, Della bustled about the kitchen like everything hadn't shifted in a matter of hours.

"Have you been at the Morrises'?" she asked.

Garrick shook his head and set the bucket of milk on the counter. "Just doing the milking. I wasn't sure if Edna would be back this morning."

Della leaned into the dough she was kneading. "I would be surprised if they aren't at Sunday services. Mrs. Morris is known to never miss."

Della hadn't been at the house, hadn't seen the near-mourning Mrs. Morris had begun.

Violet ran into the kitchen, calling for Uncle Garrick, and hugged his legs. He tossed her into the air. As she flew, for a moment, Garrick felt that same weightlessness. But then he caught her, and the reality of life slammed back into him.

He tousled her hair. "When will this sprite be doing the milking?"

Della laughed. "As soon as you teach her."

Garrick looked at his niece. "Are you ready to learn how to help around here?"

Violet's whole body wiggled with her vigorous nod.

WHEN IT WAS time for church, Garrick helped the children climb into the wagon. He climbed in after them, easily recalling when he'd been living here last how this wagon had been full to bursting. Willem and Lydia and their children had more than filled the rest of the space.

He thought of Fay. Was Della right? Would they be at the church this morning? If not, he was determined to check in at their house on the way home. He glanced back down the valley, wishing he'd ridden Dusty, but Joshua stood up, teetering on his short legs, and Garrick swooped his nephew into his arms.

This was Garrick's family. Fay thought she wanted him, but she only needed him. He glanced at Della and Bastien's backs as they rode on the bench seat. He supposed they needed one another too, but somehow it was different when it came after the wanting.

The memory of Fay pressed against his door, himself only inches away, flooded his mind. No matter how he tried to drain the image away, it dammed itself up once more, clogging his senses.

By the time the service was over and the congregation began filing out, Garrick still hadn't removed the memory completely.

A familiar young woman came over and greeted Violet, who held tight to Garrick's hand. The woman straightened and offered Garrick a dimpled smile. "I'm Genevieve. You might not recall."

Garrick gave her a nod, still trying to place how he was supposed to know her. Perhaps from the dance. "Pleased to meet you. I'm—"

The woman laughed. "I know who you are. Around here, any new face causes a fuss. I'm sure Della is glad to have you." She looked down at Violet again. "Do you like having your uncle around?"

Violet nodded but leaned closer to Garrick.

Genevieve looked back up at Garrick. "Seems everyone wants you to stay."

He supposed if news traveled fast, this woman also knew Garrick had bought land and had every intention of staying. "I'm glad to be wanted." As soon as the word left his mouth, he cursed himself. Even when he wasn't thinking of Fay, he was. Stupid, foolish man for allowing her to claim every corner of his mind.

"My pa is the blacksmith. You'll be needing a few tools when the spring comes." She gestured toward the main town. "His smithy is just west a bit."

"Thank you." Garrick smiled. This was a woman who wanted him. He could see it in the tilt of her head, the sparkling in her eyes.

Then, as though his traitorous thought had summoned her, Fay appeared at his side and took his arm. Leaning across him, she spoke to Violet. "Good morning, sweetheart."

Violet's demeanor brightened, speaking to her comfort with Fay.

Fay continued. "Hugh has a little something for you. He brought it home from Billings."

Violet twisted, her eyes scanning the crowd for Hugh.

Fay laughed, her grip on Garrick's arm tightening. "He's just over there at our wagon, waiting for you."

Violet skipped away.

Fay straightened and met Garrick's curious gaze. "It's just a bit of candy. He always brings her something."

Garrick narrowed his eyes. He didn't care what Hugh had brought home for Violet. Did her presence here mean

Mr. Morris was well enough for the family to leave the sickbed? Or was Della right, and Mrs. Morris's unwavering faith forced them here no matter the circumstances at home?

Fay glanced at Genevieve. "Morning, Ginny."

Ginny? Garrick surveyed the woman again with new understanding. It was no wonder she'd looked familiar.

Fay glanced up at Garrick, her eyes as sparkling as Ginny's, but with a mischievous glint. "Did you tell her the good news, darling?"

Darling? Garrick swallowed, suddenly wishing he could clap a hand over Fay's mouth and haul her, kicking, back to the wagon. He tried conveying all of this with his eyes, but the way Fay smiled... It unnerved him.

One glance at Ginny told Garrick her eyes no longer sparkled. She looked at Fay with a hard gaze. "News?"

"Garrick and I are engaged."

Garrick's whole body froze stiff, his arm tightening against his ribs and squeezing Fay's fingers. "I thought we weren't going to tell anyone just yet."

Fay slid her hand out of his grip to wave it in the air. "Oh, that's only so we don't steal Edna's day, but Ginny is great with secrets. Like an iron vise, this one is." Fay dropped her hand, and Garrick caught it again, entwining their fingers. Fay squeezed his hand. "He bought a bit of the Wright's land, did you know?"

"I heard." Tight, Ginny's voice held none of the laughter from before Fay had arrived. She turned her anger on Garrick and ran an assessing gaze from his hair to his boots. "He's good enough for you then? I suppose because he's a Graham..."

Garrick's chest tightened at the falsehood and the disdain that cut her words. "I'm not a Graham."

Ginny's gaze cut away from Garrick. He'd been cast off like a pesky branch on a fallen log. "The self-righteous Fay has finally found someone good enough. I guess we should be glad you're not leaving any broken hearts in your wake, not like Eloise did. Nobody wanted you anyhow."

The venom in Ginny's voice was disconcerting. Garrick shot a look to Fay, unsure if he'd really heard the cruel words spoken on the lawn of the chapel. Fay's mouth was drawn, and her throat bobbed. The spark in her eyes had disappeared, replaced by a dead blankness.

He wrapped an arm around her shoulders and turned for the wagon. "Let's go see how your pa is feeling."

Fay's shoulders drooped as she nodded.

Garrick glanced at Ginny. "It was a pleasure to put a name to the face. Fay has told me *all* about you." He held her gaze for a moment longer, hoping to convey exactly what he meant.

It was a small joy when Ginny's smile faltered just slightly before she turned it on full force and dipped her head. "Pleasure to meet you too." Ginny spun on her heel and stalked away.

Garrick slid his arm off Fay's shoulders and glanced around. More than one pair of eyes had taken in the scene. "So much for not telling anyone just yet."

Fay crossed her arms and glared at Garrick. "What were you doing, flirting with Ginny Price?"

"I wasn't flirting. She was speaking to Violet."

"Oh? Do you usually speak to a child while looking directly into an adult's eyes?" Fay lifted her chin and lowered her voice. "Do you think if she thought you single, she might ask you to pay her a call at her home this evening?"

A call? "What? No."

Fay glanced toward the wagons. "I should go. As you said, my family is such a burden, and I must see to them."

She moved away, but Garrick had long legs and keeping pace wasn't difficult, no matter how quickly she moved her feet. "I was only trying to steer you away. Ginny was speaking as though you were shallow and unloved."

"Yes, well, I've heard it all before." She shot a look at Garrick and then returned her gaze to her destination. "I didn't think she'd be so bold in your company." Fay's cheeks were pink with embarrassment. Or anger. Garrick couldn't tell which.

"She's going to tell everyone we're engaged."

Fay reached her wagon and placed one boot on the wheel. "Are we not?"

Garrick jawed on air like a fish on the shore, a hook piercing its lip. No amount of struggling would put him back in the safety of the water.

Fay climbed into her wagon and reached a hand out. "Now, press a kiss to my hand before our audience thinks we are quarreling."

Garrick's back burned with the insinuation that they were being watched. He frankly didn't care a hoot what the entire town thought of him. With the show Fay was putting on, she obviously cared more about them than she'd ever let on.

Garrick took her fingers and brought them to his mouth. Before he made contact, he stared at Fay's eyes. "I'll not kiss you until I know you love me."

He released her hand, knowing to any onlookers it would seem as though he'd actually kissed it.

He strode to Della's wagon and climbed inside, not meeting anyone's gaze. He pulled Joshua onto his knee and feigned interest until Bastien and Della climbed in and took them out of sight of the church.

Unfortunately, the Morris' wagon was on the same route and soon bounced along just behind them.

Garrick longed to hop out of his wagon and into the Morris'. The thought of her so close with all that raged between them almost made him do it. By the time they reached the turnoff for the Morris's house, Garrick couldn't take it any longer.

He called to Bastien, "Can I get out here?"

Bastien nodded and slowed the horses. Della climbed into the back with the children and Garrick climbed out. As he started up the path, he saw Fay watching him, a stricken look on her face. He jogged to catch up and hauled himself into their wagon. Hugh was driving, and he glanced back and smirked at the added weight. Lachlan gave Garrick a friendly smile, then hooked an arm around the wagon side and looked ahead, giving Fay and Garrick as much privacy as could be had in such close quarters.

Garrick leaned close to Fay, but had to speak over the crunch of gravel under the wheel. "We said we'd wait to tell anyone."

Fay darted a glance at him, and the shame on her face made Garrick itch to kiss it off. "I know."

He leaned closer so he could lower his voice. "I haven't even told Della. Does your mama know?"

Fay glanced at the front of the wagon to where her mama sat, staring forlornly out along the snowy landscape, then looked back at Garrick and shook her head.

Garrick drew a long breath through his nose. A mistake because rather than steel himself, it only served to draw in Fay's scent of vanilla and chamomile. He longed to turn and pull her against his chest like she'd done when they rode home from Pete's. Had that been nearly a month ago now that he'd held her between his arms, etching her smell into his mind with every breath?

Thankfully, before he had the chance to override his self-control, they pulled to a stop in front of the house. Pete sat on the porch, a tobacco pipe in his mouth. Mrs. Morris hurried to climb down and move past Pete into the house.

Garrick climbed down and offered Fay a hand as she followed. She met his eyes with a mixture of fear and apology. Garrick jerked his head toward the door. "Go check on him. I'll be out here when your mind is at ease and you're ready to talk."

Soon all the Morrises were inside, and only Pete and Garrick remained on the porch.

Pete drew smoke into his lungs and blew it out again, eying Garrick the entire time.

"Fay says you're taking good care of her pa."

Pete nodded, his unnerving gaze still pinning Garrick.

"Will you stay for the wedding?"

Another nod, then silence.

Finally, Pete took the pipe from between his teeth and pointed it at Garrick. "How long you two been engaged?"

Garrick laughed, the wrong reaction, but just now, the question was so impossible to answer, he couldn't do anything else. Settling his nerves, he met Pete's gaze. "She can't quite make up her mind."

"About you or the marriage?"

"Either, I guess." Garrick waved a hand toward the house. "She wants to marry me *now*, but I think she's worried about her pa and just grateful. Not in love."

Pete's brows lowered, casting a shadow over his eyes.

"Gratitude is reason enough to get married." He shook his head, disappointment emanating from his expression. "You young folks have your head up in the clouds. Love comes. It's one of the few things that grows in a marriage. You don't need it to start. You just need to be willing." Pete's face darkened as though a new thought had come upon him. "Her pa cannot hold you to a proposal. Do you need to be held to it?"

"I'll marry her as soon as she's ready."

"You said she's ready now."

Garrick nodded. "But her pa..."

"If she's been unsure before, you better strike while the iron is hot."

Garrick eyed the man with his blacksmith terminology, the idea that he hammer on Fay while she was weak. He wouldn't be surprised if Pete had apprenticed as a blacksmith in addition to all the other trades he had mastered.

While Pete's logic might be clear, Garrick still felt as though accepting Fay now would be taking advantage. Pete may not have married for love, but Della had, and now he thought of it, all the folks in Aster Ridge had married for love. Garrick knew nothing of Pete's marriage, but he knew of Della's and Bastien's, of Thomas and Ivete, of Willem and Lydia, and he wanted a love like theirs.

But then he thought of the reason Fay had rejected him. It hadn't been Garrick as a person she'd rejected—it had been his circumstances. What if Garrick could take advantage now to save her from being taken advantage of by another, unknown man? She'd been the one to press *him* into a corner. If she had the ability to think through making Ginny Price jealous, then she ought to have the sense to know her own heart and mind.

"If you aren't going to strike, I've heard that distance makes the heart grow fonder."

Garrick smirked, recalling the old adage. "Absence. It's absence that makes the heart grow fonder."

Pete drew on his pipe, the tobacco leaves glowing orange. "That's what I said." He blew the smoke, and in the cold winter air it looked the same as a regular exhale. "I've an empty cabin, and you know its whereabouts. Perhaps you should give Fay the space to make up her mind."

The front door opened and Fay stepped out. First, she looked at Pete and gave him a small smile. "Pa's awake, which is more than I can say for before you got here." She waggled her fingers at him. "I don't know what type of witchy magic you know, but I'm grateful for it."

"Grateful, huh?" Pete raised a brow at Garrick, and if the man had been ten years younger, Garrick might have had to sock him in the jaw for the insinuation. With a nod, Pete set his pipe on the rail and went inside, leaving Garrick and Fay in silence.

Garrick nodded at the door. "Do you want to be in there, since he's awake?"

Fay shook her head. "There are enough bodies in that room. My brothers are still struggling to make sense out of the idea they almost returned to dig his grave."

Her voice broke, and Garrick closed the space between them to wrap her in his arms. He held her close, the way he'd wanted to do this morning and every other time he'd seen her. He breathed her in, but it wasn't sweet because he knew she wasn't his, that every time he released her might be the last time.

Love grew, all right. At a faster pace than he'd ever have imagined. Once acknowledged, it came faster and faster. How quickly would it grow within a marriage when the security of those sacred bonds would only serve to slice away at any reservations, any insecurities?

Then she pressed away from him and his confidence deflated. Fay had high dreams. Would she ever be content with a man like Garrick? Would she regret their marriage when her family needed funds and Garrick was unable to assist? He tried to imagine them in a home of their own. But he wasn't sure she would ever see the spark of hope he envisioned. Would her heart forever be in that back bedroom, where her pa sat on the edge of dying?

As much as Willem's advice made sense, Garrick couldn't abandon his own dreams of marrying someone who loved him. Fay wanted him now, but he refused to accept anything until he was sure she was hoping for a future rather than merely trying to hold together broken pieces.

23

ay pressed away from his embrace, afraid of everything that rolled through her.

Fear.

Desire.

Pain.

Joy.

She eyed him, waiting for the anger. She'd completely gone against everything they'd agreed upon that morning. When his words didn't fly in anger, she risked a few of her own.

"Ginny brings out the worst in me. She just... I couldn't stand to watch her flirt with you. You are my fiancé. Is it so wrong to expect a bit of fidelity?"

His face twisted in incredulity. "Fidelity?"

"She gets everything. She always has." Fay's hands started to shake as memories assailed her. Ginny with a new ribbon in her hair. Ginny with a gaggle of friends around her. Ginny squealing in delight as Bobby Henry gifted her a new ribbon, the old one Fay had so admired left in the dirt. Fay, picking up the ribbon when everyone had gone. "She gets everything."

Garrick's expression softened, and he pursed his lips before speaking. "She doesn't get me."

"Not yet. She's got her sister's dimples, and those girls have claimed every other man's eye." Fay leaned against the railing, pressing the heels of her hands into the wood. The cold served to ground her, to remind her that Garrick's warm body was the last refuge her limbs should crave.

"I bought land out here. For you. I'm staying here. For you. I would have never done those things if I didn't hope for a chance. With you."

"I'm trying to give you that chance, but you are refusing it."

"For your sake." His voice rose. "Do you think I'd take advantage of the desperation you feel right now? I can see it on your face this very moment."

Fay flinched as though she'd been struck. She moved her chin, trying to dispel whatever expression he saw.

He stepped nearer, his hand lifting to cup her cheek. "It's not in the set of your jaw." He leaned closer. "It's the light in your eyes."

She blinked, glancing up at the bright blue sky, trying to absorb its innocent light, free of the weight of life.

Garrick pressed his forehead against hers and let out a hot breath. "I want you to marry me, but I want you to *want* me too, not just need me."

He stepped away, his warm hand dropping to his side. Fay took a small step closer and placed her hands on his chest. "Do you not believe it is both? Want and need?"

Garrick frowned. "I'm not sure you are capable of discerning the difference."

Fay glared at him and pushed at his chest. He didn't budge, and the action forced her backward. "You presume to tell me what I think?"

Her blood was hot, warming every extremity with its ferociousness.

Garrick lifted a hand between them as though trying to calm an angry bison. "I think I should go away, just for a bit. Let Pete here take care of your pa, let your life settle down to a resting state. Then I will happily propose marriage once more and allow you to answer."

Fay set her mouth. "We are engaged. Are you breaking it off?"

Garrick's eyes were sad. "Don't make me answer that."

But hurt raged too hot inside her. "Say it. Say you don't want to marry me."

"Fay."

She stepped closer and pressed at his chest again. She put her feet into it this time, and he took a single step backward. Immediately she wanted him close again. She hated him for doing this, for leaving her just when she'd decided she wanted him.

He gripped her wrists, stepping close again, but this felt nothing like an embrace. His deft fingers were shackles holding her in place. His voice, when he spoke, was as tight as the strings on a fiddle. "I'll not be the boots you are wearing that are too big, waiting to drag you, help-less, through a forest. You are trying so hard to be brave, and you are brave, but you're tired too. Just let Pete care for your pa. Let your heart find zeal again. Then come to me. Please come to me."

He released her wrists and bounded down the steps. He clapped his hat on his head and turned. "I'll be at Pete's."

She wanted to shout at him, to tell him that if he loved her, he wouldn't leave her just now. Not when she needed him to wrap his arms around her and hold her together. He thought her strong, but she was all bluster, a child with a pistol that isn't even loaded.

But he mounted Dusty and left. If it had been summer, dust might have concealed his abandonment. As it was, she watched until only her tears blurred her vision.

24

The next week passed with joy all around her, but she'd put a shell around her heart, and it shielded her from even the good. Papa improved each day. Though his cough sounded worse, Pete assured them that the phlegm was breaking up, and their pa was mending. Edna prepared for her wedding by putting the final touches on her dress. Hugh had moved into the Graham's guesthouse since Garrick was no longer living there.

Yet, even though she knew Garrick wasn't inside, she couldn't look at the doorway without thinking of him. Without pretending that if she just pushed through, she would see him, fresh from sleep, the wind in his shirt like a ship's sail, propelling her closer.

When the day of the wedding arrived, Fay mustered all the happiness she could, as though she'd been holding it in reserve the last week. Edna was stunning in her new blue-green frock, and her mama had traveled the two days to attend. When Mrs. Archer wasn't fretting over some small detail, she was tutting over Pete's slim shoulders and plying him with pastries.

He'd try to resist in his gruff way, saying an old man like him didn't need anything more than bones, but Mrs. Archer persisted, and Fay took genuine joy in watching Pete turn soft in her hands. Hands more than strong enough to shape a bit of tough dough.

After the ceremony, Fay sidled up next to Pete and linked her arm through his. "I'd like a dance with the man who saved my pa."

Pete harrumphed and pulled away, but Fay followed, linking her arm once more. "Edna will want a dance too. You cannot deny the bride on her wedding day."

"She's got a husband. What need has she to dance with me?" His scowl drew a laugh from Fay, and the simple action served to lift her heart.

They made their way down the boardwalk from the church and into the large building where the town held dances and meetings. It looked much the same as any other event, but this was for her brother, and when she surveyed the space, she was glad to see the faces of the folks who loved her family best.

The musicians started, announcing Hugh and Edna's entrance, and the crowd applauded their union. Hugh planted a kiss on Edna's mouth, and her shocked eyes earned laughter from the guests.

Hugh danced with Edna for a bit, then Pete turned to Fay. "Will half a dance suffice?"

She quirked her brow, then nodded. Pete pulled her onto the floor and she placed her hands on his bony shoulders.

"Mrs. Archer is right." She gave him a squeeze. "You're too thin."

"That woman is too big. She'd never last in the woods."

Fay laughed. "I think she might surprise you."

"Your man has surprised me. I didn't think he'd last that long. Or might be he's been mauled."

Fay gasped, but when she caught Pete's smile, she smacked his shoulder. "Cruel man."

Pete shook his head. "I'm not the one who sent him out there."

"You surely did. He didn't invite himself to your cabin."

Pete conceded her point with a bob of his head. "Are you sure about him? He's got some fanciful ideas."

Fay smiled. "I like his ideas. Only I hate when they interfere with my own."

Pete shook his head. "In my day, we got married for good reason. That's what makes a marriage work."

Fay's heart softened. "Your Samantha was a good woman."

Pete looked around the room, annoyance clear on his face. "She would have been on the side, chatting happily. She always loved weddings, though I tell you she had two left feet."

Fay laughed. Though she'd been rather young when Samantha passed, she remembered the woman held an unmatched grace. It was odd to think her a poor dancer. "I think you must be right. I cannot recall seeing her dance."

Pete smiled. "No, she never did. I suppose that's why she was content to marry me. I never pressed her to dance."

Fay squeezed his hand. "You are a fine dancer, Mr. Corbin."

He only squinted at her flattery, and Fay leaned her head against his chest. He might not be full and broad like

Garrick, but his wiry frame had brought healing to more than just her pa.

She looked up again. "You headed home tomorrow?"

Pete nodded. "Offered to escort Mrs. Archer to the train station, but she can't ride a horse." He spoke the words like they were filthy, as bad as not being able to open a door for herself.

"Well, she must not have need to know those things."

Pete scoffed, but Fay could tell he hadn't lost all respect for her. An idea flickered to life in Fay's mind. "She's a rather pretty woman."

Pete sniffed, but Fay could see a memory lifting the corners of his mouth.

"You could ride along the wagon, be her companion in that way. You take the road half the time anyway."

Pete frowned. "It'd be slow going. She'd likely force me to eat every hour."

"And you'll love every bite."

He laughed, and Fay smiled to have broken his tough facade.

"The real question is, when are *you* going to my home?"

Fay gulped and looked down.

"He's gained your pa's permission."

"Yes, but—"

"He's gained yours."

"Yes."

"You are engaged, and if he asked you to come to him, you should obey."

Fay bristled at the term. "Should I? What if I want him to come to me?"

"Then you'll lose him."

Fay blinked at the matter-of-fact way Pete spoke the words, as though they made no difference in the world.

"He'll have to come back. He has land here."

"Doesn't mean he'll come back for you. No doubt there are more than a few girls in this town who would gladly slide a ring onto his finger."

An image flashed of Ginny, winking her dimples at Garrick. "He loves me."

"Love only grows if it is nourished. You've been a barren field all the time I've been here."

That wasn't fair, with a wedding and a possible funeral both fighting for attention. "My pa—"

"Barren." Pete cut in, as though reasons were nothing.

The song ended, and Fay moved away, glad Pete had only had half a dance. She wasn't sure the destruction he might have done had he twice as long to do it.

As the day wore on, Fay assisted her mama and Mrs. Archer with all the small details of running and cleaning up the festivities. Everyone rode back to Aster Ridge together and made sure Hugh and Edna were tucked away in the guesthouse before dispersing to their various homes for the evening.

Fay relaxed into the sofa next to her mama. The sun wasn't even down, but Fay wanted nothing more than to climb into bed. The image of Garrick sleeping in Pete's bed filled her head, and she immediately changed her mind. She wanted one thing more, but she couldn't go after it now, not until the sun was up and she had a travel companion.

SHE ROSE IN THE MORNING, refreshed after so many hours of sleep. She'd expected anticipation to keep her awake, but instead she'd dreamed of Garrick. Her visions hadn't been filled with a reunion as she might have chosen, but instead with foggy visions of him, his face, his arms, his throat. Impatiently, she saddled Lady and Pete's horse and waited for Pete to collect his gear. He checked the saddle and she swore he only pretended to fix the girth. With a kiss to her mama, she climbed up and followed Pete down the path.

Though she was grateful for their swift departure, she couldn't help but feel disappointed that Pete wasn't riding alongside the wagon carrying Mrs. Archer. The more Fay thought about it, the more she wanted those two to find love with one another. She wanted everyone to find love.

As she urged her horse a bit faster, she hoped that was what she would find at the end of this journey.

25

Garrick rose from Pete's bed and checked his trap line. He'd caught one animal the whole week he'd been here, but somehow that was reward enough to keep him setting and trapping each day. Maybe he should have waited and bought land here, to live in solitude like Pete.

Fay hadn't come. He'd waited all week with one ear cocked to the west, waiting. Nothing. The wedding was over, and if Mr. Morris still fared well, Pete would likely be heading home today. Garrick would have to vacate the cabin. Where would he go? Back to Aster Ridge to argue with Fay? To convince her she still wanted him?

Not for the first time over the last five days, he'd second guessed his logic. He should have taken Fay to a church the very day she told him yes. He should have secured her hand then made himself everything she wanted. But now... Did he have the same leverage? With each day that passed, he was certain he'd chosen wrong. Certain that, during his time away, she'd overcome her desperation and no longer needed him. Today would be the last day of his isolation. Pete would return, and Garrick would be forced to make a decision. Or sleep on the floor.

He took his frustration out on the unchopped wood, first sawing it into rounds, then using the ax to chop it into smaller wedges. He had worked up a sweat and knew if he didn't stop soon, he would be chilled from the moisture that slicked down his back.

A nicker came from deeper in the woods, and he paused, listening. Movement showed between the trees, and Garrick set down his ax.

"Pete?" he called out.

When Pete didn't answer, Garrick's heart picked up. Had she come? He gulped and pulled a handkerchief from his pocket to wipe the sweat from his forehead. Stepping nearer the trees, he saw the familiar white boots of the Morris' horse, Lady.

Dropping his handkerchief to the ground, he bounded into the trees, meeting Fay. He was breathless, though the distance wasn't more than that between the cabin and the stream. "You came."

Fay slid off her horse, and he was glad to see she'd worn her own boots this time. Spots of bright pink bloomed on her cheeks and nose. The moment her feet met the ground, Garrick pulled her to him, crushing her with all the insecurities that had weighed on him through the week. He released her and glanced around. "Where's Pete?"

Fay waved behind her, glancing up at him under the brim of her hat. "He's checking the trapline, giving us a bit of time alone."

He glanced at the cabin. "Last time we got quite a reputation for being alone."

"Well, at least this time we'll have deserved the gossip."

Garrick grinned and looked under the brim of her hat at her wide innocent eyes, a contrast to her scandalous words. Lady shifted and Garrick knew he should remove her bit and get her a bucket of feed, but he wasn't ready to let go of Fay.

He loosened his hold, letting his clasped hands slide down to the curve of her back. "Your pa?"

Fay gave a shallow nod and leaned her face against the lapel of his coat. "He's well."

He glanced out across the snowy landscape, smiling at the last time they'd been here, how badly he'd wanted to hold her like this. "I didn't know if you would come. I waited."

She leaned away, her eyes flashing to his. "Did you expect me sooner?"

Garrick shrugged. "Well, if I had my way, you would have been on my tail."

"You think me forward, soldier."

Garrick laughed. "I think a great many things about you." He released his hands and stepped back, catching her hands in each of his. "Your pa is well." It wasn't a question, but a confirmation. She had no reason to need him now. If she needed anything, it would be had from a man who was better off than he. If she was choosing him now, she did so because she wanted him, and that idea hummed in his middle, spreading outward like ripples in a pond.

"He is well." Her voice was quiet, unsure.

"And you are here."

Her throat bobbed as she gave a single nod.

Garrick dropped to the ground, the snow crunching

beneath his knees as he squeezed her hands. "Will you heal my heart and be my wife?"

Fay laughed and mirrored his position falling to her knees in front of him. "Heal your heart? Have I wounded it?"

"Greatly." He raised her hand to kiss her knuckles but paused. "Say that you still want me even though you no longer need me."

Fay glanced at their hands and pressed his fingers with her own. "See, that is where you are wrong."

He winced, rocking back on his toes. Not the words he wanted to hear.

"I've wanted you all along. It was not until I needed you, too, that I saw the sense in marriage."

"Sense." Garrick rolled the word around on his tongue and wasn't sure he liked the taste.

Fay softly chuckled. "Perhaps we are both poor at proposals. You out of guilt, me out of sense. But do you see that we have all the reasons? Plus, the town is abuzz with my engagement. Everyone was more than surprised you were not at the wedding."

Garrick laughed. Perhaps Fay was right. They had all the logical reasons to marry, but they had the emotional ones too. He supposed there would always be elements to a relationship that couldn't quite be put into words or explained to an outsider. "The folks in Dragonfly Creek still believe us?"

Fay nodded.

"Well, who are we to disappoint?"

Fay ran her thumb along Garrick's fingertips. "I've disappointed them for as long as I can remember."

Garrick released her hands and cupped the back of her head, knocking her hat to the ground and revealing her simply braided hair. She didn't even move to put her hat back, so intent was her gaze on his. He stared into her eyes, intent and afraid to ask the question that nearly choked him. "Do you love me?"

She nodded, and he heard her swallow. He stared into her hazel eyes. Did she remember his vow not to kiss her until he knew she loved him?

The blaze in her eyes told him that even if she didn't remember, she knew what was coming.

He slid his thumb under her chin and tilted it up. He paused, grinning, before he pressed his lips to hers. Her mouth was hot against his, snuffing out the cold swirling around them, the cold he'd been battling all week without her near. He pressed closer, wanting more of her, wanting all of her, forever.

This victory was everything. Better than earning a knockout, and more hopeful than a battlefield. It was the future he never expected.

He recalled the morning she'd asked him to kiss her, the willpower required to refuse her request. To release his hold and step away from her, allowing her the space she needed to grieve her father's illness.

She relaxed her head into his hand now, and he leaned into her surrender, deepening the kiss, rising higher on his knees for better leverage. Her lips were chapped and scratchy from the windy ride here. She was no damsel. She was a strong woman who didn't fear the challenge of half a day's ride to claim the man she wanted, a woman who would brave cold and discomfort, who would do anything for her family.

"You'll be my family now?" he asked.

It wasn't until he'd said it that he realized he needed her. He needed someone who knew what a family was, who could teach him about love and devotion. Adoration and argument.

She nodded, and he pressed another kiss. He never wanted to stop, but he didn't know how far behind Pete was, and he had learned a lesson in reckless behavior.

Fay's lips whispered against his own. "Pete said we should have had a double wedding."

Garrick smiled. "Would have been easier."

"I don't want a big wedding."

Garrick looked at her eyes, wondering if this was Fay the fiancée speaking or Fay the daughter. Perhaps there would never be a discernible difference between the two. "No?"

She shook her head and then glanced behind to scoop her hat from the ground. Placing it on her head she said, "I'd be just as happy to take you to the church on our way home."

Garrick laughed. "I'm not sure your mama would forgive me. She's already given me more grace than I deserve." The moment he had the thought, he was stricken. Eloise. "Your sister won't like you marrying me."

Fay's brows twitched. "I don't think she'd care much. She's already got a husband."

She tilted her head up, her lips begging for more kisses. Garrick complied.

When they stopped, Fay whispered against his mouth. "She's got her own family now. And I'll have one too."

Garrick drew back a little. Fay was downplaying the situation. "Will our families never see one another?"

Fay rose, shaking her skirts out. Then she eyed him. "If you don't stop speaking of my sister, I'll take back all the forgiving I've done and assume you're marrying me to get closer to *her*."

The words, though meant in jest, slammed into Garrick. How many times had she played second fiddle to Eloise? He caught Fay in an embrace, a new vow whispering from his lips. "Never."

She hummed into his chest, her arms wrapped tight around his waist.

He touched her back, her hair, her arms, struggling to believe she was truly here, truly agreeing to be his.

She pressed her cheek against his coat. "You have to be okay with me helping my family, even if it means a bit of our own money."

Garrick nodded, pulling her tighter. She would always need to help her family, and they would always need her, but she had a new need now, in the way she clung to him. He supposed that was the only way Fay knew how to love, pressed between two needs, and for the first time, he had no urge to fight the order she chose.

EPILOGUE

The ground was barely thawed when Garrick started on their house. Her brothers grumbled at how many shovels he'd chewed through, digging too early in the year. Not a month later and he'd built them a simple one room house. Fay didn't mind simple, not when Papa was well and petals painted the valley.

Most days, she and the Graham children had taken to having their lunch as a picnic on the ridge overlooking Garrick's land. She'd watch her man down there toil over his home—their home. When the children got too cold, she would bundle them up and return them to their mama.

As she did, she would dream of holding the hands of her own two children. The life she had imagined with Garrick was finally within sight, and it wasn't full of the things or money she had always pictured. Instead, it resembled much of what her own family shared. It was living in tight quarters with elbows brushing at the dinner table. It was tailoring old clothes to fit the next sibling.

For the first time, she appreciated that. While what had happened to her family was awful and unfair, they had one another. Somehow, her parents had cultivated such love that Fay and her siblings had nearly given all they had to support it. That was something to replicate, not resist.

Today there would be no picnic on the ridge. As Fay sat in front of the small looking glass, she undid her braid and ran her fingers through her hair. The wavy texture didn't at all resemble Eloise's tight coils. A pang of sadness hit her heart at the thought of her sister, so far away.

Eloise hadn't been pleased to learn of Fay and Garrick's courtship and engagement. Ignoring that knowledge was no easy feat. She only hoped with time, Eloise would realize Garrick was right for Fay, just as Aaron had been right for Eloise. It didn't much matter what Eloise thought, for Fay wasn't sure she would ever see her sister again.

The trains didn't yet travel that far west, and the trip was no holiday jaunt. Folks died every time they tried crossing that wide Columbia River. It wasn't something Fay wanted to brave merely for her sister's approval.

She twisted and pinned her hair until it resembled the stylish coif from Lydia's book of dress patterns.

Her stomach fluttered to wonder what Garrick would think of her in her new dress. It was a far cry from the worn skirt and apron he usually saw her in, or even the old trousers and hat from their first adventure.

A knock and subsequent deep voice came from the front of the house.

Mama came into Fay's room. "The pastor is here."

Fay gulped and nodded.

Edna squeezed past Mama. "I only just realized by

having the ceremony here, you won't get to drive by the post office and show Ginny how well her plan to ruin you worked."

Mama tsked, but Fay couldn't stop her laughter from escaping, easing the anticipation that ran across her shoulders. "Nobody would accuse her of not trying."

Edna knelt in front of Fay and tugged at her hair, pulling pieces loose to frame Fay's face. "You look lovely."

Fay ran damp palms down her thighs and tried for a smile.

"Nervous?"

Fay gave another anxious laugh. "No."

But Edna's pursed lips said she wasn't buying one bit of it. Her eyes flashed up to Mama. "You told her what to expect...tonight?"

Fay clutched at Edna's arm. "She did, and there's no need to tell me anymore." Edna laughed outright at the desperation in Fay's voice.

Mama stepped out of the room for a second and returned with a large basket in her hands. "A tradition has been formed. This is for both of you to open together, but Edna had one thing she wanted you to open now."

Edna drew a large package out of the basket and set it on Fay's lap. "I thought you might want...well, just open it."

Fay ran a hand over the clearly high-quality box and gave Edna an accusatory stare.

"Just open it. It's from myself and my mama."

Fay lifted the lid to find a wide-brimmed straw hat. It was too small to cover much, and from the pin that was through the cap, she knew it didn't have a chin strap. This was meant as a fashionable piece.

Edna lifted it out and held it above Fay's hair. "Would you like me to put it on?"

Fay could think of what it took to get it here. Not just the cost of the hat, but money spent having such a delicate parcel sent. This was no hand-carved wooden spoon like what Hugh had surely contributed to the wedding basket.

"Edna, it's too much," Fay tipped her head to the side against Edna's hip.

Edna scoffed and helped herself to adjusting Fay's hair under the brim and pinning it into place.

Fay had to admit the look was pleasing, but the hat served no purpose. It would do naught to shield her face from the sun, and she'd be too afraid to wear it outdoors where the wind blew strong. There was only one little wooden rod to hold it in place.

"Hugh and I wanted to get a hat for Garrick, one that wasn't so small as the hat he wears from his time with the Rough Riders. One that might shield his face from the sun during the long hours he's spending on your spread." Edna's eyes sparkled, then she shrugged. "When I asked my mama to have one made, she insisted on getting one for you too."

"You got one for Garrick too?" Though it meant more money spent, somehow that made her feel less guilty about accepting this one. "How did you know his band size?"

Edna shrugged. "He wears this strip of wool fabric under his hat. Della helped me take the measurement after he'd removed it for the night."

Fay remembered the night she'd wrapped that bit of wool around his head. The night she realized how little control she had over her family's health and happiness.

"I don't need a hat. You should keep this one." Even as

she said it, Fay could not help admiring herself in the looking glass.

"Fay," came Mama's warning.

Fay stood so she could look at Edna and Mama without looking in the mirror, because her reflection was crumbling her resolve. "It's not that I don't appreciate the gift. It's only that I don't know where I'll wear such a fine accessory."

"To your wedding." Edna's voice was soft.

Fay glanced down at her new dress and touched the short brim of the hat, thinking of the floppy one she usually wore. It had never looked the same after getting so wet that first night searching for Hugh. A smaller hat for her, and a larger hat for Garrick.

She smiled thinking of her old, grandiose ideals. How Garrick had curbed them and turned them into something fitting, something beautiful.

"He's not going to recognize me." She turned her head, admiring the dainty accessory.

Mama laughed and wrapped an arm around Fay's shoulders. "He will."

She escorted Fay from the room, and Edna followed with the basket in hand.

With such a small house, the only guests that could fit inside were Fay's family and Garrick's in the form of Della and Bastien. But Della had refreshments waiting at her house for the new couple to come and accept the congratulations from the rest of Aster Ridge and any folks in Dragonfly Creek who might wish to feign pleasure at Fay finding a husband.

As soon as they were out of the hallway, Fay's breath caught as she spotted Garrick in his new hat, wider brimmed and curled on the sides in the western way. It was black, too, a shade darker than his hair, and it sat low on his forehead, the additional contrast making his eyes a more piercing blue. He smiled broadly when he looked at her, a snapping fire promising more. He most certainly recognized her. Mama released her hold and let Fay walk the rest of the way to Garrick.

He took her hands and situated them on opposite sides of the pastor. "Don't we look a picture in our new hats?" He winked and Fay's stomach flipped. Would she ever get used to the effect his full attention had on her?

She looked over the small crowd and spotted her papa. His face was still gaunt. The thinness from his sickbed hadn't yet left him. Her smile drooped then; she didn't know how many more winters he had left. They'd done their best, but age made him weaker than ever. She turned back to Garrick, finding comfort in the warmth of his hands, more callused than before with all the work he'd done to their house.

For the first time, her heart lifted. Soon, they would create a family of their own. No longer did children seem like a burden or an expense. She gazed into Garrick's icy blue eyes. Would their children have his eyes and her hair color? Some primal urge reared in her, and she wanted— needed—to bear his children. To raise them up and marry them off. To have grandbabies of her own. She almost laughed at herself, thinking of grandbabies before she'd even borne a child.

The pastor began, and Fay tried to listen, but her mind whirred with so many possibilities. She'd lived a full life. One with love and danger, drama and peace. For so long she'd thought finding the right husband was the pinnacle, the final feat to tackle. Yet standing here now felt like standing on a ridge over the valley, scanning the wide grasses to see which direction she wanted her feet to cut a path.

A fanciful thought, perhaps brought to mind by her posh new hat, but she felt like her life was just beginning. That finding the man she wanted to share it with wasn't the last thing, but the start to everything.

ALSO BY KATE CONDIE

Want free content and more from Kate Condie? Sign up for her newsletter at www.subscribepage.com/katecondienewsletter or follow her on social media @authorkatecondie

ACKNOWLEDGMENTS

Thank you to my readers whose kind words and reviews keep the imposter syndrome at bay and encourage me to keep writing. To my wonderful team —Whitney, Michelle, Kelley, Karie, Beth, Crystal, Taryn, Ariel— for their support, ideas, and hard work. Also, to my grandparents whose cabin helped me discover a love for fishing in the mountains. Without those trips to Kirwin, Wyoming, this series would never have started.

ABOUT THE AUTHOR

 Kate Condie is a speed talker from Oregon. Reading has been part of her life since childhood, where she devoured everything from mysteries, to classics, to nonfiction—and of course, romance. At first, her writing was purely journal format as she thought writing novels was for the lucky ones. She lives in Utah and spends her days surrounded by mountains with her favorite hunk, their four children and her laptop. In her free time she reads, tries to learn a host of new instruments, binge watches anything by BBC and tries to keep up with Lafayette as she sings the Hamilton soundtrack.